# Love You More Special Edition

## STACY TRAVIS

FAST TURTLE
PRESS

LOVE YOU MORE

————

STACY TRAVIS

Cover Design: Wildheart Graphics

Editing: Emerald Edits

Publicity: Valentine PR

*"Love is the one wild card."*
*- Taylor Swift*

*For the Swifties* 🤍

# CHAPTER
*One*

JAX

The yellow light breaks just above the horizon, bathing everything in that dewy glow of a new day. It feels…optimistic. Something I need right now.

"Incoming." My brother's voice grumbles from a dark corner of the tidy industrial kitchen where I'm making coffee. I know enough to put my hands up.

Or duck.

It only took one mistake of doing neither for me to learn. Back when Archer was seven to my five, and he beaned me with a soup can. He's been throwing things at my head ever since, and now, thirty years later, I try not to take it personally.

Even if he means it personally.

"Asshole." Looking down at the object I've just intercepted, I see a crumpled t-shirt with Taylor Swift's face on the front. "Why?" I ask.

"Assume it's yours."

One time. *One time* I slipped and sang a few lines from a

Taylor Swift song, and my brother's been calling me a Swiftie and making sure anyone within earshot knows I like her songs.

There's no point in fighting him. He's older and grumpier, for one thing. And trying to get him back by making fun of his shitty taste in music is barely a sport. Who cares if he's lost in the depressing grunge bands of the nineties?

I don't need to look closely at the shirt to know it doesn't belong to me. For one thing, I don't buy concert shirts. Ever. For another, the shirt is tiny. Too big to fit my seven-year-old daughter, but barely worth pulling over my head to prove it can't be mine.

"Must be one of your girlfriends left it in my room. Told me to say hi," I mutter. He knows that's not true either, but after my wife left two years ago, my family mostly avoids the taboo subject of my dating life. And ribbing him about his own lack of action shuts him up for now.

As I go about the business of slicing up yesterday's sourdough to toast, Archer's footsteps recede from the old brown barn, which sits in the middle of our family's vineyard.

Archer has a house nestled at the base of the hill that gives Buttercup Hill Vineyards its name, and I live at the opposite end of the property, where the land is flatter and the vineyards are right outside my back door. Our father and our other three siblings also live onsite, mostly around the perimeter, which gives each of us some privacy.

Normally, at this hour, I'm the only one bustling around in the kitchen, which overlooks well-maintained raised beds of tomato plants, herbs, and creeping vines that teem with squash, cucumbers, and eggplant.

We have an entire team employed to care for the produce in the garden boxes and make sure everything looks just so, but I'm not interested in produce right now. I just want a cup of strong coffee and a bite of breakfast to kickstart my day.

In another hour, half of my family will be awake and barking things at each other in the name of business and bonding, and my productivity will be sunk for the morning. It's why I always get up at four. Almost always. Just not today.

Today, I overslept. I've been sleep-deprived for going on two years now, so it's probably not the last mistake I'll make today.

Then I'll hear about it from my siblings, who don't know when to mind their own business, or my father, who's losing his mind—his words, not mine. That's how he characterized his Alzheimer's diagnosis in the days when he could still joke about it. Funny guy.

Checking the time, I groan. Almost six. I should have tidy income and expense columns, along with a few items checked off my to-do list by now. Instead, I'm pushing yesterday's lunches aside in the employee fridge, searching for strawberry jam.

"Meant to ask, have you been in to see Dad?" Archer returns with a pitcher of water, which he uses to fill three small bottles that fit into a belt he wears while running.

"Not in a few days. The nurse said he's having a rough week, barely recognizes her." I grind out the words, hating to be the bearer of news none of us wants to hear.

Archer's face falls, and he nods.

"Goes in waves like that. Maybe today'll be different." I'm telling him something he knows, and I hate that I don't feel more optimistic.

Crossing his feet at the ankles, Archer draws my attention to the brand new running shoes he's wearing. Brown with fat cushy soles and an orange logo. "You jumping on that Hoka craze?" I ask him, surprised because my brother never does anything he hasn't thought through deliberately, and I've seen him in the same brand of running shoes since college.

"Not jumping on anything. They make a good shoe."

"Yeah?"

"Yeah."

"What's special about them?"

He shrugs. To be clear, Archer shrugging is the farthest thing from admitting he doesn't know something. It's more of an annoyed tic than anything else. "Sometimes change is good."

"I call bullshit. You don't change shoes. You don't change anything."

Another shrug. Now I know he's holding out on me.

"What's that mean?" I don't mean to raise my voice, but being my older brother means Archer can frustrate me more than anyone else. And lately, he's been working my last nerve.

"You'd know if you were a runner."

"I'd be dead if I was a runner. It's too damn hot to be a runner in Napa Valley. You're just some kind of superhuman freak desert animal."

He snickers without smiling. "That's a lot of venom for six in the morning."

"It's a lot of company for six in the morning." I shrug, and I know he's aware that my gesture is just as loaded as his. He takes a step back.

"You're still mad about the thing?" he asks, drawling like I'm being petulant. The "thing" is his decision to lease some land to grow zinfandel grapes when I asked him to wait a year. I have some financial messes to sort out—in short, we've been over-spending—and he chose to ignore my request. Archer runs the winery now that our dad is unable to handle it day-to-day.

"We could've just bought the grapes. We didn't need the land costs on this year's books."

"That's why we pay you the big bucks as CFO. You'll work it out."

Except that I haven't, and he's added one more stress to a terrible situation. I take a step forward, my eyes moving from his steaming cup of coffee to his stoic face, and I have the urge to deck him. But then the view behind him overrides everything else. As usual.

Walking out of the kitchen to the deck off the backside of the restaurant, I watch three brown ducks glide across the water before turning my attention back to the acres of twisting branches. The property is nearly three hundred acres in total, large enough for us to grow most of the grapes we use in our cabernets, merlots, and sauvignon blancs.

I never miss a chance to stare at the vines. They're proof of everything that's beautiful about the universe. And the reason for all the good fortune my family has. Which means proof that I have a place in this world, even if I don't know much else for certain.

Archer knows, which is why he follows me out there. Pacing in a circle on the porch, he stuffs one hand into the pocket of a puffer vest, which he definitely won't need five minutes into his run. He's wearing it over a short-sleeved tee with nylon shorts and compression tights beneath them.

"Why do you wear two pairs of pants?"

He tips his head up; eyes narrowed in annoyance. "We've discussed this."

It's true. We have. But I can't help twisting tiny knives into his overly muscular flesh because I'm one of the few who gets away with it. Our youngest sister, PJ, being the other.

I give him a blank stare like I'm either trying to annoy him or my mind is going AWOL. He knows better than to question which one it is. That's what having a parent with dementia will do to a family. Well, it's one thing.

"The shorts have a pocket for my phone, and the compression pants prevent varicose veins." He bends down again to stretch his hamstrings, fingertips grazing the deck. Damn, he's flexible.

"You don't have varicose veins."

His expression morphs into an almost-smile. "Exactly."

He's being ridiculous. I look down at my lightweight chinos and black t-shirt, pretty certain that I'll be sweating through the fabric in an hour or less in the upstairs office with questionable air conditioning.

I'm still waiting for him to tell me why he was out here bothering me instead of doing his daily six miles around the vineyard when we both hear the distant crunch of gravel. Someone's car or truck has entered the property and is making its way into the visitor parking lot.

"You expecting someone?" I ask.

"Nope."

"Probably a new delivery driver." The new ones often turn into the visitor gate instead of continuing down the road to the service entrance.

Archer chuckles, shaking his head. "That, or Dash made good on his threat to hire you a nanny. Here she is, at the ass-crack of dawn, ready to take Fiona to school."

"That joke's getting fucking old." I've made it clear I'll be running on fumes before I trust anyone with my daughter. But I check the time. I need to wake Fiona at eight. She likes to get to school early to play four square and tetherball. Doesn't matter that the blacktop is hot as blazes in the wine country in early June. If there's a playground game afoot, my seven-year-old is there for it.

Still smirking, Archer takes off running after shedding the puffer, which he hangs on one of the Adirondack chairs where visitors will recline all day long. A glass of wine in hand, they'll stare at the view I have now and feel the sense of calm I'm chasing like a greyhound racing a mechanical rabbit I'll never catch.

Maybe someday, I will.

Our vineyard encompasses more than just acres of grapes and a tasting room. We have a casual café, a five-star restaurant, and a wine cave that stretches half a mile, filled with fermentation tanks. At the eastern corner sits an inn run by our middle sister, Beatrix, who also handles the restaurants. That leaves our youngest brother Dashiell to deal with the people side of the business— hiring, keeping employees happy with perks—and our youngest sister PJ, short for Penelope June, to manage all of our corporate media.

Beatrix is the most normal of all of us, dependable like a four-lane highway with clear signage and regular rest stops. It gives her an advantage because when the familial crazy starts flying, she's the one who can bring us back to earth. Every family needs a Beatrix.

Glancing in the direction Archer went, I momentarily wish I was into running. I'm on my road bike often enough, touring the neighboring estates, where vineyards roll over verdant hills and clapboard farmhouses dot the landscape like sheep.

It's research, checking out how our competitors' signage looks from the road, how inviting the vineyards look, beckoning in the distance. I take voice notes on my phone and photos that end up in bimonthly reports.

We have to be better. We have to be the best.

Most of the time, we are. But we've been losing money—a lot of money—and it's my job to figure out why. At the moment, I can't. And it's no use asking my father what the hell is going on. In the advanced stages of his dementia, he doesn't always give me logical answers.

In the distance, Archer runs between rows of sturdy grapevines, headed around a rather large pond replete with ducks and water lilies that have no business growing in the hot Napa sun.

When visitors tour the property, stay at our inn, dine at our restaurants, and taste different varietals of wine, they're treated to a suspended moment in time. They enter the gates of Buttercup Hill Vineyards, and worries are replaced by lazy afternoons sipping wine. Seasons become unimportant because flowers are always in bloom. It's been the mandate since my father took over from his dad, and my four siblings and I need to keep things going exactly as they've always been.

Without realizing it, I've drained my coffee. The sun has tipped up above the horizon, its searing beam now searching for my eyes as I stare east from the back porch.

And there's that car again, its wheels grinding in the gravel as though it's left and arrived for a second time. I suppose it's possible something's afoul with our signage in front, so drivers will be heading for the front gates all day long unless I fix it.

The two-story farmhouse shades half of the driveway from the sun, but it's no delivery truck.

This car is like a ladybug on wheels, candy apple red and sitting in the middle of the sandy gravel, dust still swirling like it backed up fast and hit the brakes hard. The driver's side window is open, which is why I notice her hair first. Even in the shade, it's a wild, fierce, copper-colored waterfall.

Walking down the steps to the gravel, I'm nearly knocked back by the equally piercing shade of green in her eyes. Her hair looks casually windswept, like the cover of a historical romance (My sisters are readers. I pay attention), and her eyes speak a language I know well. I've glared at my share of morons the same way she's glaring at me. I haven't the slightest idea what I've done wrong, but I can see I'm about four seconds from finding out.

The door unlatches and swings open with force. One tanned, yoga-sculpted leg kicks out, and a Birkenstock-clad foot hits the ground. The other leg follows, and I find myself looking down on a petite, frustrated woman in white cutoff shorts and an oversized purple top that falls off one shoulder.

She has a tiny purse, which she grips like a weapon. For all I know, she has a gun in there, so I'm not about to make any false moves, not when she parts her pink pillowy lips and lets out a long, frustrated exhale.

This is no delivery driver, at least not one like I've ever seen before. I really hope she's lost because I dislike the next, far-worse scenario that occurs to me—Dashiell has taken it upon himself to hire me a nanny.

# CHAPTER
## *Two*

RUBY

I can't believe I wasted a shower on this.

People are unreliable. And by 'people,' I mean 'men.' Kind, well-meaning, often incredibly handsome, and sometimes great in bed. But unreliable all the same.

Take my last boyfriend, who said he supported my career ambitions until it became inconvenient to see me only every other weekend. I didn't spend a month after our breakup playing Taylor Swift's "Red" album at top volume, only to be blown off in a different way by a different man now.

That's my primary thought as I put my car in reverse at Buttercup Hill Vineyards, where I came to interview with the no-show Dashiell Corbett. It's only my dream job he's torpedoing. No big deal.

I back up in an arc, put it in drive, and get ready to barrel down the road when I notice a man standing next to my car with his arms crossed.

At first, I think he must be a security guard simply because of his muscular build and irritable expression. Probably ready to yell at me for the noise or harass me for trespassing. I fling open the car door and step out, ready to tell him to back down.

"Sorry, we're closed." He flicks a hand like I'm a bug he can dismiss.

Nope. That's not gonna work for me. Not when I drove an hour.

If he's not a security guard, maybe he's Dashiell himself, finally rolling up. But he might as well be the devil incarnate because the stark line of his jaw and the carved chest muscles under his tight tee make me want to do things that will send me straight to hell. With zero apologies.

He's hotter than the midday sun in Napa Valley, which is saying something. I've seen people wilt from heat stroke in less brutal conditions. And this man could induce a fainting spell with the heat of his eyes alone.

Shaking that thought from my brain, I'm glad the mess of my wind-blown hair obscures what is, no doubt, a blush creeping across my cheeks. My pale, red-headed complexion is my nemesis when it comes to hiding emotions.

"Hi," I say as I push my door closed and step closer to him on the gravel drive. I'll just pretend he didn't try to flick me away.

Stretching to my full height, I'm still easily a foot shorter than the man in front of me, who keeps several feet between us like a showdown. He's creating his own shade, shielding me from what spare sunlight creeps around the house.

"Morning," he lobs back, his voice harsh and low.

"Hi," I repeat. "I'm Ruby." I want to roll my eyes at myself for stating the obvious. Of course he knows who I am. Who else would be standing out here to greet me other than the man who emailed me for an early morning interview?

He nods, eyes stony with resignation, as though he's not happy to see me. Well, that squares with an interviewer who's a half hour late and unapologetic about it. *Nice to meet you too.*

"Okay." He seems impatient, annoyed, like he's seen a few too many women of my type for his liking. Problem is I don't know what type that is, but I suspect he thinks I'm not serious about the job, and I'm desperate to set him straight. Yes, I'm still in the clothes I slept in, but that's a whole other story—I was kind of hoping he wouldn't notice. And I'm here because he asked me to come at six in the morning—early for some people, but I appreciated that he took into account the Bay Area traffic and my hour-plus commute. So why isn't he friendlier?

"Someone short-sheet your bed or something?"

He shrugs, hands deep in his pockets. "I don't even know what that means."

Suddenly, his beautiful exterior fades slightly in the sunlight. It irritates me when I can't stop my eyes from wandering south to where I can count every one of his abs through his black tee.

Straightening my top so it covers both shoulders, I try to present him with my most confident smile, while fearing that I look more like a predatory loon. The wide neck of my shirt immediately betrays me and slips, now exposing the other shoulder.

Clenching my hands into fists, I tell myself to leave it alone and keep smiling through the uncomfortable moment, which I'm making more uncomfortable by grinning at his grim face for no discernable reason. I see a flicker of amusement pass over his features, but mostly he's just staring at me.

It's fine. People are weird. I've long since accepted that.

"It was nice of you to come out, but I don't need a nanny. Sorry to waste your time." He takes a step backward.

"What?"

"Did you not hear me?" He cups a hand around one ear.

"I did. And thanks, but I have no interest in being your nanny."

His mouth tugs down. Sure. He's one of those guys who's fine telling me to take a hike, but when I turn around and reject his non-offer, he's suddenly offended. Well, too damn bad.

"Well, good. Then we're in agreement." His quieter tone lacks conviction.

I take a look around the place as my heart sinks. Because I'm clearly not getting the job I came for, and I really like what I've seen so far here.

Driving along the quiet wine roads earlier, something felt different. When I approached Buttercup Hill Vineyards, the very air around the property was different, lighter, more fragrant. I could barely see a thing in the dim early morning light, but as the sun rose, I felt an unfamiliar joy of anticipation. Like my senses knew this place could change my life.

As soon as I turned off the main road and onto the lane with the hammered tin archway spelling out Buttercup Hill Vineyards in gleaning letters, I felt like I wanted to stay here forever.

But that was before I stood before with what appears to be a surly lumberjack winemaker.

If this job prospect is a bust, I'll be zero for three this week. The first one looked promising. The ad made the job sound like I'd be helping the wine buyer at a restaurant, but it turned out to be a bartending job. Where I'd wear a revealing sailor's uniform and a hat.

The second job was more like online dating gone very, very wrong. The manager at a large wine company spent a week sending me flirty texts before agreeing to meet. When we did, he asked questions about how I liked to spend my time outside of work. Because it was a wine-related job, I reasoned, maybe he needed to know that I had an active social life.

But when he asked me about my simple pleasures and my self-care routine, alarm bells began sounding. When he asked me to play "would you rather," I got the heck out of there.

So this job needs to come through. Third time's the charm and all that.

Plus…I can't stop fangirling over every inch of my surroundings. Even though I've only seen a gravel road and the front gates of the place, there's something magical about the way it feels. It's why I cracked my windows open even though my car has perfectly good air conditioning. I wanted to see and smell and feel everything as I drove along.

The grand oak trees soar up on both sides of the gravel drive, their leaves providing shade no matter where the sun is. That must be what I'm smelling, a syrupy, sweet, woodsy smell I remember from going to camp as a kid.

The air in Napa is just different. Dry, fragrant, earthy. If happiness had a smell, it would be this place. If charm had a definition, it would be the white-painted clapboard farmhouse, which only bears resemblance to an actual farmhouse in its style because normal farmhouses aren't this large. Even from the small glimpse I have, I can tell the place is massive, two stories with green shuttered windows and a front porch big enough to hold an eleven-piece band.

To say nothing of the vineyards, which I know stretch for acres in all directions. I saw row upon row of grapevines dotted with perfect hanging bunches of grapes before turning into the driveway. The leaves fluttered in a light breeze that blew through my open window, bringing with it a new kaleidoscope of smells—freshly watered, mineral-rich soil, a faint scent of ripening grapes, the warring floral notes from lavender and star jasmine along with other varieties of heat-tolerant blooms.

Olive trees flank the front of the house, with more lavender growing beneath them, giving the place a Mediterranean vibe beneath the wine country sun. The crunch of the gravel beneath my tires. A creek lazing down from a nearby hill. No detail left to chance. The place is perfect.

Except for the man standing here with his arms crossed and a look of disdain on his pretty face. I try to ignore the way his roped forearms flex as he drums his fingers on his bicep, which swells under the fabric of a worn t-shirt.

He's tall, well over six feet, and his looming presence is giving me pause, not to mention the suspicious look on his face as lines crease his forehead and his lips press together like he doesn't trust himself to say the right thing. It would be charming if it wasn't me he was glaring at.

It's not that I need a welcome wagon, but this guy looks like he's about to tell me to turn my car around and get off his property. I wouldn't be surprised if he has a pitchfork stowed somewhere on that porch that he uses to frighten off strangers.

Only I'm not a stranger. I'm here for a reason. If his muscled forearms would stop distracting me, I'd tell him as much.

Instead, he points toward the exit with a thumb. "We open to the public at nine."

Despite my better instincts, I move toward him, my body overriding my brain. I take another step, now close enough that I can feel his coiled, restrained energy. Close enough to see a line of gray rimming his pale blue eyes. Little hints of salt sprinkled through his dark, tousled hair. Tiny creases at the corners of his eyes, either from glaring or smiling—hard to be sure.

He just told me to leave, but every fiber of my being is urging me closer to this farmhouse, closer to a dream job that isn't even on the table. I don't care.

He misunderstood, probably because I'm dressed for day drinking or touring the vineyards. That's a whole other story, and I'm kind of hoping he'll ignore my clothes if I do.

"No, no, I'm here for the other job. I was here at six sharp, like you said."

"Like I said?" He rubs a hand through his hair, pushing it away from his arrestingly attractive face before rogue pieces fall over his forehead like a stylist arranged them. "Nah. Wrong guy."

His stony stare is unnerving and a little rude, but I hold my ground, staring back.

"Aren't you Dashiell?"

"Nope." I expect him to elaborate, but he doesn't.

*O-kay…*

Finally, he seems to pull himself out of whatever trance has taken over, and he shakes his head. "I'm sorry…who are you?"

"I'm Ruby." We've been over this…

He says nothing.

"This is where you're supposed to extend your hand and say 'Nice to meet you' or something friendly that also sets proper work boundaries. And then you go and get Dashiell because I drove an hour to be here. Are you new to this?"

"New to what?"

"Peopling."

Now his lips quirk into a grin, and he begins nodding. "Oh, here we go."

I begin wondering if he's of sound mind. I know wine country people probably spend a lot of time in the sun, especially in the summer months. Maybe his brain is fried. Or he has a wine bottle shoved up his ass.

"Come on. You're not exactly a welcome wagon. That can't come as news."

He crosses his arms. "Sorry you drove all the way out."

"Sorry you're an unfriendly jerk." My hand goes to my mouth, but I fail at shoving the words back in. I watch as this man's eyes flicker in shock at my bold rudeness. I can see I've lost this job before I've even had a chance to interview for it.

Then I hear the low chuckle of laughter.

"You're laughing at me?"

He nods. "You better believe I am, Ginger. You come blazing up the lane to see my brother, whom you've clearly never met because if you had, you'd know I ain't him. Then you proceed to insult me."

He grins, and I tell myself not to notice how straight and white his teeth are. I tell myself to ignore the dimple that pops in his cheek beneath the layer of scruff that—dammit—looks way too good on him.

"That was an accident."

"I didn't hear an apology."

I blow out a slow breath. "I'm sorry." I wait for the cloud of doom to lift, but it doesn't. "Let's start over. I'm here, and I'd like my interview. And you are…?"

"Jackson," he grunts. "And I told you. There's no one here to interview you." He hefts a wine crate he seems to have just noticed, and my eyes rivet to the way his broad shoulders flex while he holds it against one hip. "Besides, I don't even know what job you're talking about. I don't do the hiring. That's my brother's job."

"Exactly. He's the one who made the appointment with me. So I assume he's here someplace, even if you're too stubborn to help me out. Is there a number I can call?"

Fishing my cellphone from the pocket in my purse, I start scanning through my emails in search of his brother's message to me with directions and the time and date of our meeting.

Sure enough, today is the day, and I have the time right. I hold it up for his brother to see, but either he has really excellent eyesight, or he's not interested in what the email says.

"You've got it wrong."

"I don't."

He's still holding the crate, and it's starting to make my arms hurt in empathy, so I find myself listing to the side as though he'll do the same and prop the crate against the wall. He doesn't. He also seems unbothered holding what is probably a dozen bottles of wine.

Instead, I'm the one who leans against the wall, letting it take my weight because, suddenly, I feel defeated. I'm going on four hours of sleep and wearing the wrong clothes for a job interview because I left my change of clothes behind. I ran out the door and hopped in my car, frazzled and in a hurry to make a good impression by arriving early. Only I forgot the very interview outfit I'd ironed and laid out on the bed.

This is what I've got, and it's not my best. In a matter of moments, this guy will pack me into my car and send me away from this lovely winery forever. My head bows in acceptance of the inevitable. I bite my lips to stem the surge of emotion from failing. Again.

Today will go down as just another in a long list of crappy episodes, and I'm almost too exhausted to fight, but I came all this way.

"I really need a win." I wince, admitting this uncomfortable secret. Not a great way to impress a potential employer. Then again, he might as well know he's dealing with a hot mess, so we avoid misconceptions later on.

"I'd like to help…" He reconsiders. "Sort of."

An uncomfortable laugh escapes me. "At least you're honest."

"I just mean that I'm not sure how much I really can help. So…" He looks in the direction of my car, and I know he's waiting for me to take his cue and leave.

But I can't. Not yet. This place is too beautiful. I want—no, I need—to try a little harder.

I can't tell if the grunt that emanates from him comes from strain at holding the box or frustration at me. He doesn't stand still long enough for me to tell, turning for the front door of the farmhouse, which appears to be the public entrance to the winery. I follow him because he hasn't told me not to.

The cool darkness spills out from the room in a rush of heavenly air that's so much more pleasant than the heat already sitting on Napa Valley. The fact that it's already hot at six in the morning should give me pause. Instead, it fuels my interest in being here even more.

I watch Jackson disappear into the dark space and fear that if I don't follow him, any chance at a job will close with the door he's about to slam in my face. So I creep in behind him and let my eyes adjust to the dim light coming through drawn blinds.

I start noticing shapes, a large desk in the center and a couch off to the side. When the lights flip on, I squint at the brightness and hold my hands up as though I've been caught stealing. Jackson scans the room as if trying to see if anything is out of place.

It would be hard to imagine him finding anything, what with the tan suede sofas that look butter-soft, the perfectly-weathered, rustic wooden coffee tables, and warm globe lights that bathe the room in a honey glow. And the plants…bunches of fragrant lavender surge from fat, glass urns, and potted olive trees frame the room. It's so homey I almost plunk myself down in the middle of a sofa when Jackson's watchful eye lands on me.

"If you could please let Dashiell know I'm waiting, I'll be out of your hair." I fist my hands in the hem of my shirt because my palms have begun to sweat, and the last thing I want is for my nerves to be obvious.

I shouldn't be nervous. Not around this guy who seems to be taking perverse pleasure in *not* helping me get to the man I'm supposed to see.

"He's asleep. It's not like he checks in with me after he comes back from a bar, but let's figure he got in late. That's why you aren't going to be meeting with him anytime soon."

"Oh. Well. That's a problem easily solved. Could you wake him, please, and let him know I'm here?"

He starts moving through the front door, so I turn on my heel and march after him. My shoes don't make much noise, which is probably why he doesn't realize I'm right behind when he whips around.

I don't have time to brace myself, but I turn my head at the last moment to avoid breaking my nose on his sternum. My cheek slams against his chest, and the hard planes of what is obviously a very well-maintained set of pecs and abs greet me like a granite rockface. His heartbeat at my ear. My hands gripping his shirt to keep from bouncing back.

His attitude may be cool, but his body is all warmth. The scent of citrus and pine hits my senses, and I inhale a little deeper.

His eyes go wide, and he takes a step back. Only then do I raise my hands between us in surrender. "Sorry. I thought you meant to follow you."

"You operate under a lot of thoughts and assumptions."

"Well, one of us does." Cant. Stop. Mouth. It will be the death of me.

"Does what?"

"You just made a thought or assumption about me. Pot or kettle, your pick, Jackson."

Shaking his head, he scrubs a hand over his face. "People call me Jax, and I highly doubt Dash meant for you to be here now."

"Really? Does your brother go around making appointments without meaning to? If so, I'd suggest medical attention, though it's not really my business. Let's err on the side of him intending to meet with me."

"Dash isn't a morning person, meaning he rarely shows up anywhere before nine. So I know for a fact he wouldn't schedule a meeting with you at six in the morning."

I can feel the corner of my lips twitch, and my eyes blink faster than they need. I'm not going to cry because some dude is too lame to wake up at a normal hour.

But I can see I won't be getting my interview.

"Oh." It's the best I can come up with as my ego deflates.

"Unless he was messing with you. Did you do something to piss him off?" Now he's smiling as though he has some idea of what that might be. Like maybe his brother asked me out and I turned him down, or something stupidly dude-like.

I glare at Jackson like *he* might be the one in need of medical attention.

"Well, considering I've never met him, I find it hard to imagine how, but I suppose anything's possible."

Without asking, Jackson takes the phone from my hand and glares at the screen. After a second, he hands the phone back, shaking his head. "He's meeting you at six in the evening. Guaranteed."

"What makes you say that?" I ask, looking at my phone where there's no "pm" after the six in question.

"Because no normal person schedules an interview at six in the morning. Especially my brother. And the fact that you showed up here ready to roll at the crack of dawn tells me a thing or two about you."

Great. I don't need to ask what it tells him, but I'm a glutton for punishment, so I do anyway. "What, that I'm abnormal?"

When Jackson doesn't say anything, his expression stony, I

nod and drop my eyes to the floor in defeat. This is what I get for wanting something, for going after it, and for feeling hopeful for the first time in a long time.

My stomach is tangled in knots of disappointment and resignation, so I turn for the door. Walking back to my car, I tell myself I don't care about his assessment of me. But just as my trembling hand reaches to open my car, Jackson's voice startles me.

"No. It tells me you're exactly the kind of person we ought to be hiring," he calls after me, striding slowly in my direction. "Stay. Talk to me."

I don't reply. Inside, unicorns are leaping over rainbows in my heart, but I won't give him the satisfaction of showing my excitement. So I do my best to play it cool.

# CHAPTER
## *Three*

JAX

Squinting at me, she tilts her head. A few strands of hair drop down in front of her eyes, and she exhales hard, blowing them off her face before they settle in exactly the same spot. My hands itch to wrap them around a finger and move them away, but I don't move.

"You don't even know me. Why do you suddenly want me to stay?"

It's a fair question, one I don't have an answer to. I don't really have a plan, which is unlike me, but something is telling me not to let her leave, so my brain scrambles to concoct a reason to keep her here.

"I'll interview you. For the job."

I shouldn't find an eye-roll charming, especially when it's accompanied by a scowl and what I'm pretty sure are muttered obscenities. But I do.

"Five minutes ago, you didn't even know there was a job to interview for. Now you want to be my boss?"

Cue exploding brain as I try to restrain myself from telling her all the ways I'd love to boss her around. Swallowing hard, I manage a nod.

"You strike me as someone who could use a little bossing." Now I'm adding sexual harassment to a job description I know nothing about.

Her eyes widen and flash at my comment, and I prepare myself for the feminist schooling that I absolutely deserve. And yet, I'd bait her over and over again just to watch what it does to her eyes.

She surprises me by laughing. Her head tips back, and she closes her eyes, which is sad because they're so damn pretty, but the look of pure joy on her face is a nice substitute, even if I have no idea why she's laughing. Or if she's doing it at my expense.

Opening her eyes, she fixes me with a new stare, but she looks more relaxed than she did a moment ago. Then she shakes her head. "That makes no sense."

At first, I think she means my innuendo, but she waves a hand and explains, the other hand reaching for her car door. "You do not want me to work for you."

"Why not?" I mean, she's right. I don't need anyone new working for me—in fact, complications of any sort will only slow down the hellish process of trying to get our business on track. I should send her along in her ladybug car and take a second cup of coffee to my office, where I belong, but I'm drawn to her.

"Why *not*?" She looks incredulous, eyes opening even wider before they scan the landscape around us. Almost like she can't help looking. And that's something I do understand.

That one small unintentional movement makes me like her even more. It's what makes me think, yet again, that she should work for us in some capacity.

People like her, who understand on a gut level what makes this place special, are the kind we need. We're not going to survive on wan smiles and so-so chardonnay. We need a passion that bleeds through every gesture, every conversation, every wine tour, and at home, where people drink our wine. If passion is going to intrude on a person's home life, it had better be worth every rude penny.

But I can't tell her I'm reading all of that into her glance. Even if I know in my bones that I'm right.

"Yes. You said you're here for a job interview, and now you're disqualifying yourself from working here?"

She huffs a laugh. "I was disqualifying myself from working for *you*."

I'm not even offended. Just curious. "Why?"

"I don't want a pity job because you feel bad that I'm too dumb to know that six o'clock means evening."

"I don't think you're dumb. I appreciate your go-get-'em attitude. It was a compliment. What job are you interviewing for, anyway?"

"Tasting room assistant." She mutters her answer like it doesn't matter, slides into the car, and drops her left foot onto the clutch. I shouldn't be so turned on that she knows how to drive a stick shift, but I fucking am.

I step into her space for reasons I don't exactly understand and make it impossible to shut the car door, gripping the lightweight frame. "I don't hand out pity jobs."

I don't hand out jobs, period. I'm not in charge of what my younger brother calls the "human capital" of the business for a very good reason. According to him and an array of others, "I make people *not* want to work for us."

Aside from that bullshit assessment, I know I should send her along and have her return at six in the evening, and yet…I don't want my younger brother anywhere near her. I'd be hard-pressed to come up with an attractive woman who hasn't fallen for his tattoos, messy hair, and bedroom eyes—but in this case, an irrational part of me wants to keep this woman for myself.

And I have no idea what job she's applying for or what she's even qualified to do. "What are your job qualifications?"

"You can't be serious." For emphasis, she turns the key in the ignition, and the car sputters to life. I feel the hum of the motor under my hand, which still grips the doorframe.

"Ruby, turn off the motor and come have a cup of coffee with me."

I'm done messing around with a cat-and-mouse game I don't understand. I hold out my hand. "What?" she asks.

"Hand me your keys."

"I'm not giving you my car keys."

"So. Fucking. Difficult," I mutter, and it earns me a smile. With an overly strong motion, she turns off the motor and drops her keys into my hand.

I notice a crystal-studded Eiffel Tower hanging from the keychain and tuck that bit of information away. She likes Paris? She's been to Paris? Someone she knows brought her a keychain? This isn't her car or set of keys?

I'm grasping at anything to know more about her, and I can't fathom why it matters to me.

After shoving the keys into my pocket, I present her again with my hand. At first, she looks confused, but then she gingerly puts her hand in mine, and I help her out of the car. She gives the door a swift bump with her backside, and it slams shut. This woman…

Leading her back toward the entrance to the farmhouse, I launch into tour-speak, the throwaway two-minute introduction to the family winery that I know by heart. My father had all of us work as unpaid tour guides in our teenage years.

I think it was his way of indoctrinating us into the culture of the place he'd spent his entire life building while getting some free labor. Sounds like my father. For a moment, my mind drifts back to how he was in those days—before he became an overbearing tycoon who suffered no fools. And before the more recent days when those very qualities I hated began fading from sight, making me yearn for them just a little bit.

But I don't tell Ruby any of this. Instead, I lead her back

through the reception area, where guests queue up for tours and wine tasting.

"My grandfather founded the vineyard using a strain of grapes from a region in France where *his* grandfather grew up and farmed his family's land for his entire life. There's still a small winery in the Loire Valley run by a distant cousin," I tell her, leading us up the stairs where guests aren't allowed.

At the top, a wide landing yields to hallways leading in three directions.

We follow the middle route, lit by skylights running the length of the building and taking us past windows that look out over the vineyards. The creeping vines fan out in neat rows as the yellow morning light dances on the pale edges of twisting leaves.

When we reach the doorway of my office, I point to a grey velvet button-tufted couch I never would have picked if anyone had consulted me about décor. Which is probably why no one consulted me.

I make the mistake of looking at my computer before we begin talking. "Dammit." The outburst comes before I can restrain it.

"Everything okay?"

"Yeah. Just financial stuff. Numbers in the wrong columns?"

She laughs. "You mean losses instead of gains?"

"Something like that." Exactly like that, but I shouldn't be telling that to a complete stranger.

"Sounds stressful."

"You have no idea, Ginger." I shut my laptop. If I can't see the red ink right in front of me, maybe I'll stop sharing my business problems.

Ruby perches on the edge of the cushion, knees together. Glancing at her bare legs, I wonder why she chose to wear shorts to a job interview. Then again, she thought it was logical to show up at six in the morning, so I roll with it.

"Let me see your resume." I swallow a yawn that's a direct result of not finishing my coffee and sit behind my desk.

"I didn't bring it. Dashiell has a copy."

"Dash isn't here."

She gives me a look that reminds me of Fiona, who, at age seven, has already mastered a withering stare capable of melting steel. "I can see that. So, what? Do you want me to recite my career milestones for you?" She stands up and stretches as though getting ready for a thespian throwdown. "Would you like it to rhyme?"

Her ballsy sass would have no place in a normal interview, but I like it. I'm so used to people meekly saying yes to me and cowering under my glare. She doesn't give a shit about any of it, and I find it refreshing. If completely confounding.

"Sure. In iambic pentameter." My sarcasm flies unchecked because I know she can handle it.

"Are you always such a grump? Are you this way around your kid?"

"How'd you know I have a kid?"

Another withering look. "You thought I wanted to be your nanny, remember?"

"Right. As to your other questions, yes to the first, no to the second. I'm a very good dad." I don't know why it feels important that she believes me, but it does.

Her look has turned to skepticism. "Okay. Let's not get off-topic. What incisive interview questions do you have for me?"

"Tell me about yourself. What qualifications do you have for the job you want?"

"That's two questions."

"Never said it wasn't."

Nodding slowly, she seems to be assessing whether she likes my questions well enough to answer them.

"I don't want the job."

She's either nuttier than a Christmas cake, or no one's told her this isn't the way to ace a job interview.

"Sorry?"

"Working in the tasting room is not the job I want, but it's a job I'm willing to do. Mainly because I've dotted my last "i" and crossed my last "t" as a receptionist in corporate America while taking online classes at San Francisco Wine School to become a sommelier. I studied everything I could, but the only real way to learn is by apprenticing and working with wine in person."

Stretching my legs under my desk, I school my expression so she doesn't see that she's surprised me with her directness. But I can be direct, too, and this interview is over.

"You're overqualified, and in my experience, that never bodes well for an employer or an employee. You'll get frustrated, and that'll make me frustrated."

She huffs. "I get the feeling that's your natural state. Besides, I won't be working for you."

"Indirectly, you will be. I handle the business side, and employees are my business."

"Then you should know I'm an excellent employee. I have a plan. Pay my dues in a tasting room, work my way up to sommelier, run my blog, and make my own wine." She pauses and seems to weigh her words. "I mean, I'm already doing that, but whatever," she mutters dismissively."

"What?"

"Nothing."

"You just said you make your own wine. Is that true?"

She shrugs. "Yeah. Closet winemaker. Literally." She points to herself.

"What's that mean?"

Pressing her lips together, she assesses me, maybe wondering how dumb I really am. "It means I make wine in my closet. I pressed a batch of grapes last night and strained out the juices. But this morning, I checked the hydrometer that sits in one of my fermentation containers to see if the sugar levels looked right."

"And if they don't?"

"I run the risk of making vinegar instead of wine. But you know this, being a vintner, of course." She side-eyes me as if making sure I'm not a wine impostor.

I'm still stuck on the last three things she said. "You make your own wine," I say, ensuring I heard her right.

"Yup. Science nerd here. Making my own wine. Don't judge."

I shake my head in disbelief. But I'm riveted. "And how was it?"

"What?"

"The sugar level."

"Just below one, which meant I needed to add a little extra sugar. The grapes I chose were risky because they're a more sour variety, but I'm experimenting. That's the whole point."

"You just dump in some sugar, and you get wine?" I know a lot more about wine than I'm making it seem, but I want to know her methods.

"Not exactly. I dissolved granulated sugar in warm water and added it little by little until it seemed right. I may have rushed the process because I needed to get out the door and on the road. Which is why…" she says, looking down at her lap, "I forgot to bring my change of clothes for the actual interview. These are what I slept in."

I should be a better guy and not look right at her chest, where it's now quite apparent she isn't wearing a bra, and at her slim legs, which I've been staring at since she got here.

Either she doesn't notice my salacious look or she's used to it because she keeps talking.

"Anyhow, I figured I could explain all that to your brother and tell him about my other experience, so hopefully, I'd get the tasting room job I want."

"Bad idea," I tell her.

"Excuse me?"

"Just a dose of radical honestly. Why would you want to spend your day being a glorified bartender?"

The air leaves her lungs like I've slugged her. "I hardly think of it that way."

I tip back in my chair, fanning my hands out to show her I'm being reasonable. "Pouring wine for people all day? Polishing glassware? Seems like bartending to me."

Just then, the sun moves high enough to cast a beautiful pinkish-orange hue over the room, and we both follow the light, which paints the oaks gold. We gaze in silence at the magnificent trees.

Warm light hits her face, making her cheeks glow a rosy pink. I didn't think a woman could be more beautiful, and she's shattered that fallacy without even trying.

I'm about to give her a list of reasons why she's wrong for the job when my phone rings. My dad's nurse tells me he's awake and lucid. Better than he has been in weeks. And he's asking for me.

It's been getting harder and harder to see him. Every visit feels like he's slipping away a bit more, sometimes not knowing my name or who we are to each other. Who we were.

The lucid days sometimes feel hardest because they dangle a filament of hope, only to snatch it away in the next minute, the next visit. I keep losing him over and over again.

And now, if he's asking for me, it's because he wants to talk about the business, which I should take as a sign he's feeling okay. He never was one for chitchat.

If he's having a good day, I need to get there right now.

Job interview over.

# CHAPTER
*Four*

JAX

"I come bearing pastries." My sister Beatrix stands in the foyer of the family house holding a bag of almond croissants. Her gray-blue eyes are alert, like she's been up for hours, but I know better. She smiles to cover a yawn. Dark brown hair swept into a sleek ponytail, which brushes her shoulders and always makes her look ready to tackle something.

I know she has croissants in the bag because she always brings them from Sweet Butter, the café that's on everybody's way between home and work.

And she knows I like them.

"You thought I needed a chaperone?" I roll my eyes. I can smell the buttery pastries from here.

"I thought we should listen to the doctor."

"I'm not sure how it helps to have two of us lobbing questions at him when he's already confused."

We ascend the grand spiral staircase to the second floor and walk toward the wing where my dad has been spending all of his time lately.

I reach for the pastry bag, but Beatrix holds it away in order to make some sort of point. "Oh, I didn't realize you got your medical degree. Was that at www.quack.com?"

Apparently, there's no use arguing with the doctor or my sister. I understand that two people will remember interactions with our dad differently, which might be fun info for a doctor to mull—I'm just not sure how it helps my dad. "Whatever. You can come."

"Oh, thank you, kind sir," She gives me a sarcastic curtsey and hands me the pastry bag.

Unrolling it, I inhale the scent of almond paste and powdered sugar. This day has not gone according to plan in so many ways already that it's not going to kill me to eat a pastry. Or two. I bring the croissant up to my nose and take a bigger whiff before biting through the flaky layers.

"You have powdered sugar on your nose." Without looking, I know Beatrix is rolling her eyes.

"Stop doing that. Fiona's started rolling her eyes at me, and she probably learned it from you." Thinking back to Ruby, I decide I must be a magnet for eye-rolling females.

My sister waves a hand dismissively and sips from a paper coffee cup. "Hardly. Girls are born knowing how to do that. All you did was give her a reason. Something guys are born knowing how to do."

I'm not about to start debating gender studies after putting my foot in my mouth once already this morning. Which brings my thoughts back to Ruby. I wonder if she'll really come back and talk to my brother or if I've sufficiently scared her off from working here with my perma-scowl and bark.

I let my thoughts linger on the image of her lean legs crossed at the knee and how carefree she looked when she laughed. I kind of hope she comes back.

"Why are you here?" My dad's voice bellows across the bedroom when Beatrix and I appear in his doorway.

Even diminished by the onset of Alzheimer's, he's a large,

intimidating man with sharp blue eyes that look confused more and more of the time. I notice that his full head of salt-and-pepper hair is longer than usual, and his perpetually clean-shaven face has a couple weeks of growth on it.

It's why my siblings and I have the sole interaction with him when it comes to all business aspects of the winery. When his dementia advanced to Alzheimer's two months ago, he was deemed "non-compos mentis"—not legally responsible for the things he says or does. That's when my siblings and I were awarded power of attorney to make all decisions for him and the business.

"Good morning to you, too." Beatrix smiles at his gruffness because it's a sign he's having a good day. When he's uncharacteristically kind, it generally means he doesn't know who he's talking to and is remembering the early days when he and our mom were still married.

"Hey, Dad."

"To what do I owe the honor?" Dad sits up straighter at the large work table in the middle of his bedroom. The four-poster bed has already been made, and his nurse hovers in the corner of the room, failing to make herself as invisible as I'd prefer.

As he eagerly awaits the answer to why we've come, my heart deflates. He asked for me, and if he's already forgotten why, I may have lost my window of lucidity.

His deep chuckle startles me. "I'm kidding, Jackson. Let's get down to it. There's going to be another big financial hit on next quarter's books, so I need you to prepare."

My heart, buoyed by my dad's clear mental state, clenches even harder at the financial news. I glance at the nurse, making sure she looks capable of handling a heart attack because I may have one.

"What do you mean? We already did that *this* quarter." Maybe he's confused. Maybe he forgot.

My dad nods. "I know. And you handled it, so I know you'll handle it again."

I get a side-eye from Beatrix because I only sort of handled it, and she doesn't know the details. I'm still working out what to tell shareholders. And I sure as hell won't know what to tell them next quarter to keep our stock from tanking.

"Dad, I need some details. Why are we taking these losses? Nothing's changed in our business model."

He examines his hands before tucking them behind his head and tipping back in his chair. The nurse sprints over to him, and he casts her a look of disdain. "I'm not falling over." He rights the chair and levels me with his blue eyes.

"I don't want to get into that today," he says.

"Dad, I think we have to."

He looks down at the newspaper on his desk. "I've been at this a long time. Just do what I'm asking."

The family-owned winery was started by our grandfather, who barely had four pennies to rub together. He was a seasonal worker for over a decade at vineyards that abutted his blue-collar suburb and saved every dollar until he could afford to buy a half acre of his own land.

The story is posted on a gold-lettered wooden plaque in the visitors' sitting area of the tasting room, but most people have heard the story before they ever come in the door—how our grandfather talked one of the vineyard owners he worked for into selling him the tiny plot, how he talked a French relative into sharing a cutting from a heritage grape varietal not found in California.

And then the rest—how our father took a small boutique winery that only a few people cared about and built it into a behe-moth with hundreds of employees onsite. How he grew it into a massive retailer of wine to every major grocery chain in the coun-try. A lot of people have things to say about him selling out, but he never gave a damn, and by now, the operation is far too big to put any horses back in any barns.

My siblings and I are charged with keeping his legacy alive and profitable while he withers outside of the public eye. In fact, his Alzheimer's diagnosis has been kept under wraps for the better part of a year, thanks to our youngest sister, PJ.

"Dad, I need information, or I can't do my job." I take a step closer, hoping there's something visible on the desk that will explain things. There's only yesterday's New York Times and a stack of other unread papers.

"See? That's going to be a problem." His blue eyes slice through me like lasers.

"What?"

"You're off your game. Find an assistant to handle the other distractions in your life, for the love of God. Work comes first."

This again. By "distraction," I know he's talking about Fiona. My siblings and I were raised by nannies so we wouldn't be similar distractions to him, and I don't want that for my daughter. Once I get Fiona up and off to school, I'll drink a gallon of coffee and make up for the missed hours of work.

"I don't need help. We're managing just fine."

"You're coming apart at the seams. Have you looked in a mirror lately? You look like shit—haggard and mopey."

I nearly choke on the air entering my lungs. My father may have made a near-fatal error when it comes to our winery's finances, but his chief concern is how I look. I take it as a sign that he's doing okay, all things considered. Maybe he has more of his faculties than it seems.

"I'm fine, Dad. What would really help me is for you to stop telling me to expect new losses every quarter."

He shrugs. "Cabernet harvest didn't yield what we thought. It costs money to fix these things. It's the business."

But it's not. It was never the way our business ran, and it doesn't make sense now. We grow all the cabernet grapes we need, we care for the vines, we pick, we make wine. It's been the same for decades—a profit machine led by the strength of our vines.

Beatrix nudges me and tips her head ever so slightly toward Dad. I see what she's noticing. His gaze has left me and now hovers somewhere over my shoulder. He stares at a family portrait, the last one of him and my mom with all five kids before they got divorced. It seems to calm him when he's struggling to remember things, even though they haven't been married for over fifteen years.

I'm probably fifteen years old in the portrait, and all of us kids are smiling like we're suffering in the matching suits and blue dresses our parents made us wear. We had no idea our parents' separation was in the works or that our mom would end up moving back to Chicago and leaving us in the care of a rotating brigade of nannies.

When he focuses on me again, a bit of the fire in his eyes has dimmed. He points a long finger at me. "The hamster in there is running himself fucking ragged. You're either going to burn out or make a mistake with numbers, and I don't want to see the hell storm that follows either one of those." He flicks his fingers in the direction of my skull.

"I'm good."

"Not what I hear from your older brother."

I feel my blood pressure ratchet up, and Beatrix takes a step closer, putting her hand on my shoulder. "Let it go."

Our dad doesn't always remember who said what. Mostly, we don't badmouth each other, but meddling is in our blood, according to our mother, a midwestern, no-nonsense woman whose mother was a professional matchmaker.

As such, Grandma had strong feelings about our father and apparently warned our mother to stay as far away from him as possible. "He'll be a cheater, that one." That only encouraged the twenty-one-year-old rebel I only caught glimpses of on occasion. Most of the time, our mother was too weighed down by the responsibilities of heading a household, and eventually, when my dad proved our Grandma right, our mother left.

"Just handle it," my dad says, lifting a sip of coffee to his mouth. He puts it down with too much force, and it spills into the saucer, unleashing a string of curses and ends in a coughing fit.

The nurse comes over and picks up his water glass. He ignores her until he's finished coughing. Then he snarls, "I can pick up my own damn water glass."

He chooses a different newspaper, the pink pages of the Financial Times. When he moves his coffee cup aside and starts to read, Beatrix and I take our cue to leave.

Dad never says goodbye. He hates wasted words.

# CHAPTER
*Five*

RUBY

Twenty minutes after Jackson disappears with barely a goodbye, I find myself still standing in front of the winery, unable to bring myself to leave.

If I really want the job Jackson tried to convince me I'd hate during our fake interview, I need to come back at six and talk to his brother. It kind of chaps my hide that he knows I drove here, and he won't do anything to help me out, as in wake his damn brother up and make him interview me now.

I understand how business works, however, and I'm not such a prima donna that I expect people to drop everything for a woman who appears unable to tell time. But he could have at least tried.

On the far side of the farmhouse, I hear the rumble of car motors, which means people are arriving to work. I move slowly, wanting to take in the sights and sounds of the winery this morning as the place wakes up and purrs to life. It feels like an insider view that could possibly help me later in my real interview. The more feeling I have for the rhythm of the place, the better I'll be at fitting in here.

I linger a bit longer, figuring eventually, Jackson or someone else will come out and tell me to move along. But no one does.

A few minutes later, I grow even more bold and walk a few paces down the drive to study the tall oaks I've been admiring from afar. The trunks are so large up close that it would take three of me with linked arms to encircle one of them. I stare at the leaves, perfect like paper cutouts, curling at the edges.

It's already coming up on eighty degrees, but I don't mind the dry heat. I can understand why grapevines dig into the sandy soil and grow here.

*So now you're a plant? You are losing it.*

I follow the curve in the drive around the hedge of rosemary and notice the entry point in the maze of plants. Walking the curving gravel path, I inhale the flowering rosemary and lavender planted in planters at the center of the maze, where water in a tall urn fountain burbles at the top.

I should go. There's a fine line between fangirling a potential place of business and creeping around like a lunatic. I probably already crossed that line when I debated hugging an oak, but we can't all be perfect, can we?

Eyeing my little red car, I make a beeline. Before I can open the door, I hear crunching on the gravel behind me and a shy voice.

"Hi."

Turning, I see a tow-headed girl in a knee-length hot pink tee standing barefoot on the drive.

"Hi," I respond, glancing behind her and to the side to see who's with her. Maybe a family drove up like me, intending to beat the traffic, and their daughter slept in the backseat. Now, she's awake and ready for an adventure in the hedge maze.

But as far as I can tell, we're the only two out here.

"Is that your car?" Her breathless question comes with wide eyes as her small finger points.

"Yes, it is. Do you like it?"

Nodding enthusiastically, she skips over to take a closer look. "It's like Luigi from *Cars*."

I laugh. Having seen the movie years ago, I recall the little blue Fiat with his Italian accented sass. "It *is* like Luigi. Is he your favorite?"

Another enthusiastic nod. "He's funny. So is his friend Guido."

That movie is nearly two decades old, so someone made an effort to show it to her. As a woman raised with very few racecars and girl power in my life, I appreciate it. And given the conversation an hour ago with Jackson about a nanny, I wonder if he's her dad.

Casting another glance around, I figure I'll see him or some other parent finally catching up to the little sprite, but other than birds, we're alone.

"Do you need help finding your parents?"

Her head tips back as she laughs like I've just said the most ridiculous thing. She twirls, and her shirt flares around her hips, catching the light like a blooming flower. "Could you really *do* that?" She makes it sound like I'd be revealing secrets behind a magic act. Producing the assistant who disappeared inside a box.

"Maybe. I could try."

She shakes her head, which sends her messy blond locks scattering into her eyes. "People already tried."

"What people?"

"My dad, mostly. He tried really hard. But if a person doesn't want to be found, it's pretty hard to find her." She taps a finger against her lips like she understands the profundity of her words. I'm taken aback by her adult-level insight, and I wonder again if Jackson is her dad. Might explain a few things about his stoic demeanor if people have disappointed him in the past. It makes me want to cut him some slack, even though he tried to burst my wine-country bubble earlier.

"Is Jackson your dad?"

Nodding, she treats me to an adorable jack-o-lantern smile. She has gaps between all four of her front teeth, like each one is free to roam wild until more crowd them into submission. "Are you and my dad friends?"

"I met him earlier. Bet he's an awesome dad, isn't he?"

She nods soberly. "Except when he bosses me, which is most of the time."

"That's what dads are supposed to do," I tell her. "My dad did a lot of bossing." It's not a lie. I just don't tell her that I haven't seen my dad in nine years when both of my parents were killed in a car accident. It's the last thing a girl with only one parent wants to hear.

"You're funny." The smile returns.

"No, I'm Ruby. Funny is my next-door neighbor." This cracks her up, and I revel in the unbridled joy of being a kid, hearing a dumb joke, and laughing with abandon. Her head drops back as she giggles.

"I'm Fiona. Shh, don't tell my dad I just told a stranger my name."

"Normally, you shouldn't do that. It's super dangerous. And you should never keep secrets from your dad. But...we'll keep just this one between us. How does that sound?"

She nods her head, her sleep-rumpled strands of hair falling into her eyes.

Just then, a fat June bug buzzes through the air near Fiona's head. Swinging her head back, she squeals and runs to hide behind me.

I watch the flying beetle zoom its clumsy way around my own head, bobbing and weaving and buzzing as it goes. The garden lights have dimmed now that the sun is out, so there's nothing obvious to attract the bug. I swat at it, but it doesn't take the hint.

"I don't like it..." she says behind me. I look and find her covering her eyes with her hands and peeking through her fingers.

Watching the round bug's path, I try to follow it with my outstretched hands, but it's moving in the erratic way those beetles do. "Hang on, let me get it."

Swooping after it, I manage to capture the bug in my hands. I feel it rattling around until it finally gives in and sits in my covered palm. "It's okay, you can look."

Cautiously removing one hand at a time, Fiona moves out from behind me, checking to ensure that the coast is really clear. I show her my clasped hands. "You're holding it?" The awe in her round eyes tells me I can get her over the fear of big bugs if I direct her the right way.

"Right in here." I hold my hands to my chest like I'm guarding a secret. Fiona leans closer, inspecting my hands for gaps where the bug might fly out.

"Is she trying to get out?"

I smile. "She seems pretty calm right now. It's dark in here, so she's probably taking a nap." I slowly move my hands closer to Fiona. "You want to hold her?"

She shivers. "I-I'm not sure."

"She's big for a flying bug, but small compared to you. And she's way more scared, I guarantee it."

Fiona nods. "Makes sense." She still looks hesitant, and I don't want to force it.

"How about this? I'll show you something cool that June bugs can do, and if she keeps hanging around near us, you can try to catch her next."

"Yeah. Okay." More enthusiastic nodding.

I start rattling my hands, shaking up our little June bug, who already had enough trouble flying straight. "This won't hurt her. But she'll be confused for a second." When I let her go, she flies in several goofy loops before straightening out and buzzing around the rosemary bushes to our right.

Fiona bursts out laughing. "No way. You made her dizzy."

"Just a little. But I promise, it doesn't hurt. I looked it up to find out. We used to do this as kids all the time, so I wanted to be sure it was okay."

She looks at me with awe, the way kids often do when they try to imagine what adults were like as kids their age. I see the questions scrambling in her head, all the things she wants to ask about being a kid "in the olden days," but before she can articulate one, the June bug comes buzzing back.

"I wanna catch it this time." She races after it when it flies back toward the rosemary. The hem of her long shirt bounces as her feet hit the tiny rocks on the drive. The bug flies the other way, getting more excited by the pursuit.

"Come over here, Fiona. Stand still. Let her come to you." She does as instructed, and sure enough, the June bug settles down its flight enough that Fiona can reach out and cup it between her small hands.

"Ooh, it's tickling me," she squeals before leaning down to talk quietly to the bug in her hands. "Don't be scared. I won't hurt you."

I watch her contemplating what to do next. She looks up at me. "I'm scared to let her out. What if she flies in my face?"

"She won't hurt you. Worst that could happen is you get a bump on the nose." I reach over and tap her nose to demonstrate.

"Okay, then lemme give her a little shake." She rattles her hands twice and sets the bug free. Almost like the beetle knows it's responsible for a good show, it lurches forward, makes a tumbling loop, then flies off toward the rosemary again, bidding us adieu.

"That was so fun!" Fiona jumps in the air and flings her arms to the sky. I'm envious of a seven-year-old's ability to find so much joy in tiny things. I feel so weighed down by my job search and the need to earn a paycheck that I've almost forgotten what it feels like to have fun playing with a bug.

I've also almost forgotten that we've been out here for a while, and there's still no sign of Jackson. If she lives here with him and he's gone off to work, I wonder who's taking care of her.

"Do you need me to help find someone? An adult?"

"For sure not. I escaped!" Her glee is almost enough to make me want to go along with whatever she's up to, but the adult in me knows better.

"Maybe it's time to go back. Not too cool to run away from home. Even to play with bugs."

She sticks her bottom lip out in exaggerated defiance and shakes her head. "I didn't run. I walked. I live over there." She points into the distance, where I can't see anything but vineyards. A part of me has no trouble believing this moppet thinks she lives among the wine grapes, at least in her imaginary world.

"Oh, then, maybe I should walk you back." I look down at her bare feet. "These rocks don't seem too comfy on the feet."

"Nah, I'm used to it. I don't need shoes."

"Yes, you do." The deep voice rumbles from behind me, but by now, it's familiar after I spent nearly an hour talking to her dad. His voice sends a ripple of delicious heat through my veins. The gruff hum of his words dances over the surface of my skin.

"March yourself back inside, young lady, and get dressed like I told you."

The girl's face immediately transforms from mischievous to pouty, with those long eyelashes only kids have fanning out over her cheeks. She blinks with dramatic, epic sadness designed to win over scolding adults. I wonder if Mr. Burlypants will buy it. "I just wanted to see the red car." Her voice is part whine, part plaintive heart-stopper.

He shakes his head like he's seen this drama production before, but the corner of his mouth can't fight the pull of a smile. The tired irritation I saw earlier stands no chance against the love he feels for this girl, and my heart twists watching him fail to resist her.

I'm intrigued by the softer, tender-hearted side he kept hidden earlier, and I find myself wanting to see more of it.

"Fiona…" It's a warning wrapped in a hug. She knows he's no match for those long lashes and imperfect teeth. "I asked you to get dressed. I did not tell you to come outside in your pajamas and talk to strangers about their cars."

I bristle at being called a stranger, even though I know he's teaching her a lesson about trust and safety. I want to tell her—

and him—that I'm friendly and trustworthy, but this isn't about me. "He's right," I tell Fiona, even though I kind of love how spirited she is despite her grumbly dad.

"Fine." She stomps off, making an effort to kick the small river stones as she goes. Then she stops, turns back to me, and gives me a shy grin and a wave. "Bye, Ruby." Her voice drips with dramatic sadness.

I can't help but smile as she plods toward the farmhouse, but Jackson's eyes are on me, not his daughter. "You find this funny?"

"Not funny, but she reminds me of how I was."

"Shocker, you were a handful," he mutters. I wish the raspy growl of his voice didn't do things to my insides that put me in danger of making bad decisions.

"Still am." He might as well know it.

That earns me a chuckle, at least. "I don't want to keep you." Guess I'm being run off his land.

"Okay, then…thank you for the interview. No matter how intimidating you tried to be, you sort of failed. It was a *pleasure* meeting you." I grin, raising an eyebrow so he'll know exactly how I feel.

"It was, um, *interesting* meeting you."

Jackson nods, bidding me goodbye for the second time this morning and extending his hand in invitation. It redeems him slightly that he's offering some civility now. I reach for his hand, prepared to close the door on him, delightful as his daughter may be.

Our fingers brush before my palm settles in his. His much larger hand engulfs mine as his calloused palm sweeps across the softer skin of my hands. All I feel is heat.

From the moment his skin glides over mine, I feel it—a delicious vibration over my cheeks and down my neck. A chill, despite the heat outside. A welling feeling that I want this man's hand on me in more places. Everywhere, all at once.

We shake, but I'm the one who's shaking, unsteady on my feet when I'm someone who always knows where I'm going.

He turns back in the direction Fiona went, probably planning to give her another lecture about talking to strangers and walking outside without shoes on. But what he doesn't understand about girls like Fiona—and me—is that there are always plenty of people in our lives telling us to put on shoes and act like a lady.

There aren't nearly enough who let us walk around barefoot on rocks that aren't sharp enough to kill us but are hard enough to teach us a few things.

I had to learn the hard way, but Fiona doesn't have to do it like that. I don't know where her mother is, and for once, I hold my tongue and focus on the issue at hand. Fiona needs to be a kid, and with her dad all wound up about his business concerns, she's at risk of learning to make spreadsheets instead of kitchen science experiments.

He can't just hire some stern older woman who will suck the fun out of life. I should know. I was raised by one until I was old enough to raise my sister and myself.

Which is why I call after him.

"I could be your nanny." The words have left my mouth before I have a chance to edit them. Or delete them.

He stops, but he doesn't turn around. I watch his shoulders slump in defeat. Then he shakes his head and tips it up to look at the farmhouse. I can imagine him counting slowly to ten so he doesn't blow his stack.

Looking over his shoulder, he seems calm but confused. "What did you just say?"

This is my chance to backpedal and tell him I said something different than what we both know he heard. I should do that. Instead, for reasons I don't entirely understand, I double down. "I offered to be your nanny. You said you needed that, and you've also, um, made it clear I'm not right for the other job, so…"

"So…?"

"You could hire me."

My heart pounds in my chest, but not because I'm afraid he'll say no. I'm afraid he'll say yes. I don't want to be anyone's nanny.

I have a degree, and I intend to build a presence in the community as an authority on Napa vintages.

I can't rightly say what is making me go for broke with him, but I also can't force myself to take the words back. I feel possessed.

His confused expression gives way to stoic resolve. "I don't need a nanny. We've covered this. You also told me you don't give a flying rat's ass what I think about your qualifications for the other job if you recall."

"I do. But I also recall you saying that people in your family think you need a nanny, and now that I've met Fiona, I'm offering."

He scrubs a hand over his face, and I notice the fatigue in his eyes that I hadn't focused on earlier when I was busy tumbling into their depths. Maybe he's just tired of me, but I sense that there's something else he's not saying, even after he spilled a small amount earlier.

"You don't like to ask for help," I observe.

His laugh comes out like a bark, but his eyes soften, telling me I'm right. "What makes you say that?"

Shrugging, I walk toward the front door of the farmhouse. He has no choice but to follow me if he wants to hear my response.

"Maybe I recognize a fellow sufferer." I shove my hands into the pockets of my shorts, a signal to myself to stuff any additional details away. He waits for me to elaborate, but after a moment, he understands I don't plan on saying more.

He shakes his head. "Sorry. I'm not letting just anyone take care of my daughter."

"Of course not. I'll supply background checks. I know CPR and first aid, and I've been fingerprinted and cleared by the California Justice Department. Had to do all that to take care of my sister." His eyebrows pop up as I recite my qualifications.

"You want to be my nanny," he says, trying the concept on and wriggling as though it's an itchy coat.

"No. I want to be a sommelier. And I want to work here. So I'll do whatever it takes to accomplish that, even working in the tasting room. Even working as your nanny. Besides, I like your daughter." I don't mean for the last part to come out sounding as though I don't like *him*, but from the way Jackson frowns, I can tell it does.

He comes a few steps closer just as the breeze kicks up, hitting me with a light scent of citrus and pine that isn't coming from the oak trees. When Jackson crosses his arms, shoving a fist behind one round, hard bicep, I try not to notice, but not noticing Jackson Corbett's body is like standing in a thunderstorm and trying not to get wet.

"Look, I'll come back for the interview with your brother later. If he hires me, that'll get me closer to a sommelier gig. If you hire me too, that will actually cover my rent for the apartment I want. Two jobs without a commute between them. Win, win."

Only not. Because driving an hour each way to get here and working two jobs will likely lead to my early demise. But, I'll cross that bridge…

"This makes no sense, Ruby."

"I know." I wish I could present a logical argument, but I'm going on instinct here, and something tells me this man needs help more than he's willing to admit. And my own set of demons makes it impossible to keep from wanting to be that person. It will be my downfall one day, but not today.

"How would that even work?" It's the crack in his steely armor that I need. Not that I have any idea how to answer his question, but his slight thaw gives me a moment to spitball.

"I guess I'd have two jobs. If your brother agrees to hire me, that is. I'd work in the tasting room in the morning while Fiona's at school and pick her up in the afternoons and entertain her until you're done with work. Cook dinner…I make a mean caprese sandwich. Presumably, you'll finish up earlier if you're not running around to afterschool activities with Fiona and trying to do your job."

"Caprese?"

"Tomatoes and mozzarella. My favorite." He's squinting at me like I've lost my mind, but it makes sense to me.

Jackson shakes his head. "You'll be exhausted. Fiona is exhausting."

"She's seven. That's her job, to work your very last nerve and look adorable doing it."

Shaking his head, he exhales a laugh that seems to be all the air he has left. The man is cooked, and it's barely eight in the morning. I feel bad for him, even if he's not the best people person in the world. Given what he has resting on his shoulders, it's no wonder.

"You seem like you know a lot about it." Jackson rubs the back of his hand across his forehead, wiping a light sheen of sweat that can only be brought on by a kid trying to be mischievous.

"I chased after my younger sister when I was in high school and she was about that age. It's been a few years, but this isn't new to me."

Jackson looks in the direction where Fiona disappeared as though he can see her. And because he knows her better than I do, he can. She creeps from behind one of the potted olive trees that flank the porch and stands to her full height, which barely exceeds the top of the pot.

I chastise myself for not realizing she didn't go inside after she was told to do so. My little sister wouldn't have done it either. Maybe I'm a little rusty at this kid business. Not that I'd dare reveal it to Jackson now that he seems to be considering hiring me.

Oh, but he isn't considering it. Not when he's shaking his head and biting down on his lower lip so hard I fear it might bleed. "Okay," he says with a pained look that says he's between a rock and a hard place. And for the life of me, I can't understand why I'm dying to be there with him.

Except that I do. I already like Fiona, I need the money, and I want to be involved in the winery. I have career goals and pride.

But I don't have time to tell Jackson that because he's already walking back toward the house, calling after him, "If you get the job this afternoon, come see me, and we'll discuss an arrangement."

And then I'm standing alone in front of Buttercup Hill Vineyards, wondering what the heck I've done.

# CHAPTER
## *Six*

JAX

An hour after sending Ruby away in her jelly bean of a car, I've gotten Fiona dressed, fed, and organized for school. Sort of.

"I hate this shirt. Why are you making me wear it?" She tugs at the poofy sleeves of a white shirt one of my sisters bought for her.

"Because there's a law in the country that says you need to go to school wearing clothes."

"Is that really a law?" She sticks her bottom lip out and stands with her legs wide and her hands on her hips. When did every female start channeling superheroes?

"No."

"I like Ruby. She's nice." Fiona turns her wide eyes up to me and grins.

"Great."

"Is she coming back here?" My daughter has a habit of hearing things she isn't supposed to, so I'm not sure how much she caught of our conversation.

"Pick out a pair of shorts and put them on. I'll be downstairs."

I shouldn't take out my morning's frustration on my daughter, but I'm frustrated with everyone at the moment.

I've not only sort of agreed to hire a nanny, but I've agreed to hire a woman who will likely make my life crazier than it already is.

I shouldn't worry. The chances of Dashiell hiring her are slim. I know how Dash works, and if he's bringing in one woman to interview for the tasting room job, he's probably bringing in twenty more. Ruby's odds of getting the job are slim, especially once Dash sees her resume. She's overqualified, and for all we know, she's a mole sent by one of our competitors to discover what makes Buttercup Hill the industry stalwart.

A couple years ago, when he was newer at his job and more naïve, he hired a woman he'd been dating for just over a month. That was a bad enough decision right there. But when she turned out to work for Wood Street Vineyards, our biggest competitor, my father ripped him a new one and told him to find his priorities or get out.

He'll take one look at Ruby's resume, and his radar will kick in. He'll send her on her merry way, and I'll never have to make good on my bullshit offer to "discuss an arrangement."

Jesus. I can't believe I said it like that. Makes it sound like I'm soliciting her to be my professional escort. Didn't seem to bother her, so maybe I shouldn't worry so much.

But like I said, it's probably a moot point because Dash will see right through her. "Never hire someone who doesn't want the job they're being hired to do. It will only lead to suffering for both of you," he told me one day when we were fantasizing about having different jobs at the winery.

My background is in psychology, which makes me far better suited for something other than numbers. I can read people. That is, when I'm not exhausted and grumpy. Dash, on the other hand, studied communications. Or rather, he did very little studying at all and nearly flunked out of college because he spent so much time skiing in Tahoe and so little time studying. Our father gave him an ultimatum—come work in the family business or get cut off and see how that feels.

Then he made Dashiell the employee-facing member of the team so he'd have a daily reminder of how many people would kill to work at our company.

He pulled the same shit with Archer, who's the numbers guy in the family. He should have my job sweating over the bottom line and trying to balance columns that refuse to behave. But that would be too easy. Giving a person a job they're good at? Not my father's style. He wanted each of us to "stretch and grow." Or, if you take a more cynical view, he wanted us to struggle and argue with each other and make sure no one could claim superiority in any way.

We took the cynical view.

With our sisters, Dad was different. No, he didn't find them jobs suited to their skills—because the chauvinist in him didn't believe they had any skills. So he gave them what he considered unimportant roles that they couldn't screw up too badly. But because my sisters are badasses, it's largely due to their talents that the company hasn't fallen apart in my father's absence.

If only his mind were sound enough to see the irony.

"I have some advice for you," I tell Dashiell when he pokes his head in my office to ask if I want to grab lunch. "There's a woman you're interviewing later—don't hire her."

"Hiring advice from the man who hates dealing with people? Quick, let me get my laptop and fire off a rejection letter." He raises an eyebrow behind his tortoiseshell glasses. His hazel eyes flash, and his cheeky grin pops a dimple in each cheek. With his bedhead and lazy smile, he can charm the pants off of most people. Just not me.

"Trust me on this. She's not a match."

Picking up a stapler from my desk, he opens it and closes it again with a snap. He does it once more and watched me wince at the *snap*. Being the youngest male in our family can't be easy, but Dash has learned every trick in the book on how to irritate us back when we were kids, and he's still using the same playbook today.

"Who's the woman, and when did you date her?"

"Her name's Ruby, and the answer to the second is *never*." I get an uncomfortable twinge in my gut when I say it. I've never laid eyes on her before this morning, so it shouldn't make me feel sad to say we've never dated. It shouldn't make me feel any way.

"What's the deal, then?"

"She showed up at the wrong time, and I met her earlier. Just think she's not the one." Again, that twinge in my gut.

He shrugs. "Okay, thanks for the tip. You can tell me all about it over lunch."

I wave him away. As in, *go away, you little gnat*. He does this almost every day, and each time, I send him away. It's been like this since my wife left, and I took over shuttling Fiona around. He knows I've been burning the candle at both ends for the past two years, and he never misses a chance to ply me with food if I've skipped a meal.

"I'm not hungry."

We're lucky to have two highly-rated restaurants on our property, not to mention that I have a kitchen at my house. It would be hard to plead starvation around here. But day after day, I find myself in the weeds with work, and I generally skip lunch.

"Liar."

"Asshole."

"I brought you a sandwich."

"Thanks."

He nods. "Just don't want you fucking up the books. Low blood sugar'll do that."

"Hasn't happened so far, and I skip lunch plenty."

"Don't even say it. You've been lucky, is all." He's not wrong—I shouldn't be making financial decisions on no sleep and barely any food. And, unfortunately, he's wrong because I haven't been lucky, not lucky enough to turn dad's business losses into gains before anyone's the wiser.

If I can get through the investor meeting next month without anyone looking too hard at a one-time charge that caused our quarterly profits to plummet, maybe I'll have a prayer of righting the ship by the end of the next quarter. That is, if I can figure out what my dad was doing that cost us so much money.

My eyes move to the sandwich in Dash's hand because he hasn't made any moves toward giving it to me. He sees where I'm looking, puts the sandwich on the desk behind him, and crosses his arms.

"You gonna give me that?" I gesture to the sandwich with a nod.

"Trixie told me you and Dad got into it this morning about financial problems. You gonna tell me what's going on?"

"Not today, I'm not." Not when I don't have an explanation that makes sense.

"When, then?"

"Don't worry about it."

Slowly, he pushes himself away from the desk and walks the wrapped baguette sandwich over to me. He holds it away like a carrot he expects me to jump at and watches me. "Why do you guys all think withholding food is the best way to get me to do something?"

"Because it works."

"Not today, it doesn't. I'll tell you about our finances when there's something to tell. Until then, go away and let me do my job."

He holds the sandwich closer. It smells like honey mustard and dill pickles, and my mouth starts watering.

"Fine." He turns on his heel and leaves my office, sandwich in hand. Seems to be a pattern today—everyone's got attitude—including my damn stomach, which growls at me for the lost opportunity to eat. But only one person comes to mind whom I wouldn't mind seeing again, despite the sassy attitude.

I wonder if Ruby is stubborn enough to ignore my advice. Yeah, I kind of hope so.

# CHAPTER
## *Seven*

RUBY

There are worse things than spending all day in Napa Valley. My sister has been telling me for years that I was missing out by working and studying so much, and I'm not about to tell her she's right, but…maybe she's right.

The day unfolds right out of an Instagram reel of quick cuts advertising the best of the region. Sunny side-up eggs at a roadside breakfast spot where I share a picnic table with a small posse of Harley Davidson aficionados. They spend an hour telling me stories about the cross-country road trip they took that landed them in Northern California. They're spending a day wine tasting before heading to the coast and driving along the winding highway road above Big Sur on their way to Los Angeles.

I spend my next few hours driving the wine route, popping in and out of wineries but not doing much tasting. I visit two small hotels, hoping to find something in one of their gift shops to replace my ratty shorts and sandals for my afternoon meeting. I don't want to blow my chances by showing up looking like a babysitter.

The first shop has only bathing suit cover-ups and hats, along with tote bags, tees, and golf shirts emblazoned with the name of the hotel. The second only has mugs, wineglasses, and, oddly, an assortment of flip-flops.

I try a few varietals at Cakebread Cellars and Frog's Leap because they're a couple of my personal favorites, but mostly, I'm trying to get a sense of how they run their tastings.

I've done my research over the years at wineries in every town I've visited, but I'm a little behind on my knowledge of Napa because it's so spread out.

Standing behind a group of women, I take mental notes. They look to be about my age—mid-twenties—and they're on their way to being drunk before noon. They squeal louder than they probably realize as one of them drops a glass onto the stone floor.

"Don't worry." A tasting room assistant in a brown t-shirt dress almost the same color as her hair puts on gloves and whips a broom out from behind the bar to scoop the broken glass. I make a mental note about safety, speed, and thoroughness.

The women, who all wear matching pale pink shirts emblazoned with "I Do crew" on the front, don't miss a beat, getting the dropsy sister a new glass and toasting with full glasses of chardonnay. The brunette in the middle of the throng wears a tell-tale bridal veil and a shirt that says, "I was told there would be strippers."

Par for the course at wineries, where not everyone is looking for top notes and wood barrel aging. I file that observation away as well. The better I can show Dashiell Corbett that I'm prepared for whatever their guests throw my way, the better my chances of landing the job.

A couple hours later, I stop at the Napa General Store for a sandwich and ask if there's any prayer of finding a clothing store in the area with something more appropriate to wear for an interview.

"Duck Feather. They have an absurdly fabulous gift shop," the cashier advises, her sleek lavender ponytail brushing shoulders bared by a pale pink halter dress that looks like exactly the thing I ought to be wearing to a job interview.

"Any chance you bought that there?" I ask, peeking over the counter to see more of the dress.

She looks down. "Ha. Not there, but I'll bet they have something like this. Best gift shop in the area."

I thank her for the tip and take my sandwich to go. It's just shy of three, and my ambitious plans to cover more of the wine route are foiled by the heat of the day. The thermostat in my car reads ninety-one degrees, and I know it won't cool down much before evening.

Turning down the long drive of tiny Duck Feather Vineyard feels promising. It's always fun to find these hidden gems among the more well-known growers. Sometimes, they only produce a few dozen cases of wine per year, but some are so good they have waiting lists to buy what they produce.

Maybe I'll get lucky at Duck Feather, a winery I've never heard of with a sign so rustic that it looks like someone painted it by hand.

The yellow clapboard house that serves as a tasting room and gift shop is small and charming, a fraction of the size of Buttercup's farmhouse. Inside the tasting room is a four-foot burnished wood countertop with two barstools made of metal and cowhide. I bypass the wine and browse in the adjacent shop.

Every shelf is adorned with Duck Feather merch, from baseball caps and tee-shirts to wine bottle stoppers, coasters, and tea towels. There's more here than I've ever seen at the most well-known wineries. I guess Duck Feather is trying to put itself on the map this way.

A whole other section is devoted to clothing that could hold its own at a beach resort or restaurant lunch. It's a smart business move for a small wine producer because, no doubt, people come to Napa and realize they aren't dressed for some of the finer restaurants they may want to visit.

After buying a pale blue maxi dress, I slide onto one of the barstools to sample Duck Feather's wine.

"You like the sauv blanc?" The man working the tasting counter wears a white button-up shirt, open at the collar, and a pair of khaki pants. His smile is kind, if bored. He's probably already asked this question several dozen times today, and probably everyone has a version of the same answer. "Yes." "It's good." Most people don't come right out and say they hate a wine unless it's not what they're expecting—overly sweet when they want something dry or heavy when they want something light.

"It's nice. Light." It tastes faintly of grapefruit, and it's mild enough that it goes down easily. On a hot day like today, I could drink a lot of it without realizing it until it's too late.

I keep notes on every wine I've tasted in an app on my phone designed to let me mark and find wines by winery and vintage, write down details about the various awards and scores they've received, and jot down the way the wines are made.

My own set of notes goes into a different file—details about who I was with when I tried the wine, whether I tasted it or drank an entire glass, whether my friends liked it. Then I go farther down the rabbit hole and write down obscure facts that only wine nerds care about—the top notes, underlying flavors like cherry or chocolate, details about the kind of wood used in the storage casks, fermentation times, soil conditions—any details I can scrounge up that fall outside the normal information a person could look up online.

That's the gold. That's where I separate myself from other would-be sommeliers who have different palates and might choose different wines to go with certain foods. I'm banking on my taste setting me apart. Someday.

I take a second sip of the pale white wine and swish it in my mouth. Normally, I'd make use of the spittoon bucket, but I swallow the whole mouthful.

"Refreshing, right?" he says, leaning over the counter and putting his elbows down close to my glass.

I take another sip and nod. "Goes down easy. Probably too easy, right? You get a lot of people here who just want to get drunk and don't really care about wine?"

He rolls his eyes. Probably seen his fair share. "Most people."

That's what I was afraid of when I answered the ad for the job at Buttercup. I don't want to be a glorified bartender like Jackson said. "But some are here because they care about wine, right? That makes it all worthwhile."

He shrugs. "I guess. I mean, we get a lot of blowhards, too, people who think they know. 'Oh, I'm tasting cinnamon and old vines.' Not sure you can taste the age of a vine."

"Maybe some people can." I don't want to sound like a blowhard, but I think he's wrong.

"Yeah. Not me."

"Do you need to know a lot about wine to work here?"

Another shrug. "It's a script. We learn about the wines here, and I know what to say when someone really goes in for the detailed info."

I can't help but feel disappointed. Of course, it makes sense. For some people, a job is a job. Doesn't matter if they're bartending in a hot bistro or pouring small tastes for day drinkers at a winery. I try not to let the idea kill my enthusiasm.

"You want a refill?" The man winks. "We're not supposed to, but you're cute. I make an exception for cute."

He pours before I answer and pushes a glass toward me that's nearly filled to the rim. "Thanks." I have no intention of drinking it. The last thing I plan to do is get behind the wheel of a car with alcohol in my system, given that my parents were killed by a drunk driver.

"Don't mention it." He wraps a bar towel around his neck and grins.

I give him a once-over. Objectively, he's handsome—all his features are in the right place. Angular nose, pretty green eyes, a dimple in his cheek when he smiles. I almost feel like yawning, and it freaks me out.

What happened to me? One hour with Jackson Corbett and my homing device for attractive men is completely broken.

That does not bode well for me, especially since I've offered to work for him. It's one thing if I get hired by his brother to work in the tasting room. I probably won't even see Jackson. But I had to go and offer to be his nanny. Clearly, the heat has wilted my brain.

I'm so caught up in my thoughts while I sip the crisp sauvignon blanc that I miss half a conversation I didn't realize I was having. "So that's when I started working here. Tips were better at the bar, though. You having a leisurely day?"

"Doing research. Killing time." I tell him about my job interview, only sort of paying attention.

"Yeah? Didn't know they were hiring." I follow his gaze through the open door of the tasting room and can see the unmistakable hill that gave Buttercup its name.

"I'm so turned around. Is that Buttercup right over there?"

"Yeah, we're neighbors technically, but not really since their entrance is all the way around on the other road. I doubt they know we exist."

I'm saved from having to prop up his ego when his co-worker summons him to retrieve a bottle of wine. While he goes to a corner where wooden wine crates are stacked three high, I pour the remains of my wine into the spittoon and slip out the door. "Thank you!"

Never have I ever run so fast from a guy that good-looking. Something is definitely wrong with me.

Walking through a small flower garden behind the tasting room, I realize how sleepy I am after waking up so early, driving around all day, and being in the hot sun. There's a very welcoming hammock hanging from another oak tree—the theme of the day.

It takes my weight easily, and when I close my eyes, it feels awfully nice.

———

"Holy shit." A butterfly landing on my cheek startles me awake, and then I startle it. The orange Monarch flutters away as I puzzle through what just happened. Wine… A guy winking at me and pouring…

Then, *gah*! I'm due at Buttercup Hill Vineyards for my interview.

"Shit, shit," I say to no one, flipping myself out of the hammock and landing on one knee. Fortunately, there's grass beneath me. Of course I didn't set an alarm on my phone because I didn't plan on falling asleep. And now it's…a quarter to six.

I hoof it down the path to my car while recalling what the man said earlier about the Buttercup entrance being on a different road. My car sits in the shade of an olive tree, and I whip open the door and shove myself into the driver's seat. I have ten minutes. Because of the way the roads wind around the low mountain behind Buttercup Hill, it's ten minutes away, nine if I gun it.

I gun it.

On the drive to the vineyard, I practice some deep breathing and try to make my heart stop racing. Between my accidental nap and my pre-interview nerves, I'm a hot mess, speeding down the highway and praying no motivated police officers are waiting in a hidden driveway, trying to fill a ticket quota.

Sneaking a look at myself in my rearview mirror, my fears are confirmed. My hair is a hornet's nest of red waves everywhere, and there's no hope of taming it. I'll have to ignore it and try to compensate with some red lipstick that might distract from my sleepy eyes.

"Focus here. Listen to what I'm saying," that lipstick needs to convey. I give myself the eye-roll I know my mother would give if she were here.

"I know," I tell her ghost. "I know."

_____

The long drive from the highway has eighteen oak trees on each side—I count as I change out of my shorts and into the blue sundress, hoping there are no hidden cameras catching me. Planted ten yards apart to give their branches ample room to spread, the trees are a couple hundred yards of shady welcome for visitors.

The space opens like curtains flung open to the morning sun. A broad circular drive takes cars on a loop past the tidy rosemary hedge maze, where visitors can drop their cars at a valet station that's currently unattended. Most wineries don't have valet parking, but most wineries don't usher guests through an archway of grapevines into a week's worth of wine tasting, pampering at the bed and breakfast spa, and fine dining at two restaurants.

The Corbett family has built a destination winery, and the entrance gives off a "your vacation starts here" sort of vibe.

The farmhouse itself fans out in all directions with vineyards as far as the eye can see. By the time I get to the door, a sweaty dribble runs down my back. I'm about to open the door to the winery when it swings open, and I find Jackson standing there.

He doesn't look pleased to see me, tipping his head to the side and grimacing. "You again?"

"Nice to see you too," I quip, trying to push past him into the entryway, but he blocks it with his broad shoulders, leaning his forearms against the doorframe like a cactus. If I want to get around him, I need to slither past his muscles.

"Six in the evening. Right on time." I hold up my phone as proof.

He shakes his head. "I made a bet with myself that you wouldn't stick around twelve hours later for a job you don't want."

"Sounds like a sucker's bet either way." I give him my brightest red-lipped smile and slide beneath his elbow, brushing his lats with my hand as I pass by and sending shivers down my spine.

The cold air inside the room hits me as soon as I enter, which is a good thing because he just set my hand on fire.

Once inside, I don't need to check in with a receptionist or otherwise announce myself because Dashiell Corbett is there waiting for me. He looks like a younger, less polished version of Jackson, if Jackson shed his computer for a surfboard and had pale blue eyes like the sea. One stray lock of hair hangs down over his forehead, obstinate.

"Ruby?" he asks.

Extending my hand, I shake his. "Yes. Hi."

"Dashiell Corbett. Thanks for being here. Heard there was a mixup earlier."

"Yeah, my fault."

He dismisses the thought with a flick of his head, which succeeds at tossing the lock of hair out of his face. It falls back immediately. "Appreciate you coming back." He gestures around the entry with a flick of his fingers in both directions. "This is where people come to check in for tours and tastings. Pretty much the staging area for everything that happens next around here— shuttles to the restaurants or the inn, walking tours, the whole lot."

He talks as he ushers me down a different hallway than the one that led to Jackson's office. "Mostly offices over there, but here's the part that always gets a lot of oohs and aahs from our guests."

He hauls a heavy barn door along the iron rod that holds it over an archway. Sweeping it aside, he reveals a small wine cave, its walls heavy plaster with arched cubbies where wine barrels sit with candelabras on top. The air in the room drops by at least ten degrees, and for the first time all day, I feel a chill. And equal parts awe.

Nodding at my wide eyes, Dashiell nods. "Right? Show-stopper."

"It's gorgeous." I step farther into the room and take in the wrought iron chandeliers, circular with candle-shaped lights twinkling atop them. Rustic wooden benches line one wall of the windowless room, which somehow doesn't feel dark because of all the sparkling lights and large swaths of backlit stained glass.

Dashiell walks me closer to one panel, pointing. "You know how churches often tell the story of the saints in their stained glass? This tells the story of our family and the winery." He nods and points me to the next panel, where fields of grapes are pictured under a sunlit sky with a lone farmer gazing at the harvest. "It's a little much," he admits quietly.

"It's perfect for this room, and I'll bet people love it."

"You've got that right. Tourists eat it up. You give 'em a story about early California folklore, dustbowl days, and hearty Americans working the land and dreaming of better days, and they're all in."

The difference between Dashiell and Jackson is like night and day. He has such an easy rapport and a clear enthusiasm for the customer-facing side of the business. I can immediately understand why he's the one conducting interviews and Jackson is stuck crunching numbers in his office.

But instead of feeling more drawn to Dashiell's easy way, I find myself thinking about Jackson, wondering what he's doing right now. Wondering if it was an accident that he happened to be there when I arrived just now.

And that's plain crazy since I only spent an hour with him, and he mostly tried to dissuade me from coming back for the interview and taking the job.

I run a hand over the rough-hewn bar top that contains a homey display of silver picture frames, each showing the farmhouse and grounds in different eras. There are family photos as well, and I find myself trying to pick out Jackson in each one when Dashiell starts talking again. "I understand my brother advised you against this job."

"He had strong opinions," I confirm.

Dashiell nods. "I'm of a mind to disagree with him in matters of staffing, so that works in your favor."

"Ah, so it's a good thing he told me to take a hike."

"But he's also right. You're overqualified for the job. You don't need to study viniculture to pour wine for guests all day, and I don't want you to get bored and quit in a week."

I stumble over my words, confused. "Bored? You don't need to worry about that. There's so much here to keep me interested, believe me. Please don't count me out because you're worried about what I might do."

Dashiell raises an eyebrow at that and picks up his phone and scrolls. When he finds what he's searching for, he taps the screen and shows it to me. It's a picture of the room we're standing in, only it's filled with dozens of people. He flips through to other screens, all showing people enjoying themselves in different parts of the winery estate, but it's chaos.

I've looked through the website from top to bottom, and all the photos there are well-lit perfect images showing the right number of people smiling and sipping wine in the tasting room, walking through the vineyards, happily exploring the kitchen garden behind one of the restaurants. But these are Dashiell's personal photos, all showing messy scenes.

"This is what no one will tell you until you take the job. It's madness. We're incredibly busy, and the company mandate is always 'the more the merrier,' so it's only going to get busier through the summer and once we roll out our new vintage. People have been waiting."

"I know. I'm waiting, too."

He nods. "Right. You're invested."

"I am. And I applied for the job because I want to do it, not because I want it to lead to something better. I mean, of course, I do want that… someday…when I've earned your trust…"

He holds up a hand to stop me. "I get it. You don't have to butter me up. Take the job. Start on Monday. Jemma will show you the ropes. She works for my sister, Beatrix. You'll meet her too, kind of a dynamo, kind of a Type A nightmare." He looks around the room, hefts a large coffee table book from a corner of the bar, and hands it to me. "Some weekend reading to get you in the mood before your first day of training."

"So…that's it?" I spent more time arguing with Jackson earlier about my qualifications, and he wasn't even my interviewer. I feel like I must be missing something.

"That's it. You're hired." He starts walking me back to the reception area. "Your training will include a tour of everything, but if you read through this book, you'll know more than your tour guide. And I have a feeling you will."

"Awesome. Thank you." I feel like doing a little dance, but I restrain myself. I don't want to do anything to jeopardize my good fortune. But now I need to find Jackson because if I didn't just sell my soul by agreeing to be a glorified bartender, I'm definitely going to do it being a babysitter for the world's biggest grump.

But he has an awesome daughter, so I'm in.

# CHAPTER
## *Eight*

JAX

Fiona sits on my bed, eyes glued to the TV where Frozen plays for the eleventeenth time. I feel like a terrible parent for setting her up in front of a screen instead of taking her outside to practice on the roller skates my sister gave her for her birthday, but I need to work, and she's set for at least an hour and a half.

I didn't need to go through the front door of the farmhouse to walk to my office. There's a perfectly good entrance in the back of the building that takes me on a shorter route, so I'm not sure why I took the long way.

*It's because you wanted to see Ruby again.*

If that's true, it's a matter of good business practices. If there's a chance I'll end up hiring her to work with Fiona, I want to give her another once-over, make sure she shows up when she says she will, ensure that I wasn't just overtired and addled when I agreed to her ridiculous proposal this morning.

Yeah. I've been thinking about her all day.

It's the sassy, world-be-damned attitude she seems to have about everything. That's refreshing. Most people who want something from our family or the Buttercup Hill business kowtow to me and tell me exactly what they think I want to hear.

Maybe Ruby doesn't have much experience in corporate settings, or maybe she just doesn't care. Either way, I'm interested.

The sun has dropped low enough that the oak trees do their job of cooling down the air beneath them. I walk down the front drive to where it forks and leads to a large overflow parking lot. It's where the valets take the cars when the winery is teeming with guests, and just beyond it, there's a covered garage where I have my SUV.

I'm itchy to walk over there, hop behind the wheel, gun the engine, and race the hell out of here. I'm staring wistfully in the direction of the lot, unable to see my ride, when I feel a tap on my shoulder.

"You lost?"

I know it's Ruby before I turn, and not because I recognize her voice. It's because the second her finger touches my skin—those tiny taps—my pulse quickens, and I hear the rush of blood in my ears. It makes no sense that I'd feel pinpricks of heat crawling over the back of my neck simply from her light touch.

And yet I do.

I hate that a woman could have this effect, and at the same time, my body craves more of it. So much more. Dating isn't something I do. Ever. Where would I find the time, between working twelve-hour days, being a full-time single parent, and protecting her from the emotional fallout of my ex leaving us abruptly?

Women are nice to look at and flirt with, but that's as far as it goes. So, what is it about *this* particular woman that makes me want something different?

I look over my shoulder to find her standing in that damn Wonder Woman pose she took earlier. And one look at the way her hair drapes over her shoulder in messy waves makes me turn the rest of the way around. It's like her hair from this morning went through the spin cycle over the course of the day in the sweaty, hot sun. It's just-fucked hair, and I like it.

For a moment, I imagine myself running my fingers through it to see if it burns my skin. That's the way it looks—like flames. I can't help but wonder how her hair got so messy. Maybe she has a fuck buddy in the area. Or maybe someone back at home.

Which makes me wonder what her hair would look like spread out over the pillows in my bedroom like the dark, moody rays of a sunset.

*Fucking stop it.*

"Nope, not lost. Just fantasizing about getting lost," I tell her, suddenly more interested in staring at her than getting in my car. At least not without her in it.

"Ha, I know how that goes."

"Yeah?" She didn't give me that impression earlier. Then again, I was too busy whining about my business problems to ask. Because I'm just that kind of asshole, apparently. I'm surprised she indulged me for as long as she did. In fact, I'm surprised she's standing here now, "Care to elaborate?"

She shakes her head. "Nope. Not today." She smiles and waits, but then her enthusiasm gets the better of her, and she blurts, "I got the job."

The sight of her has highjacked my brain cells, and all I can do is stare and think about what I could do to her for one long night that would result in her hair looking just like this.

"Aren't you going to say congratulations?" She taps her foot impatiently.

"Of course. Congrats. Hope Dash didn't ask irritating questions that have nothing to do with the job. He can get off on a tangent."

"He was fine. Barely asked me anything. In fact, I kind of think the fact that you warned him against me worked in my favor. For future reference, if you want to tank someone's interview, make your brother think it's all his idea."

Now she has my attention. "Wait, he told you I tried to tank your interview?" Doesn't sound like Dash, but maybe Ruby has the same kind of hold on him that she seems to have on me. The thought makes my skin crawl.

Her lips quirk into a knowing smile. "No, but you just did. Why, Jackson? I thought we were doing so well. Where's the radical honesty I was led to believe I could expect from you?" Her voice is plaintive, teasing, as she wrings her hands.

"I'm sorry. But I read your resume, and I still think you'll hate pouring wine all day."

"I won't. It's the perfect job. I have my reasons."

She looks so definitive, crossing her arms in her powerful woman stance, that I decide to take her word for it. "Okay, then. Look forward to bumping into you from time to time."

The fantasy of my car and the open road is still calling to me. Of course, I'll be walking back inside the house to take care of Fiona and work after she goes to bed, so my wistful thoughts are the only respite I've got.

She puts out a hand like a stop sign. "Wait. What about the other part? You need someone to help with Fiona, and I could use the money. Didn't we have a deal earlier?"

Cocking my head to the side, I take her in again—all of her this time. "Hey, you changed clothes."

She looks down at the dress she's wearing and smooths her hands over the skirt, which only draws my eye even more to the curve of her hips. The blue sets off her pale skin and riotous copper hair in ways that make me feel more alive than I have since my wife left.

"Yeah. I had a few hours to kill before my interview, so…" She fans her hands to the side and juts a hip out. I stifle a groan.

Her green eyes are merciless, peering into my soul in a way that should be illegal. The pink apples of her cheeks are so round and perfect that I want to take a bite out of each one. Then my eyes drop down to her pink lips and stay there. I imagine how they'd taste, sun-ripened like a summer berry. Like the jam I had this morning.

She's windblown and worn by a day that's already lasted more than twelve hours, and she's even more beautiful than she was this morning. More real. Like a carefree woman who belongs on the back of a horse in a field or gliding on a porch swing with gin and juice in a Ball jar.

I'm feeling worse for the wear, but she seems willing and eager to keep going. I know from looking at her resume that she's twenty-seven, which gives me a handful of years on her.

I sort of thought she'd forget about the nanny position if she got the other job, and a part of me knows it will be a test of my patience to have her working for me. Not to mention the parts of me she's brought back to life in a matter of hours. I can't afford to think about what effect she'd have on me after days. Weeks…

It's dangerous territory, and I know better than to take risks where my daughter is concerned. To say nothing of my heart. She's elicited feelings from me that are better kept under lock and key.

"I'm not hiring you as my nanny."

"What? Why? Fiona loved me."

"Yeah, maybe a little too much. She was running around all afternoon trying to catch bugs. She wants to have a bug habitat in our house now so she can observe them and become friends with them."

She nods, walks past me to the porch steps, and sits on the top one. Suddenly, my legs feel as tired as my brain, so I sit next to her, careful to keep enough distance between us so that my dick doesn't get any wild ideas about my intentions.

"Cool," she says. "Amazing, actually. She was scared this morning, and now she wants to be friends with bugs?"

"Doesn't seem so amazing to me." I try to get away with the lie, but my face betrays me, cheeks pulling my mouth into a grin at the image of Fi conquering her fear of bugs. "Fine. It was kind of awesome that she got over her fear, as long as she doesn't raise a bug army. Don't let it go to your head."

"A bug army will be great. You'll see." She bumps me with her elbow. I feel the same twinge of electricity sear my nerves, and it makes my back stiffen. I should have sat even farther away.

I stand up and move so I'm outside of elbowing distance. "Look, I don't want the help because I'm a stubborn guy, and I feel like I should be able to handle everything. Especially parenting."

I don't know why I'm admitting these things to her. I don't admit my shortcomings to anyone. And of all people, I shouldn't admit them to someone I don't know. And yet, she makes me feel comfortable getting things off my chest. Admitting it feels like a relief.

She nods. "I get that. I'm the same way with my sister."

"Your sister?"

"Yeah, I kind of raised her from the time she was thirteen. Our parents died."

No wonder she's so patient. So good with spirited girls. "Wow, I'm sorry."

"It's okay. It was a long time ago."

I suck in some air and blow out a breath because, I swear, looking at this woman makes me forget to breathe. "I want to do it all. But the reality is, I can't do it all. At least not well."

She nods, long and heavy movements as though it pains her to admit something she isn't saying out loud. I don't get the feeling she's agreeing with me, but I think she understands. Like she has personal experience.

"I get that."

Makes me want to know her better. But the last time I invested in a woman was with Fiona's mom, and look at where it got me.

It also makes me edge closer toward believing what my family has been saying for a year—I need help.

"Yeah?"

Smiling, she stands up and fishes her keys from her purse. "Yeah. It's what working women have been saying for—I don't know—forever?"

"How about this: we do a trial run for a week or so, see how it goes?"

"You're really resisting this. Hard to accept help, huh?"

At this point, I don't feel like either of us needs me to answer.

The light is fading fast from the day, and now it's dusky enough that I know she'll have better visibility on the road. I do the thing I know will have implications for me in more ways than one—I extend my hand toward hers.

"Thank you for considering taking this on." What I really mean is that I'm grateful to her for taking *me* on. I know I'm a work in progress, but she doesn't seem fazed by it. "I'll see you tomorrow."

"Deal. I'm off to Berkeley, but I'll be back with all the Mary Poppins energy in the morning."

When she puts her hand in mine to seal our arrangement, I feel it again—the electric zing that tells me I'm in deeper than I understand.

This buzzing heat when I touch her skin is something I've never felt. I'm not going to want it to fade away. Only it has to because she's my employee now. Maybe that fact will force reality through my damned brain.

It *has* to. Reality is the only option I've got.

# CHAPTER
## *Nine*

RUBY

"You got it?"

My sister trudges from one end of the room to the other, wiping the sleep from her eyes. Her blond ponytail that started on top of her head now lists to the side with frizz surrounding her face like a swarm of gnats.

She didn't take off her makeup last night, so she has eyeliner smeared under her eyes and the faint glow of red on her lips. I don't ask her where she was because I know the answer: at her boyfriend Tim's fraternity, where she sleeps when they're not fighting, leaving me the place to myself.

I don't need to ask how things are going any more with Tim because I always know. If she wakes up here, there's trouble in paradise, soon to be resolved with an apology for saying something insensitive. His emotional quotient isn't exactly the highest, and every fight ends with a half day of sex in his single at the squalid frat.

I point her in the direction of the French press, where I've saved her a cup of coffee after drinking two myself.

She's not a morning person, and somehow, she's signed up for a ceramics class that meets three days a week at eight in the morning.

No mistake there. No one is holding classes at eight in the evening.

"I don't feel well," Ella whines.

"Yeah? Hangover?"

"No. I didn't drink last night. I felt crampy."

I know Ella's cycle the same way I know my own, and it's too early for her period. "Maybe you ate something?"

"So much something. We had Thai food from the good place."

"Well, that probably explains it. Now get thee into thy shower."

Normally, her boyfriend Tim has the job of waking her sleepy ass up in the morning. Or not. I have no idea if she's actually passing Italian. It was part of the deal we made when I moved into her place—she'd keep quiet and not reveal to the university that I'm illegally crashing in her dorm every night, and I wouldn't hassle her about her grades.

It takes every bit of self-control not to comment when I know she's pulling an all-nighter to get a paper written, but I promised. All the more reason to work two jobs and find my own place, so I can boss her around like a proper older sister. Plus, I'm sick of living in her space, and it's time for me to get my own apartment.

"Wait, tell me about the job. When do you start?"

"I've been working there for two days already," I tell her, astounded that she's so clueless. "Do you not read your texts?"

She picks up her phone from on top of a milk crate that doubles as a bedside table and squints at the screen. She tosses it on the bed with a shrug. "I thought I responded to these."

"Ella, you're so full of shit. You just acted shocked that I got the job, and I told you about it three days ago."

"Did I respond?" Slumping against the wall, my sister looks at me for the available millisecond before her eyes drift shut. She's *so* not a morning person.

I walk over and flick her forehead. "Ow." She takes a swipe at me, but with her eyes still closed, she misses by a foot.

"Wake up. Get in the shower." I give her a nudge in the direction of the tiny bathroom, where the mirror is still fogged from my shower a half hour ago. It's a quarter to seven, and I'm about to head out the door, but I need to make sure she's awake and on her feet before I leave.

Ella staggers into the bathroom and slams the door behind her. It's the last I'll probably see of her for another few days, which is fine by me. "Love you, El," I call after her as I scoop my canvas tote over my shoulder.

"Love you too." It's the clearest thing she's said this morning, and I know she means it. We're all we've got, and even though we were born with diametrically opposed circadian rhythms, she'll always be my ride-or-die.

Closing the closet door on my viniculture experiments, I take a sniff of the air to make sure it doesn't smell like wine. The last thing we need is to have the university inspect the dorm and kick Ella out for fermenting wine in campus housing.

Not that it's overly forbidden. We checked all the fine print before I ever rented my first hand-corker, and there was nothing in Ella's dorm contract that mentioned fermenting alcohol. Then again, it probably doesn't come up a lot.

All the more reason, though, that I need to sock away money from my jobs so I can get my own place eventually.

# CHAPTER
## Ten

JAX

"Daddy!" Fiona flies into my arms when I open the front door. It's earlier than I usually get home, six on the dot. But after having Ruby take care of Fiona every afternoon for a bit over a week, I'm surprisingly caught up on work.

I've even managed to get more sleep. For the first time in two years, I don't feel like a worn out half-human at the end of a work day.

I still haven't figured out how to make up for half a billion in losses, but I have a few new ideas. If I'm not a walking zombie at work, it ought to help me come up with more.

I swing Fiona in a circle and deposit her in the chair she sprung from a moment earlier. "How was your day, lovebug?"

"Great, Daddy. Well, not really. School was so boring." She rolls her eyes. "But Ruby and I made three dozen cookies, so now I know multiplication, and we're not even learning that in school." Her amazed eyes are so wide it's almost comical, and I want to know more.

"Tell me. What can you multiply?"

Another eye roll. "Oh my gosh, Daddy. Everything." She dashes to the stove and beckons me over with a sweep of her whole arm. Ruby is in the kitchen, organizing our refrigerator, and my heart skips a beat when I see her there. Glowing, hair messy, and wearing those damn short shorts. I'm getting used to the feeling of my chest tightening every time I see her. Getting used to walking around with pent-up frustration that, for once, has nothing to do with my job.

"Hey," she says, shoving her hair behind her ear. My hands twitch because I want to do it for her. "How was your day?" The moment I ask the question, I realize how intimate it sounds, like a partner coming home after a long day at the office. My eyes shoot to Ruby's to see if she heard it that way.

But she's busy in the refrigerator and barely reacts. I can't decide if I'm relieved or disappointed.

"Good. The usual."

She's about to say more, but Fiona's excitement rules the day. "Daddy, look."

Fiona takes two steps up onto a small stepstool I didn't know we had and peers over the stove.

Standing next to her, I look at three cookie sheets with a dozen chocolate chip cookies on each one. I reach for a cookie, and she slaps my hand away.

"Fiona, we don't slap people or treat them disrespectfully. Especially not your dad," Ruby says before I can reprimand my own daughter.

She tips her head against my side. "I'm sorry. I didn't mean to hit you, Daddy. I'm just too excited about multiplication."

Words I never expected to spring from my daughter's mouth.

I have no chance of staying mad at Fiona, especially when I haven't seen her all day, so I hug her tight. "It's okay. I'm glad you're excited."

Fiona picks up a spatula and wields it like a maestro. "Okay, here we have three rows of four cookies." She points at the first cookie sheet. "Three fours equals four plus four plus four."

Looking at me to make sure I'm following her logic, she waits for me to nod. I glance over and see Ruby's smile.

"Got it," I say.

"Good.

She goes on to explain the ways to multiply six and two, nine and four, twelve and three. My daughter rattles off multiplication tables like a champ as I stand there with my mouth agape that Ruby taught her in one afternoon.

It's why I don't notice Ruby come up behind me with a red smoothie she must have made earlier and put it on the counter. "Hot day. Thought a strawberry-mango smoothie might hit the spot."

It's not her job to cook for me. Once she gets Fiona fed, she hustles her into the tub or shower and has her ready for bed when I get home. But after just a few days, I find myself coming home a bit earlier so I can watch Ruby in action. I claim I'm still working, just using my office that's right off the kitchen, but the truth is that I like seeing my daughter and my nanny together.

*You sure it's not just to ogle the nanny?*

I like watching her wrangle my daughter's spirit, and it's a relief to have someone else lay down the law once in a while. My siblings are great at pitching in when they have time, but their jobs are as intense as mine. As a result, pitching in doesn't happen as often as we'd all like.

"I'm off to take a shower," she says, already adopting Ruby's speaking style. An ache hits my heart. She's growing up too fast. Wasn't it just yesterday that she'd only take a bath?

"Okay, Fi. Sounds good." My enthusiasm doesn't sound as convincing as I'd like. Ruby reaches for my hand and squeezes it as she passes by on her way to chase Fiona up the stairs.

A shock of awareness races through me at the feeling of her skin brushing mine. My chest contracts just as she turns to look at me, a silent acknowledgment that it's all okay—my daughter is still only seven, and I need to relax.

So why is my blood rushing through my veins and crowding sound from my ears?

It's because she surprised me. I didn't expect to feel her soft palm graze mine and that unexpected squeeze. That's it.

And my pulse isn't racing right now because she knew I was having a vulnerable parenting moment and knew exactly how to reassure me.

Or, fuck it. It's all of those things.

While Ruby is upstairs helping Fiona, I talk myself down because it's my only option. By the time she comes back to tell me Fiona is in bed and wants me to read Amelia Bedelia to her, I've calmed my breathing and reined in my pulse.

And by the time I've finished reading, Ruby has cleaned my kitchen from top to bottom. "I have a cleaning person. You don't need to do that," I tell her.

"You're cleaning person coming tonight?"

"No," I admit.

She shrugs. "I don't mind doing it. It's nice to wake up to a clean kitchen."

As she's walking toward my front door, I'm struck by the feeling that I don't want her to go, not yet. My mouth takes over before my brain can catch up.

"Do you have any plans right now?"

She looks around her as though there might be a party she's unaware of. "Now? I was going to drive home to Berkeley." I know this, too. Saw her address at the top of her resume, which was when it impressed me even more that she arrived here at six in the morning that first day.

The birds that were chirping have been replaced by crickets and the low rumble of cars on the main road. It's that time of day when it's still too light for headlights to make much of a difference, but dim enough that it's a little hard to see. I don't want her on the road in that tiny car right now.

"That's a long drive after a long day."

She shrugs. "They're all long days. I'm good with it."

"Have you eaten? Dinner?"

Shaking her head, she starts putting the cookies into a container. "I'll grab something when I get home."

"It's a good hour drive. There's a decent burger place up the road, and I'm antsy to get away for a bit." I'm not sure what the fuck I'm doing. Asking her out? No, I'm not doing that, especially when she's still on her trial run with this job, and now, I really want her to stay. So I'm just being considerate.

Or am I? She's had a long day, and I'm making it longer.

Her eyes go glassy at the mention of food. "Burgers?"

"Pretty much all they have, but they're great."

"Wow, that sounds amazing. What about Fiona's bedtime?" It warms my heart that her first thought is about my daughter, but I'm also highly aware that she's not so swept away by me that she's lost touch with sensibility. Which means I need to ratchet my libido right down to the ground where it belongs.

"My sister's coming over," I lie, but I make good on it by texting Beatrix.

> Me: Hey. Can you hang with Fi for an hour? She'll be in bed, and if you're lucky, she'll stay there

> B: Sure. You still working?

> Me: No, but I need to clear my head. Heading out for a bit

> B: Ok. Don't rush. I'm good. I'll be over in five

> Me: Thanks

> B: Seriously, don't rush

I gesture with my head in the direction of my car. "Come. Take a drive with me."

She bites down on her lip, hesitating. "Does this mean you're hiring me?"

I bark out a laugh at how fixed she remains on her end goal. And how suspicious she still seems of me.

"Relax. This isn't a test. Yes, I will hire you, okay?"

She does a little dance with her fists in the air. "Okay, awesome. I don't know if you're aware, but you're a little hard to read, Jackson. I wasn't sure if you liked me or not."

*Ginger, you have no idea.*

It's probably for the best that Ruby can't get a read on me. Otherwise, she'd know just exactly how much I like her, and that wouldn't bode well for her. Or for me.

Shepherding her with a wave of my arm, I walk us away from the farmhouse and over toward the parking lot. She walks beside me, never questioning where I'm taking her.

I stop and put a hand on her shoulder to halt her motion. She turns, face turned up, expectantly. "Ruby, no. This is how it's gonna go down. You and I are going down the road to get some food, and once the glare is out of the sky, you can drive home. Then, you'll get some sleep and come in at eleven tomorrow."

She huffs a disbelieving laugh. "I can't come at eleven. I need to set up the tasting room with Jemma."

"Trix can pull someone from the restaurant to do that for two hours. We do it all the time. If you're going to work for me, I can't have you burning out. Two jobs and a commute isn't easy."

"I'm still new here. I don't feel like I should be getting special treatment from you. Not a good look."

"It's no one's business why you're coming at eleven. Like I said, we move people around all the time. It'll barely be a blip on anyone's radar."

She closes her eyes on a long blink. When she opens them, she nods, but I can see the conflict on her face. "I don't like letting people down."

"I get it. I'm the same way."

She nods. "Okay. Thanks for having my back."

"Yeah."

Except I'm not sure having her back is the reason for my

generosity. I want her. I barely know her, but I know that. I can't have her, so there's no point in entertaining the thought, but I'll be entertaining it plenty when I'm alone in the shower later tonight.

I'm completely, irreversibly fucked, even as I resolve to act like a grownup and stop thinking about her. If I didn't admit it to myself before, I'm forced to acknowledge it now—having Ruby work for me is going to test every last bit of my resolve.

# CHAPTER
## Eleven

RUBY

I feel like I'm living in a Taylor Swift song.

Hot guy driving fast down a dark road. Can't have him, shouldn't want him, but oh…I do.

I allow myself to entertain the idle fantasy of how the rest of the song would go because he's my boss, and fantasizing is as far as this can go.

It was awkward enough when Beatrix came to the house to watch her niece and realized Jackson was leaving with me. "Oh, I've been wanting to meet the woman who's made my brother less grouchy for the first time in a hundred years," she'd said. But I felt like what she really meant was, "Jackson, why are you taking the nanny out for a drive?" I know Jackson doesn't go out with women, so I didn't want his sister to think anything was going on between us.

I found myself over-explaining. "I haven't eaten, and he's just being nice." Or maybe I was convincing myself.

"Back soon, Trix. Thanks again." Jackson ushered us out

without further explanation and grumbled something about his sister being nosy.

Now that we've hit the open road, which is quiet, save for a few sets of headlights that approach every couple minutes, he seems like he's coming back to life. The winery is closed. Fiona is supervised. He's left his office. These all seem like good things.

I notice his hands relax on the steering wheel, and he drapes one arm out the window.

"Thanks for doing this with me." His voice is a sexy rumble. In the few minutes since Jackson's Jeep tore out of the parking lot and down to the main road, he's relaxed visibly. His shoulders sit about two inches lower, and he's rolled his neck a few times.

The night air is still warm. It's nice to have the windows open, though it means my hair has blown around quite a bit. I finally tied it up in a topknot, but loose strands fly everywhere. Jackson cast me a disapproving glance when I did it, but I had no idea if he disapproved of the knot or the cascade of ridiculous hair that blew into his face more than once.

"No problem. I'm always up for hopping into a truck with a guy I barely know and driving down a dimly lit highway where no one will hear my scream. Too bad my phone died. I had a lot of promise, you know. Shame it had to end this way."

He shakes his head, but I see the hint of a smile pull at his lips. It's the first sign of levity I've seen from him all day, and I like how it looks. I also like that I can bring it out in him with my gallows humor.

"You seem like you needed to hit the road. Do you always feel like this after a work day?"

He nods. "Pretty much."

I can't help but laugh. "Have you ever considered doing something else?"

His gaze turns pointedly toward me, then back to the road. "No. Not exactly an option."

"Why? Because no one else is capable of doing the job?"

"No, because it's a family business, and it's been drilled into me since birth that I'd work here."

"Huh." I don't say more because I'm mulling this idea over, and I don't like it.

His shoulders are tensing up again, and I don't like that either, so I decide to change the subject. Grudgingly. Because I really do want to talk about this some more, but I can see it stresses him out.

I suppose I'll have other opportunities because I see him every day, even if it's just for the handoff of Fiona from me to him at the end of his workday. I tell myself I'll find a way to make him talk some more.

Staring out the window, I can't see much, and it's so dark on the highway without lights that I can see him turn to look at me in the reflection on the glass.

I don't bite. He can look at me all he wants, but I'm still thinking. Specifically, I'm marveling at how different we are, and yet we're in the same place—stuck in a situation that isn't ideal because of our loyalty to family. Not an unusual story by any stretch, but still…it connects us.

He turns back toward the road—he has to because…driving. "What's that mean?" he asks, finally.

I shrug.

"Come on, Ruby, don't hold out on me. Radical honesty, remember?"

Rolling my eyes, I look at him. His profile might even be more beautiful than the head-on view of him. It's more subtle, jawbone cutting a clean line from his strong chin, muscle ticking in his cheek, lips set in a firm line that I know would give way if I kissed him.

I shake that thought away, not even sure where it came from. I haven't considered kissing a man in ages. Not the right time in my life. I need to stay focused.

Besides, he asked me a question.

"I was just thinking. Wondering what it might be like for you if you gave up the spreadsheets."

He laughs. It's so unexpected that I jump in my seat. He turns down another road, loops around, and pulls into the back parking lot of what looks like a roadside stand. The kind of place that sells beef jerky and dried fruit. Nothing about the ratty shingled roof over what's practically a lean-to says excellent food. But he lives up here, so I trust him to find us a good place for a burger.

That, or he plans on murdering me by the dumpsters lining the dirt lot where we've parked.

"Oh, Ruby. I'm a gentleman in the streets, a freak in the spreadsheets."

I bark out a laugh at his corny humor. "You are full of surprises, Jackson Corbett...but I'm being serious."

Shutting off the engine, he turns toward me. "So am I. I don't actually hate spreadsheets. It's the mistakes of people who came before me that I can't stand. And I have a big enough ego to think I can clean them up."

"Well, that's just plain dumb." If he wants radical honesty, he's getting it.

He nods. "I know, Ginger. I know."

"Okay, I'm not gonna belabor this right now, not when you're taking me to a scary-ass dark corner of the world from which I may never be heard from again."

"Ginger, I'm not kidnapping you." He spreads his hands out wide, and in one palm sits his cell phone. "Phone a friend, look at the GPS so you know where we are. I swear, I'm not trying to freak you out."

"Dude. Relax, I was kidding. And my phone's not really dead. I keep a spare charger, anyhow." I extract a little backup battery pack from my purse and show him. "We're good."

Throwing the door open on his side, he's out of the black Jeep before I can say anything more. A second later, he's yanking open the door on my side and extending his hand to help me down the high step.

With his hand on the small of my back, he leads me around to the front of the stand. It has an open awning, and I half expect to see boxes of produce lined up, all freshly harvested from some unseen farm. But instead, there's a hand-written menu describing different types of burgers. And a list of lemonade varieties. That's it.

"Best burgers in the area," Jackson confirms.

"I'm taking your word for it. Do they have anything besides burgers?"

He turns to me, concerned. "Jesus, I'm an asshole. I didn't even ask if you like burgers."

I'm so shocked at the tortured way his forehead creases that I almost can't respond. He seems nervous or unsure about his food decision, such a contrast to the smug, confident grump I met all those mornings ago.

"Relax. I love a good burger. I was just hoping they had fries, too."

He nods. "It wouldn't qualify as the best burger place if they didn't have excellent fries, too, at least in my book."

"Okay, then. Let's eat."

———

A half hour later, we've devoured a burger apiece, and we've ordered a second plate of fries with ketchup and mustard.

"I'm still a little suspicious of this mustard thing," he says, spearing a dollop of ketchup with a fry and popping it into his mouth. "Is that a childhood thing or something, liking that?"

"It's a mustard thing, liking it. And it goes with everything, fortunately for me."

He takes another fry, swipes it through the dish of yellow mustard, and studies it a moment before eating it. I watch him chew and try not to get distracted by the line of his jaw and the muscle in his cheek that I've never found so sexy on a man. I could watch him eat the entire plate of fries in some combination of food porn and cheek porn.

There are a few people sitting on barstools along the side of the place, which has a soda fountain and a sign advertising "the world's best root beer floats," but we're the only ones in the area of tables near the dirt parking lot.

"What?" he asks, wiping his mouth on a napkin and leaning his chin on his fist. It feels intimate, sitting here at a table under a metal umbrella beside this roadside gem. Now that it's dark out, the moon cuts a swath of pure white across the table, stars blinking to life above us. It feels intimate—romantic—and I tell myself to stop imagining things.

"Thank you for bringing me here."

He gazes at me with his chin on his hand and says nothing at first. I almost think he didn't hear me because it seems like he's not planning to do anything except stare at me. His gaze trails over my face as if he's memorizing the shape of my nose or the curve of my cheek before flitting to my mouth and back to my eyes. Almost like he can't keep his gaze from wandering.

It's not unnerving because I'm just as interested in staring at him. I take in his five o'clock shadow, the way his blue eyes pierce the air between us, his eyelashes, unfairly long and thick. Eyelids lazy when he blinks.

I feel the connection in the bottomless pools of blue but also in a place deep in my chest, a plum line running straight to my core, lighting me up.

It should feel weird to lock eyes for so long, but it doesn't. I almost feel like I'm being given a gift, being allowed to drown in the sight of him.

His eyes search my face, and for the briefest moment, I think he's going to lean in and kiss me.

He clears his throat and takes a sip of his drink, breaking eye contact. Then I remember how exhausted he is. Clearly, I was imagining the moment as more than it was.

"You're welcome." It comes so long afterward that I almost forget what he's referring to, but then I remember that I'd thanked him for bringing me.

"So, tell me about Fiona's schedule. What does she need each day, and how else can I help?"

He doesn't answer. I know he heard me because his shoulders have crept up another inch, and that doesn't make sense. She's the opposite of the job he seems to dislike.

"Jackson…"

"What?" He stays focused on the plate of fries.

"Anything else I should know about Fiona? How can I help you out? That's what I'm here for, so take advantage of me."

His mouth twitches at my unintentional innuendo, but he doesn't look at me.

"Hey." I tap his hand, which rests on the table. After a few taps, I leave my finger there, and he looks down at it before meeting my eyes. "What's up? Why'd you need to hit the open road? Is it the financial stuff? Is there anything I can do?"

His eyelids drop, and I get ready for another stony silence. But when he looks at me, he's focused. I notice an untouchable emotion veiled there.

"You're the first person to ask me that."

"Ask you what?"

"What I need."

Nodding, I feel a pang of sadness at what he's telling me—that he's always doing what he should, doing what he needs to do. But no one asks him what they can do to ease his worries and his burdens.

I'm about to offer more—I don't know what, exactly, but something—when he shakes his head.

"Nothing you can do, thanks. Except…maybe it would feel good to get this shit off my chest to someone who doesn't have a horse in the race."

"Your family?"

He nods. "Them, accountants, investors. I'm not looking for advice, but I've been holding everything in for so long, I feel like something's gotta give."

"Don't let the fuckers win. Talk to me. Maybe you'll feel better."

He smiles at that, and haltingly, grudgingly, he begins to talk. "Cone of silence?" I nod. He nods. "It's what I alluded to the day of your interview. Our accounting is off. We have expenses that don't make sense. I'm having trouble getting my dad to talk about them, and I think he's the only one who knows where the money was spent."

"He won't tell you?"

"He...no, he won't." He opens his mouth, and I wait for additional explanation, but he shakes his head. "It's complicated. He may have made a mistake. I don't know. Maybe keeping me in the dark is his way of protecting me."

I nab two fries, dip them in ketchup, and offer them to Jackson. His lips part, and I gingerly pop them inside, thumb grazing his bottom lip as I do it. I feel his breath hitch, and it makes my heart beat faster.

Swallowing down the urge to touch him again, I look away, dip two more fries in mustard, and eat them myself.

Two of the cars that were in the lot near us have left, and we may be the only ones still here. I'm aware of my looming commute home, but this feels like stolen time with a man who holds his cards close.

"Anyhow, the clock is ticking, and I need to find a way to find profits no one has thought of or creatively balance the books so shareholders don't pummel us. And I'm pretty much in it alone."

"That's stressful." I'm starting to understand why he's so surly and grumpy all the time, and it makes my heart twist in my chest. It's a lot for anyone to carry around.

"Yeah."

"Can you talk to your siblings about it? Maybe they know things that can help since you're all managing different parts of the business."

"I don't want to involve them in my problems."

"Jax..." His hand flinches under my finger when I use his

nickname. Before I can lift it away, he turns his hand over and wraps his fingers around mine. It feels like a bullet left a gun aimed straight at my heart. Like my hand is his lodestone, keeping him tethered and comforted in this moment. A lifeline.

I'm certain he can feel my pulse quicken, but he says nothing. So I continue. "You have a stronger work ethic than probably anyone I've met. You can figure this out. If you need me to come earlier in the morning and take Fiona to school, I can do that if it gives you more time to work."

"No." his growl leaves no room for interpretation.

"So, how can I help?"

"You already are. I'm grateful to have you taking care of Fi—it's a tremendous load off. The rest...I'll get to the bottom of it."

He crumples up the wrappers from our burgers and offers the tray of fries to me a final time. I shake my head, and he takes our trash to a bin. I feel the void when his hand leaves mine, but he seems to pay it no mind, so I tell myself the meaningless gesture was temporary comfort. For him, not me.

I have more questions, but I can tell he's shared all he plans to for now. It gives me insight into why he's so tightly wound, so I tuck away the information like gold nuggets.

We settle into the Jeep, and he pulls onto the road. I look behind us, where I see only darkness, and I feel certain we're going the wrong way.

"I'm new to Napa and all, but isn't Buttercup that way?" I point over my shoulder.

"Yeah. I'm taking you to Berkeley."

I shake my head, thinking I must have misheard him. "What? No. My car's at the winery."

"Okay, but your day's already gone off the rails because of me. You're tired. Let me drive you the rest of the way, and I'll send a car for you tomorrow to come back to work."

"Jackson, that's absurd. I'm good to drive. I'll grab a cup of coffee on the way."

"No. End of story." He makes no move to find an exit ramp

and turn us back in the direction of the winery. This man is as stubborn as a mule.

I lean back against the seat and study him, appreciating him a little more with every interaction.

As to the mule thing...I guess it takes one to know one.

# CHAPTER
*Twelve*

JAX

It's the right decision.

I'll pay for it in the morning. Hell, I'm already paying for it because I'm looking at three hours of work I could have been doing if I didn't feel a spontaneous urge to bolt off the property and drag Ruby with me.

"This makes more sense." I'm telling myself more than I'm telling her because it makes no sense. I don't do things like drive Buttercup Hill employees to their houses an hour away.

She has a hold on me, and it scares the fuck out of me.

"I'm still curious about the wine operation you've got in your closet, Ginger."

I'm looking at the road, but I feel her gaze on me. "That your way of inviting yourself up to my place, Jax?"

"It wasn't, but I ain't saying no." And…she's my employee, so I add for clarity, "Just offering to walk you to your door. Want to make sure you get in alright. The closet wine is just a curiosity." Although, if we were different people—if she wasn't my employee, and I wasn't such a jaded asshole, then maybe…

She laughs, tipping her head back against the headrest. "Maybe next time, when I don't have to be up again in seven hours." I can't decide whether I think she's actually entertaining the idea of inviting me up or giving me the brush-off.

"Is it going okay in the tasting room? You're not bored?" I grudgingly change the subject.

She shrugs. "Not bored. It's good. People are nice."

"People?"

"You know. People who come for tastings, the other Buttercup employees. Jemma's easy to work with. It's all good, Jax. Don't worry."

I do worry, though. If the job isn't stimulating, and if it doesn't put her on a path to becoming a sommelier, she might leave, and the more I know her, the more I hate the idea of that.

The hour-long drive back to Berkeley passes like it's five minutes instead of fifty. We talk and talk. It's just easy with her.

"Take the next one." She points to the green freeway sign ahead, so I signal and glance to the right before changing lanes. I take the opportunity to look at her before my eyes go back to the road. She seems uncertain, eyes darting around as we near the freeway offramp, and not nearly as calm as she seemed earlier when we stopped for food.

We exit at Ashby Avenue and drive toward campus. I don't get down to the Bay Area as often as I'd like, but seeing the Indian and Korean food places lined up next to gastropubs makes me realize I don't get to many places at all these days.

Ruby points me down Telegraph Avenue, which takes us from culinary diversity to funkier old-school Berkeley, where I'm surprised at how many storefronts are vacant.

"This is me," she says, pointing vaguely at a street. I look at the weed store on one corner, a burned-out former record store across the street, and an old swath of crime scene tape blowing in the breeze. I shoot Ruby a side-eye.

"*What* is you?"

"This spot. You can drop me here." She starts to open the door, but I hit a button, and the locks slam shut. Her look of annoyance would be comical if I wasn't sitting here looking at a corner that's clearly seen its share of crime.

"Not dropping you here."

"So why'd you offer to drive me home?" The innocence of her question runs smack into the worldly, old-soul version of her that I've been getting to know. Granted, I've spent my life in the silver spoon world of a family wine dynasty, but it doesn't take street smarts to see that she probably shouldn't be walking around alone here at night. Does it not seem dangerous to her?

"I mean, this doesn't seem particularly safe, Ginger. Where do you live, exactly? I'd like to get you as close to the front door as possible."

I'm not expecting her to laugh, but the musical chime of her giggles warms my soul, even if she's laughing at my expense. "I didn't realize you were such a housecat."

"What?" I turn off the ignition and turn in my seat to face her.

"It's not that scary out here in the world, I promise."

"Are you honestly telling me this seems safe to you?"

She looks around, taking in all the same landmarks I just did. Biting her lip, she seems like she's debating making a run for it. I'm prepared to chase her.

Instead, she nods. "Okay, keep driving."

Now I'm confused. "Driving where?"

Gesturing with a nod, she indicates that I should turn up Channing Avenue, so I do. She directs me to turn a few more times, eventually landing us in front of a high-rise collection of buildings that I recognize as university dorms. It's decidedly safer looking, well-lit, and located in an area where students walk up and down the street carrying backpacks.

"How about here? Better?"

"Are we just playing a game here? You're trying to placate me with a nicer drop-off spot so you can walk three blocks back to the other area by yourself?"

She looks at the ceiling of the car and huffs out a long exhale.

"You're infuriating."

"*I'm* infuriating? I'm not the one who's rolling the dice with safety. I'll drive you back to the other spot, but I'll be parking and walking you to the door to make sure you get in, and I won't leave until I hear the deadbolt lock."

She turns to me, eyes challenging. "I really hope you don't plan on being this overprotective with Fiona."

"You'd better believe I'm going to be even more overprotective. That is, if I even let her leave the house at all." I'm only partly kidding. It isn't lost on me that Fiona is on track to grow up to be the exact brand of independent, infuriating woman that I'm looking at right now. I both love it and hate it.

Ruby rubs a hand down her cheek like I'm working her last nerve, but I don't care. When it comes to my daughter, I don't compromise. "Okay, you may be the very best dad in the history of dads," she admits. I'm not expecting this about-face, which makes my heart squeeze unexpectedly in my chest. This woman both confounds me and comforts me in equal measure.

I lean as far away from her as I can within the car and open my window because I've broken out into a sweat.

"Thank you," I manage.

"You're welcome." She flicks a hand toward the building to our right. "This is where I live. You might as well know." I've parked under the wide canopy of a flowering cherry tree that still has some blooms left, and I realize exactly why I insisted on driving her tonight. I'm not ready to be free of her, and the ride was just an excuse.

She's humoring me the same way Fiona does when I tell her to do something she deems unnecessary, like wearing slippers when her feet aren't cold. To her, I'm an old, grumpy dude who works too hard and comes up with random rules.

I look at the signage on the front of the place, just to be certain my initial assessment was correct. "This is a dorm. Don't tell me that in addition to working two jobs, you're also a fulltime student?"

"No, but my sister is. I live with her."

"In a dorm?"

She shrugs. "Technically, she lives in a single, but no one ever checks, and I'm only here to sleep. And honestly, she's barely here because she stays with her boyfriend a lot. It works."

There's so much I want to unpack here. She's twenty-seven years old and just signed up to work two jobs, and she lives in her sister's dorm. It screams financial insecurity, but it's not obvious why.

It's also none of my business, yet I'm too fucking stubborn to leave it at that.

I can leave it at that for now until she's ready to tell me more. I do know that much about Ruby—she only talks when she's ready, but then she doesn't hold back.

A kid with dreadlocks and a beanie rides by on a skateboard, and a pair of girls in sorority sweatshirts stand on the sidewalk just outside my car, oblivious to us. Ruby watches them with vague interest.

She lives here. She sees this every day, but to me, this is a world long gone by. I haven't been on a campus in years, let alone lived in a dorm.

Still, there's not an iota of self-consciousness about her living situation or a sense that she feels sorry for herself. It makes me check my privilege yet again because I want to raise my daughter to be more like the woman in my front seat, and I don't know how to do it.

Ruby has been watching me for my reaction to her confession, and I make sure to school my expression. The last thing I want her to see is judgment. She starts to squint at me, and after a moment, her hand reaches out, and she rests two fingers against my cheek. I immediately flinch at the contact, which shoots a current down my neck, slices through my chest, and dead-ends at my dick.

She has got to stop touching me. I won't survive it.

"Oh, good. I was afraid for a second that you'd stopped breathing."

One hundred percent correct. I had, but not for the reasons she thinks. "I was just listening."

Nodding slowly, she points to my door, where I've commandeered the locks. "Can you release me, please? Like you said earlier, long day. I should get some sleep."

"If you swear this is where you actually live, I will set you free."

She holds up two fingers. "Scout's honor." I pray that she doesn't sweep those fingers against my cheek again.

I also pray she does.

"Can I walk you to your door?"

I get an eye roll. "You worried about dorm safety?"

"You never can tell."

"Fine. Let's go." She doesn't give me time to come around and open her door, swinging it open and hopping out with her tote bag slung over one shoulder. She waits for me to come around and escort her to the dorm.

I feel a hundred years old walking up to a college dorm, fully aware that Fiona is far closer to being college-aged than I am, and that also makes me feel ancient.

We pass a smattering of students sitting on benches and talking in the well-lit courtyard. In the common area on the ground floor, students sit at four-top tables or recline on couches. Most of them seem to be studying. All of them wear earbuds.

When we reach the bank of elevators, Ruby turns to me. "Okay, I think I'm good here." I get her message loud and clear, and I shouldn't need reminding. She doesn't want me to walk her to the door. This isn't a date. I've ensured her safety, and my job is done.

"Okay, just making sure. Text me when you get inside," I tell her, taking a step backward so I don't do something stupid. Like pulling her against my chest and kissing her.

She gives me a soft smile before the elevator doors close, and she's gone.

# CHAPTER
## Thirteen

JAX

PJ is the one to bring me a sandwich today. The sibling habit of forcing lunch on me hasn't stopped, despite the fact that I sometimes take breaks myself these days and make my way down to the test kitchen for a snack.

I think they just like an excuse to visit.

"It's the arugula and brie one. I know you like it."

"Thanks, Peej. Did you bring one for yourself?"

She fans herself with a manila folder she's holding, making the bangs she recently cut fan up over her forehead and drift down with each wave of her hand. I've never known my sister to wear her hair the same way for more than a year at a time. Bangs, color, cut—she's always trying something, and she almost always claims to hate what she's done. The bangs were a breakup cliché she fully admitted to falling for.

"Nope. I only have a sec." She opens the folder and runs her finger down a printed piece of paper, searching for something. "I'm figuring out tables and seating arrangements for the IMA event, and I need to know who you're bringing."

I groan at the reminder that I need to attend the Industry Movers Association dinner in a week. Our father insisted we all join the organization back when he was in charge of our financial future, and it means we all have to go to the group's events every month.

Sometimes, they're not terrible. We've had Bill Gates and other luminaries come as guest speakers to run roundtables on best practices for innovative businesses. Those events are great and always inspiring.

Unfortunately, most of the events are just dinners or obligatory weekend trips to hobnob with the other group members. The idea is to forge connections and grow Buttercup Hill Vineyards while helping media outlets and venture capitalists grow their businesses. One hand washes the other.

Once a year, we end up with an event at one of our restaurants. Attendees love it because they can bring a guest, and they're treated to a private tour of the nearly-mile-long wine cave and tastings of vintages no one else has tried. Everyone leaves with a case of wine and bragging rights about the experience.

Our sister Beatrix runs the whole thing, and PJ handles all the media and publicity. That can mean splashy magazine spreads or social media videos of celebrity weddings where the who's-who of Silicon Valley or the entertainment industry show up and need to be photographed looking fashionable and blasé.

Even though she's a pro at wrangling big names at events larger than this one—three hundred-person weddings are run of the mill at Buttercup—making sure all the niceties are in place for industry titans always gets her britches in a twist.

"Do I really need a guest?"

I know the answer, but I ask the same question every year in hopes of getting a different one.

"Let's not play this game."

"I haven't invited anyone, but I will."

She shakes her head, tapping her pen on the list in her hand. "I need a name today. How about Mallory Rutherford?" I don't mean to cringe at the mention of Mallory's name, but it happens anyway.

"No. Not her."

"Why not? You guys still make a nice-looking couple, and the *Times* will be here for media shots. You might as well look the part of industry titan."

"There are four more of you who can look like titans. I just want to drink a gin and tonic in a corner, shake a few hands, and get the hell out."

"Invite Mallory."

"It's too complicated."

A deep laugh rolls from PJ. "Why, because you won't be able to keep your hands off her? I'd say that's a good kind of complicated." She's right. Sort of. She's recalling a hot minute when Mallory and I hooked up at a party right after my wife left. I was drunk and very willing. But it was never going to be more than a one-night thing, though in my depressed drunkenness, I'm not sure I communicated that well.

"It's not. Besides, she'll be there anyway." Her parents own a massive piece of land with a small winery that half the Napa Valley vintners are dying to buy. They've never been willing to consider an offer, but Mallory will take over eventually, and she's been teasing everyone with plans to sell. It's part of how we ended up together that other night. Started out as her laying out her future ideas for the estate and me thinking it could be a shrewd financial coup if I could pull it off.

Seven gin and tonics later, she was in my bed, no potential deal was on the table, and I was filled with regret. I haven't seen her since then, so if anything, I should be avoiding her at the event, not walking in with her.

"Exactly. Better if she's on your arm. And besides, maybe it'll put us higher on the list when she wants to sell."

"Now you're out of your depth. Stick to PR." It's a low blow, but we each have our bailiwicks, and the finances of the vineyard aren't hers. Neither, for that matter, is who I do or don't bring to an event.

"Maybe I'll just bring Ruby. She works for me. I'll pay her to go."

I don't meet my sister's eye because I know she'll judge me, and I'm trying to play this off like the thought just occurred to me.

A lark. A whim.

Focusing on my computer screen, I pretend I'm thoughtfully composing an email, but instead, I'm gritting my teeth, waiting for her to give me her opinion.

My casual declaration is met with silence. Here we go. If she has an opinion, she's not going to share it because that would be too easy. It would allow for an actual discussion. An argument, even.

I can win an argument. I can't win against silence.

PJ is good at this.

Never one to suffer fools, she can wait a person out forever. She can win arguments without saying a word. Her steely stare is enough to have me thinking twice about what I've said, reasoning myself through the opposite scenario, and deciding I agree more with that view.

"Did you hear what I said?" I ask, finally, knowing full well that Ruby will probably balk at the idea of being paid to go to an event, feeling like it's charity.

"I heard you. Did you hear yourself?"

"Um, pretty certain that's not the point since I said the words."

She hops up on the corner of my desk and crosses her ankles, leaning back on her hands. If I want to see her face, I need to get up from my desk and walk around to the other side.

"What?" I don't have time to wait out her silent treatment or read any tea leaves to find out what she's thinking.

"You can't bring your nanny to the IMA event."

"She's not just my nanny. She happens to work for Buttercup, and you yourself said she was one of the best assistants you had the night she helped you at the Bloomfield wedding."

PJ looks at her list again as though it will reveal what she should say.

"Look, you know I like her, and yes, she was great at the wedding...but this is a business decision. Like I said, you'll be photographed, and this dinner is always a media zoo. I can't have any accidents. You need to be with someone...appropriate."

By which she means that she can't have people attending who might be wildcards, like my young nanny, who might get tongues wagging about whether I'm back on the eligible bachelors list after my marriage flameout.

Honestly, the last thing I need is people talking about me at all, let alone speculating about my personal life. For that reason, she's right about Ruby. Even though spending an evening with industry blowhards sounds a whole lot more palatable with her by my side. Still, I bristle at the idea that PJ would dismiss Ruby for not being sufficient.

"She's plenty appropriate enough," I say, feeling the heat creep up the back of my neck as I defend her, while praying my sister doesn't read my thoughts and realize just how attractive I find Fiona's nanny.

"You cannot bring your nanny as your date. The gossip mill will be rife with talk about you and the family. You need to keep up appearances, and the talk among the grapevines is that Mallory will inherit her parents' estate within the year. That makes the two of you a very interesting couple, and we could use that kind of press."

PJ may be the youngest, but she acts like my mother sometimes. Maybe the Corbett men need a little mothering, but I'd just as soon put my sister in her place.

"I wasn't aware this was a cotillion. Why do I need to be part of an 'interesting couple?' Next, you'll be proposing an arranged marriage as a business move."

"It's not like that." She laughs, but I don't see the humor. Far from it.

"Really? Feels that way. Happiness is disposable. I should just whore myself out for good publicity, all in the name of the family business." My voice is quiet, strained. That's what happens when I'm seething with indignation.

She knows when she's crossed a line, but we couldn't be more opposite in how we deal with things.

Swinging her legs like a gymnast, PJ uses the momentum to propel herself off the desk. She stands toe-to-toe with me, which doesn't make her any scarier, though she clearly thinks it does. "I told you. It's about optics. If Dad were able to make his case, I know he'd see it the way I do."

Closing my eyes, I have to admit she's probably right. And I hate it when she throws the "what Dad would do" into the equation. It makes me feel sad and guilty and angry at the same time, and then it makes me agree. She knows this.

"Will it really make the "optics" that much better if I pal around with the awful Mallory all night?" I roll my eyes.

"Yes, it will. And stop air quoting."

I force out a ragged sigh. "Fine. I'll do it, but only because we can't afford any more negative publicity right now. Between our numbers being off this quarter and Dad's health, we need to keep a united front. If schmoozing Mallory gives us that, I'll do it."

"Thank you."

But she doesn't leave. "Tell me, Jax. Why is she awful?" PJ probably doesn't really care about the answer to this question now that she knows she's getting her way.

She makes a note on her list and heads for the door, so I shrug and make up a lie. "I dunno. Maybe because she has nothing to say that doesn't involve being a nepo baby and inheriting her family's estate."

PJ seems satisfied with my explanation. But I'm fully aware of the real reason I don't want to show up with Mallory Rutherford on my arm—because she isn't the woman I want to be there with.

She isn't Ruby.

# CHAPTER
## Fourteen

RUBY

"I know that you have a job," my sister says from underneath a thick yellow quilt covered in fat daisies with smiley faces on it.

"Impressive, missy. I've been there three weeks already."

Flipping the covers off her face, she treats me to a view of her closed eyes, still covered in blue shadow and a beehive of hair piled on her head. Loose tendrils spill over her forehead, and she swats at them with a black press-on nail. "I know."

"So let me have the bathroom."

"No."

The point of this argument is that her alarm started blaring a minute after mine, and she's claimed dibs on the shower. I need to get in, get out, and get to Napa, so I'm not having it.

"Do you also know that it's six-thirty? Why are you up? You don't have to be on campus until eight, and it's a ten-minute walk —twenty if you stop at Café Strada for coffee."

It's her "guilty pleasure," as she calls her foolish coffee habit. The stipend that comes with her work/study scholarship doesn't leave enough spending money for daily cups of four dollar coffee. She only has coffee money at all because she's dating a guy who doesn't think twice about paying for her dinners.

Just for emphasis, I let the electric kettle's whistle blare for a bit longer before running it through the French press. Fifty cents a day when I buy the beans at Trader Joe's and grind them at the store. I calculated it.

The smell of brewing coffee will make my sister think twice about spending her money on coffee, even if it won't change the outcome. Habits are built one day at a time. I can't tell her what to do because she'll never do it, but I can drop very subtle hints, and eventually, she'll think it's her idea to drink the coffee here.

Ella rolls over and off the bed, which makes the mattress slip from its box spring. If she's aware of it, she doesn't care. Zigzagging through the small room with its university-issued four-drawer dresser, tidy desk, and orange chair, she looks like a drunken sailor on rough seas.

"You okay there?" Laughing at her movements, I wait for the coffee grounds to steep.

"I'm fine." The bathroom door slams, and I realize she still hasn't answered my question about why she's up so early. I can't think of the last time she's gotten out of bed without me making a lot more noise to wake her.

While I wait for the coffee, I check on my wine in the closet. The latest batch sits in the fermentation bucket under a cloth. It's only been nine days, and I need to wait a bit longer because there's no froth yet on the top. That means it hasn't finished, and if I take it out now, there will probably be sediment in the wine, which is the sign of a very amateur winemaker.

I'm no amateur.

I'll check it again tomorrow and see if it's ready to strain. Then, the real waiting begins while it goes through a much longer fermentation process. But I'm getting ahead of myself.

For now, I need to extract my sister from the bathroom so I can get ready for work.

"Ella." I pound on the door and get no response. "Come on, I need to go."

The bathroom door opens a crack, and she peeks through. "What?"

"I told you, I need to get going. Your class doesn't start until eight. You have time."

She flings the door open and sweeps into the room. Now she looks fully awake, hair tied back with a shoelace, face pink and freshly washed. In her hand, she holds a pink stick that I recognize all too well. My eyes go wide, and I lean forward to peer at it, nervous about what I'll see.

"It's too soon. I don't know anything yet." She seems calm. Wide awake but calm. She moves gracefully through the room and sits on the edge of the bed. The mattress slips to the floor, but she doesn't seem to notice.

"Are you okay?" I don't ask for details. Details don't matter as long as she's okay.

She nods. "But that's why I wanted to get up before you left this morning. I need you to do this with me. If I'm preggo, I don't want to freak out alone."

"Of course not. I'm here." I plop down on the sunken mattress. She scoots closer to me and puts her head on my shoulder. Wrapping an arm around her, I feel like I did when we were kids. The eight-year age difference was enough to make me feel like a parent to her when our parents died and I got custody of Ella.

We wait together, intentionally not looking at the pink stick, which Ella has placed on the orange chair.

"Coffee's probably ready. You want a cup?" I ask.

She smirks and nods. When I get up to pour it, she stretches out on the bed. "You were going to lecture me about saving four dollars and drinking this, weren't you?"

"Um, yeah. But now I can lecture you about something else entirely. Are you on birth control?"

"You know I am."

"And?"

She shrugs. "I don't know. Sometimes I take it later in the day, but I'm good about it. Trust me, I'm not looking to be a mom."

"Now, or ever?"

She rolls her eyes. "Now."

I hold out my hand with a cup of coffee right as a timer sounds on her phone. Ella sits up, takes the coffee, and leans over to reach for the pregnancy test. She holds it in her fist, not looking at it. "Ready?"

I nod. "Whatever it says, you know I'm here for you, right?"

"I know. Thank you." Ella takes a big breath and closes her eyes. She sits there for so long that I start to worry she's fallen asleep. But then her eyes pop open, and she opens her hand. Leaning toward her, I look at the tiny plus sign on the test.

My heart starts pounding, thinking about the implications for Ella. Does she want this? Can she handle it? Can I support her and a baby?

Then I look at her.

She nods. "Okay. I had a feeling. Okay." Her breathing quickens a little, and tears well in the corners of her eyes.

I'm going to be late for work, but I can't leave her here like this. "I'm here, El. We're going to get through this, okay?"

She wipes her eyes and nods. "Yeah. Okay. Thank you." The tears continue to fall. "I'm not sure why I'm crying. I mean, I love babies…they're so cute, but…this isn't what I planned on. Not yet."

"It's okay, sweetie. You don't have to defend yourself. Do you want me to… I could call in sick and hang with you today. Would that help?"

Shaking her head, she starts to cry in earnest. Big tears spring from her eyes and roll down her face, and she makes no attempt to wipe them away. "No. Don't do that. You need to make money, especially if…Oh gosh, Ruby, I'm so sorry."

Pulling her in for a hug, I smooth her hair. "Sweetie, don't apologize. I've got this. We're good." She clings to me like a koala high in a eucalyptus tree with no way down. "First things first. Let's make an appointment with your doctor."

Ella wipes away her tears, but new ones spring forth in their place. She nods. "Okay."

"Okay." I wrap her in a hug.

"You should go to work. You love your work, and you've spent so long trying to get to where you are. Be happy." It's the first time she's ever said anything about my late nights studying and part-time jobs at wine bars. I never knew she noticed. All this time, I've been wondering if she's been half asleep when we're in the same room, and she's been listening. Because she's my sister.

"Really?"

"Really." She kisses me on the cheek, crawls back under the covers on top of the lopsided mattress, and puts a pillow over her head. The coffee cup dangles from her hand.

I pull it from her grasp and put it on the desk. Her fingers hang limply, and after a minute, I hear the telltale steady breathing that tells me she's fallen asleep. That's my sister for you —even when she's freaking out about being pregnant one minute, she can fall asleep on a dime.

# CHAPTER
*Fifteen*

JAX

A few weeks into my nannying arrangement, I'm starting to feel like a human being again. A human being who goes to work, finishes nearly everything, and comes home at the end of the day with some energy to spare. Not to say that I don't wake up in the middle of the night plagued by problems I still can't solve, but at least I have available brain cells now to try and solve them.

And I look forward to coming home and ending my day with my girl. Much as I hate to admit it, my siblings were right. I'm a better dad to Fiona when I'm not running on fumes. Better because I hired someone to help me out. Better because I admitted I can't do every last damn thing myself.

The financial problems at the vineyard haven't disappeared, but I'm starting to get a grip on them. We're in debt to an investor, courtesy of my father, who borrowed nearly a billion dollars on behalf of the company. I still don't understand why, but the dominoes continue to fall as I find how much our company's business is affected in ways it shouldn't be.

It's a problem for tomorrow and the next day. For now, I'm

happy to be walking along the footpath that leads from the farm-house to Sweet Butter, the more casual of our two restaurants, by way of the one-mile loop around the lake.

Ducks drift on top of the water, leaving shallow trails in their wake. A mother leads a passel of babies that I wouldn't know about if I'd driven to and from my office like I've done for the past year. No time to be wasted taking the scenic route.

Only now, for the first time in ages, I notice whole swaths of our property that I've ignored. Lily pads float at the outer rim of the lake, star-shaped pink flowers sticking up like little sentries. A frog croaks somewhere in the distance, and one of the ducks flips its tail feathers up as it dives below for a small fish.

When I was a kid, I used to ride my bike around this lake—over and over again with Dashiell hot on my heels and gaining on me. The day he proved to be faster was the day we stopped racing.

The memories feel distant now, partly because we've all been called into service by our dad, and we all feel obligated to do right by him, even if he doesn't know the difference. Some inherited rule follower gene, apparently. But as I walk now and take in the evening air, ripe with the scent of grapes nearing their peak for picking, I let myself breathe deeper and have a moment of peace.

A glider passes by overhead. It usually happens in the early mornings when the winds are low, but this one is flying late after-noon. Fertilizer isn't my purview, so I don't pay much attention.

Even though I can't ask my dad what he's done and what he was thinking, life feels better right now. I try to avoid thinking about the reasons because I'd have to admit that some of my newfound joy is wrapped up in seeing Ruby every day. It's not just the help with Fiona that I appreciate. It's *her*.

Today, I told her to hold off on making dinner because she offered to take Fiona for a late horseback riding lesson. My daughter has been begging me for riding lessons, but I haven't had the time to take her during the week. Ruby never seems to run out of energy.

As a thank you, I'm stopping at Sweet Butter to pick up food for us. I know Ruby will try to run off as soon as I'm in the door, claiming that Fiona and I should have father-daughter time, and sure enough, she does.

"Come on. You two should have some time together," Ruby says when I plop the bags on the counter and suggest she stick around to eat with us. She starts rifling through the takeout containers, taking out an arugula salad, a caprese salad, a charcuterie platter, and a fried squash blossom appetizer before she shoots me a look.

"You expecting guests?"

I shake my head.

She's only unpacked one of the bags, and already there's more food here than two people could possibly eat, especially since one of them only likes noodles this week.

I take over unpacking the second bag, laying out containers of pasta arabiatta, spaghetti with meatballs, plain buttered noodles, and eggplant parm. There's enough food for us to eat for days, but I don't know what Ruby likes, so I erred on the side of too much.

"Come on. Stay for dinner. And don't tell me you've already eaten because we both know that's bullshit."

"I ate at the horseback riding place," she says, unable to keep from cringing at the lie as she says it.

"Yeah, I'm sure the carrots and hay were delicious."

I get an eye roll that rivals my daughter's, and she bites her lip while she mulls my offer. "Really? I'm not imposing?"

"It's not imposing when someone invites you, Ginger." I say it quietly enough that Fiona doesn't hear. If she gets wind of the nickname, she'll take it and run with it. And I prefer having Ginger all to myself.

*The nickname. I'm talking about the nickname.*

"We have lots of time together, don't we, Fi?" I ask, knowing how much Fiona adores Ruby. If there's a chance of having her stay for dinner, she'll agree to anything I say. Which would be a good time to get her to step outside the noodle zone, come to think of it.

"Yes. Plenty." Again with the eye roll.

"Fiona, it's not cool to roll your eyes at your dad," Ruby tells her. After all the times I've seen Ruby do the same thing, I raise an eyebrow at her. *Really?* She starts to giggle and puts an arm around Fiona. "Just *try* to do it a little less, k?

Fiona saunters over to me. Wrapping her arms around my waist, she buries her head in my stomach. "I'm sorry, daddy. But we do spend lots of time together. I was just agreeing."

"I know. It's okay," I tell her. "So would it be okay if Ruby stays for dinner?"

"OMG, Daddy, yes."

Before I can flip out at her use of texting language, Ruby steers me into the kitchen, where she starts laying out the food on our mismatched plates and platters, making the whole spread look even better. "Pick your battles, Daddy," she says quietly. "She'll lose interest in that expression long before you win her back after nagging too much."

She's probably right, but I barely hear her. I'm focused on the ripple of heat that shot straight to my cock when she called me "daddy." Yes, I know how wrong that is.

Fiona has been racing around the house like a zephyr since I came in the door. The kid has more energy than a puppy, and somehow Ruby manages to keep up with her. But tonight, I'm determined to give her a break, so I stomp over with exaggerated steps, arms crossed over my chest.

"Who likes noodles with butter?" I ask, grabbing Fiona and flipping her upside down.

"I do!" she squeals, thrashing around. "Put me down, daddy." When I lower her down head first, she erupts in giggles. "Kidding. I was just kidding!"

Throwing Fiona over my shoulder, I continue stomping around, this time heading for the stairs to make sure she showers and gets into her pajamas before dinner. Ruby watches the two of us like it's dinner theater, and I turn back and point a stern finger at her. "Please open a bottle of wine and pour yourself a glass. We'll be back in ten minutes."

————

"I am sooo full," Fiona says, sticking her belly out and stroking it in large circles. "I can't eat that." She points at the lone sprig of broccoli on her plate, the one green item I added to her beige dish of noodles.

"Guess you're not getting dessert." Spoken like the unfun parent I am.

"Bet you can't eat that piece of broccoli faster than I can eat mine," Ruby says, holding up an even larger piece that I'm pretty sure won't even fit in her mouth.

"Can too," Fiona says, picking up the broccoli and reminding me, yet again, how competitive she is and how hard that will bite me in the ass someday.

"Yeah? Loser gets the smaller bowl of ice cream."

And they're off. Fiona shoves the entire piece of broccoli into her mouth and chews, with Ruby reminding her, "mouth closed while you're chewing." Hearing Ruby give my daughter parental advice makes my heart swell even more for her.

Ruby's taking small, dainty bites of her sprig, all but guaranteeing that my daughter will swallow and digest her vegetable before she finishes half of it.

"I win!" Fiona announces, fist in the air. She pushes her chair back, legs dragging on the wood floor, and races to the freezer to find the ice cream.

Ruby drops the remains of her broccoli on my plate and mutters, "I don't really care for broccoli, if I'm honest."

And yet, she ate it for my kid.

Her rueful smile crinkles the corners of her eyes. "Don't tell."

"Never."

She gets up to make sure Fiona doesn't spoon too much ice

cream into her dish and adds a few raspberries on top "for color." I know she's trying to get Fi to eat more produce, but she doesn't need to try. Fiona looks at her like she hung the moon. If Ruby wants her to eat fruit, she'll eat fruit.

A full feeling blooms in my chest, but it has nothing to do with the giant meal we just polished off. This woman moves something inside of me that I'd long ago left for dead.

It's an ache of desperate yearning and also a glimmer of hope. I can't get enough.

I lean back in my chair and swirl my wine in its glass. The syrupy legs drip as the wine settles, a sign of good fermentation. Ruby picked a good bottle. Not expensive, but good in a way that sneaks up. Something that a lot of people pass over because it's not a Buttercup reserve or a limited edition. Just a good, solid, dependable wine.

I pour a bit more into both of our glasses. Wishful thinking. I know that as soon as Fiona goes to bed, Ruby will race out of here like she always does.

It's well past Fiona's bedtime, and she knows it. She's suddenly quieter, despite the sugar rush from the bowl of ice cream she practically inhaled. After she helps Ruby put the dishes into the dishwasher, she comes behind me and wraps her arms around my neck. "Thank you, Daddy," she whispers.

"For what?"

"For letting me stay up." I hug her back, never a doubt in my mind that she's the best thing to happen to me, regardless of what happened between me and her mom.

Ruby kisses the top of her head before I shuttle her up to bed with the promise of an extra story in the morning if she doesn't come back downstairs three times for a drink of water or a forgotten thought she "needs" to tell me.

"Fine. But what if I really need something?" she asks with a yawn, barely able to get the words out before her eyelids droop.

"I'm here, lovebug. Don't worry."

She opens her mouth to regale me with a final thought, but exhaustion leads her down the road to sleep.

When I come back downstairs, Ruby has finished cleaning up the kitchen, even though I told her to leave everything for me to do later.

"You are terrible at following instructions."

She laughs, carrying a stack of washed and dried plates to the cabinet. "Hey, did anyone ever point out that your plates don't match?"

"Yeah, it's been noted." The kitchen is spotless, and Ruby moves to the couch in the family room next to the kitchen and lets out a long breath. "It's also okay to admit you're wiped out."

"I'm wiped out."

"Fi will do that to a person." The mention of my daughter's name makes her smile. It's that kneejerk thing that happens when someone's crept into your heart, and just thinking about them when they're not around makes you happy.

I've noticed Ruby having that reaction to Fi's name, and my daughter gets equally giddy when I mention Ruby. Fiona and I share that affection for her. Apple doesn't fall far.

I find myself tempering a smile every time someone makes an offhand comment about Ruby. Just yesterday, Beatrix was talking about something that happened in the tasting room. "We had a party bus drop off twenty sorority sisters for the afternoon. Coulda been a shitshow, but Ruby handled it," Trix said. I fought a grin at the image of Ruby at work, and I worried that my affection for her is obvious to anyone paying attention.

Standing still in my kitchen, Ruby cocks her head, listening for any sign of Fiona rustling upstairs. "Think she's asleep?"

"Oh, yeah. You did the impossible. You tired her out."

"Ha. Okay, my job is done."

"She loves you," I confide. "In case you were thinking about abandoning us, don't do it. I might survive, but Fiona…not a chance."

Ruby laughs gently, as though the effort of laughing harder is too exhausting. But I'm not really kidding. Fiona and I have come to need Ruby more than I ever thought possible, and it concerns me. I don't want anyone getting hurt, least of all Fiona.

Ruby pops the last of the takeout containers into my fridge.

"Ginger, you're off the clock. Stop cleaning up."

Satisfied that the kitchen looks neat, she nods and pushes her chair back. "That wine was good, by the way."

"You had three sips," I point out.

"Driving." She points to herself with both thumbs. I respect that she's so responsible. "Three sips was enough to know it's delicious."

"Glad you liked it. Old vines." I hold up the bottle and look at the label, which has the older design of a hay-filled wagon against a sunrise. Our new logo—a simple buttercup that looks like it's sketched on the craft paper label—is better for our brand, but I miss seeing the old one and still have cases of wine in my cellar from the older vintages.

"Nothing like that in the tasting room. Hope I didn't rob you of something precious."

Every time she says something like this, it reminds me that she thinks about everything this way, in terms of cost and value and scarcity. Meanwhile, I uncork a hundred-dollar bottle of something I like without thinking about it. Makes me feel like the silver spoon asshole I am. Just what my father raised me to be.

"Even if it was, you're worth it, don't you think?"

She moves to the couch, so I can't see the expression on her face when she answers. "On my good days, maybe."

"They should all be good days, Ginger."

I get a muffled grunt of agreement. Or dissent. Can't tell.

Noticing our half-filled wine glasses still on the table, I reach over and grab mine, along with Ruby's full water glass and the bottle. Ruby is sprawled on half of the couch, so I put the glass down on the wood plank coffee table and sit in a leather chair opposite her.

"So what got you interested in wine, anyway?" I ask. Probably should have been the first question when I fake-interviewed her, but like I said, I'm not good at interviewing people.

She laughs. "Isn't that obvious to someone in the wine business?"

"Not at all. I didn't have a choice. It's a family thing."

Turning her head to look at me, she levels me with a truth stare. "You always have a choice, Jax."

Her words strike me, as they often do, as a revelation. So obvious, and yet I'm generally so oblivious to this kind of truth. "Is that how you live your life? Making choices according to what you want instead of what you're supposed to do?"

I expect an eye roll. Because of course she does. Someone like Ruby charts her own course. "Yeah, that would be a no," she admits. "Family tends to blur those lines between wanting and doing. It's disappointing at times, but it is what it is. You get it."

I do. And yet again, I feel like a jerk for assuming she's free to chart her course without the obligations. She just hides her disappointment better than me. "Feel like elaborating?"

"Sure." She tells me more details about her parents dying in a car accident. "Drunk driver. No life insurance policy, not much money. So I got a job." She shrugs like it's normal to get custody of a sister at nineteen and find a job to support them both.

"Hang on. That's a lot. You just…got a job? Doing what?"

"I worked as an office temp. It was great because my classes were mainly on two days, so I could take full shifts on the other days, and the pay was better than minimum wage."

I know I'm not doing a good job of hiding my shock, but I can't help staring at her with my head tilted forward and my eyes wide. "You stayed in college and worked too?"

"I had to. I mean, the school was amazing and gave me a scholarship so I could afford to stay. But I needed to support both of us. Needless to say, I don't have, like, an IRA or whatever. Not exactly saving anything."

I reach for her hand, which seems like a minuscule gesture, but she grips it tightly. Eyes moist, she looks more vulnerable than the woman I see every day. Her grimace tells me she doesn't enjoy recounting the story, and I feel even more gratified that she trusted me with it.

"No one would expect you to have an IRA," I say gently. The idea of retirement savings is almost absurd. She lets out a small laugh.

"Yeah, I guess. I'm lucky that Ella has paid housing, but I do realize that dorm living is not a long-term solution. Hence the two jobs." She exhales. Then blinks and shakes her head. "Oh, and my sister's pregnant, so there's that."

"*What?*" I feel like the whiniest asshole for complaining about my job or my life when she's been carrying all of this on her shoulders. Holding her hand doesn't seem like nearly enough, but I'm her boss, and I can't do half the things my heart is urging me to do. So I put my other hand on top of hers, cupping it between mine.

"Yeah. I'm taking her to the doctor. We'll deal with that when we know more." She shrugs. She actually shrugs, like it's all going to be okay. But how can It be? Maybe because she just faces things head-on and makes it okay. I'm stunned.

When she finishes talking, she looks a little less exhausted, as though unburdening has relieved her of something.

"You're so fucking amazing." I need better words, more eloquent words, but these are all I have. She blushes.

"Thanks."

I want to lighten her load without making her feel like it's charity, but I have no idea what to propose. "Can I do something to help you?"

"You already have. This job is getting me on the road to renting my own place."

I could do so much more. I could *buy* her a place. But I don't want to risk insulting her.

"You don't look comfortable," Ruby observes as I try to arrange my limbs so I fit into my chair. It's a massive failure, and I end up slumped over my lap with my elbows on my knees.

"Yeah, it was a mistake to buy these." I gesture at the matching chair next to mine. Not bad enough I have one of them—they came as a pair. "The idea of having this library look in here seemed cool, but the chairs are hard and not that comfortable."

Ruby's head swivels around, and she takes in the tall bookshelves that flank the wood-burning fireplace and nods. "It does have that feel. You need a pipe, though, if you're really going for the Sherlock Holmes vibe."

"Just a pipe? Short of that, I've nailed it?"

Her laugh is heartier this time. "Totally." She pulls herself into an upright position and scoots to a corner of the couch, patting the now-empty cushion. "Here. I can't be the only one sitting in the lap of luxury. Doesn't seem fair."

My brain sticks on the mention of "lap," because I'd like to haul her onto mine, but instead, I move to the opposite corner of the couch and sit. She turns to face me and brings her feet up to cross them underneath her.

I pick up her water glass and hand it to her, letting our fingers brush because I need the contact, even if it's just this. Electricity. Fire. Lust.

Every damn time.

Her eyes snap to mine, and she swallows hard before casting her gaze away and taking a sip from her glass. I'm aware that I'm staring at her lips as she drinks and wanting…her.

"Can I ask you something personal?" She winds a strand of hair around one finger, then lets it go. It spins but maintains its curl. My hands flex. I want to get my hands in that hair, but I can't. Things are going so well with Fiona, and I can't fuck it up by driving her nanny away with my inappropriate behavior.

My thoughts are racing out of control because I've told myself so many times that I can't have her, and now I can't think about anything else.

I'm so distracted—so utterly captivated—by the proximity of her on my couch that I mutter "sure" to her question without really hearing it.

"Why did she leave?" Ruby asks. Then I'm brought back to earth. We've never talked about Annabelle, and I'm not sure I want to. I don't talk about my ex-wife with anyone.

"Who?" I stall and feign ignorance while I decide whether I'm willing to let her into this messy part of my life.

Not surprisingly, she doesn't let me get away with my shit for a single second. "Looking like you do, I'm sure there's a long list." Her hand goes to her mouth, and her eyes squeeze. "Sorry, that was rude."

"I wasn't offended." My dick jumps in my pants at the thought that she finds me attractive.

"You don't have to answer the question. Unless you want to."

For reasons I don't completely understand, I do want to tell her. Everything about the way I react to Ruby is instinctual, and half of it catches me off guard, so I'm as lost as she is. Case in point, when anyone else asks me a question I don't feel like answering, I deflect it or shrug it away.

With Ruby, I feel like I want to give her the truth.

"She said she wasn't cut out to be a wife and mother." Rehashing those words is a gut punch all over again. Doesn't matter how much time goes by.

Ruby waits. I don't elaborate. I'm not sure how much more there is to tell.

"Is that all?"

"It's also why I don't have matching dishes. She took them when she left, and I never wanted to own another set. Felt like a reminder that she didn't want to be here."

"I can't imagine how she could leave now that I know you and Fi."

The air leaves my lungs, because in a few short weeks, it's not just Fi and I who've made an impression. She's burrowed deep into my dreams, and the waking moments that aren't spent worrying about finances are all spent on her. And I still want more.

"Yeah, that's why I won't risk another relationship. My

daughter deserves better." I say the words to remind myself what I know is true, even though it makes my chest ache. I'm also offering Ruby a warning, telling her I can't ever give her anything long-lasting or substantial. I just can't.

Even though right now, I want to risk everything for the woman next to me.

I slide closer to her on the couch, close enough that I can hear her breath hitch. But after a brief look of surprise, her eyes flash with recognition. Her hand falls to the space that remains between us on the couch.

She leans on it, edging herself a few inches closer.

Chin turned up toward me, eyes clear. Challenging.

My senses are overwhelmed by all the ways I crave her, all the places my hands are desperate to touch her, but I focus on her mouth. The way her tongue slips out to lick her bottom lip.

She's not telling me this is a bad idea. It's the only remaining scrap of hope that could stop me from taking what I want. And it's gone.

"Ruby…" It's a warning and a declaration.

She nods.

I can't stop staring at her lips, which still have a faint trace of the berry pink lipstick she wore all day. All I can think about is kissing the rest of it off of her. She knows. Understanding in her eyes. Complicity.

Mesmerized, I reach a hand out and trace the apple of her cheek, trailing my finger down her milky skin, memorizing every freckle.

"Daddy?" Fiona's voice calls out. "I can't sleep."

Air crowds my lungs. Ruby jerks back, out of my grasp.

"Shit." Inarticulate, and it's not even a fraction of my disappointment.

Ruby backs away. At this point, she's practically plastered against the arm of the couch.

I can't ignore my daughter's cry.

"Go," she says.

Nodding without conviction, I close my eyes in one last-ditch attempt to hold onto the moment. Then I let it go.

"Yeah," I agree.

Ruby stands up first, giving my legs the power to do the same.

In a millisecond, she has her purse and sweater in her hand, all traces of her presence in my house disappearing while I watch numbly.

"I'll see you tomorrow, Jax. Sleep well." She moves toward the door.

Fiona calls for me again, and I head upstairs to her room. I hear the motor of Ruby's car hum to life, and the last iota of hope bleeds away.

But one thing is certain. If I sleep at all, I'll be dreaming of a kiss that never happened. A kiss I can't get out of my fucking mind.

# CHAPTER
## *Sixteen*

RUBY

It takes me half the drive down to Berkeley for my pulse to slow enough so I can breathe normally. My hand comes to my cheek, where Jackson ran his finger down my skin, setting every inch of me on fire as he moved.

I feel hollow, as if I've lost the life force that normally fills me up. It makes no sense. Yesterday, I left work feeling exhausted, as usual, from working all day and chasing Fiona around the vineyard all afternoon. Now, I feel energized, buzzing with a sense of possibility.

If Fiona hadn't woken up, I might still be on Jackson's couch. The look in his eyes and his gentle touch would have turned into a kiss. No question there.

He told me he didn't want to have another relationship again after what his ex did. He laid that information out very clearly. And I took it as the warning it was.

This out-of-control, pesky attraction has no place in my life. Do I really want a fling? Is he just looking to screw the nanny?

Keep me as a convenient plaything because he's not over the loss of his wife?

As I drive through darkness on my way home, I have a hard time convincing myself that's true. From what I know of Jackson, he doesn't do anything lightly. He doesn't make mistakes.

Which is why it's probably a good thing that Fiona called him upstairs before he touched me anywhere else because I might not have stopped him. Wouldn't have wanted to stop him.

That's a problem because not just one but two jobs hang in the balance, and I need both. What's more, I like both of my jobs. Coming to Jackson's house after working in the winery lets my mind relax after cramming it full of details about vintages and tasting notes from each visitor.

After just a month, there's a noticeable uptick in my income now that I've deposited a couple of paychecks. I can't jeopardize that.

I find myself tracing the same path down my cheek, trying to recall exactly how Jackson's hand felt, but it's not the same. And by the time I get home and crawl into bed, fatigue has taken over, and I drift into a deep sleep.

———

Jackson makes no mention of what almost happened when I see him the next day. He's so utterly casual and normal that I almost wonder whether I imagined the gentle way his finger grazed my cheek. The look in his eye.

Maybe I had a streak of paint on my skin after doing art projects with Fiona, and he was merely wiping it off. Then my active brain mistakenly conjured some sort of romantic connection where there wasn't one.

After all, he's my boss, and his marriage ended badly. He's fiercely protective of Fiona, and he has a full plate at work. I doubt he's looking for complications.

For a few days, I sneak glances at him when he walks in the

door, wondering if he'll offer some tacit acknowledgment that we had a moment, even if it was something he regrets.

But there's nothing.

His sole focus is Fiona, who he greets like she's the summer rain on his parched soul. "Fi!" he calls when he opens the door. That is, if Fiona hasn't heard his car pulling up and come racing down the stairs of her own accord.

"Daddy!" she cries with equal zeal. They're so entwined with love that it fills my heart. I remind myself that I'm the nanny, not the missing piece in his family circle. I have my own family to worry about, and I need to keep my priorities straight.

By the end of a week, things feel back to normal, and I do my best to forget about the salacious dreams I keep having every night.

I try and I fail.

I tell myself to try harder.

Then, I down a second cup of coffee each afternoon when Fiona is having her snack in the kitchen. As much as I try to be the Energizer bunny and push myself along on sheer adrenaline, the two jobs are beginning to wear on me.

Each day, I work on my viniculture, wake my sister if she's sleeping in the dorm, and get myself to Napa by nine. My six-hour shift in the tasting room has only two fifteen-minute breaks, and then I head to Fiona's camp and pick her up. I agreed to stay until eight each night so Jackson has time to finish everything and get home to hang with Fiona and put her to bed.

He almost never stays at work that late, even if that means he brings his laptop home and works later.

I try for a quick handoff so he has as much quality time with Fiona as he can get.

"No, stay a bit," he always says. I haven't outright told him that money is tight, but after seeing that I share a student dorm with my sister and hearing about my past, he's gotten the memo.

"I don't want to intrude on your time together," I always say. It's our little politeness dance, waltzing around the subject of why he wants me to linger—so I'll earn another hour's worth of pay, even though he doesn't need me once he gets home.

"You're not intruding. Just stay."

So I do. And it stops feeling unnecessary. I realize I look forward to the hour or so when the three of us are in the house together. It feels normal in a way I haven't experienced with my family in such a long time. I lean into the feeling carefully because I know Fiona and Jackson are not mine to keep.

Today, Jackson is home before six in the evening, the sun still bright and hot in the sky. I hear his tires crunch on the drive and feel my pulse speed up in anticipation of seeing him.

*I just like him as a person. I enjoy his company. That's all.*

Fiona hides behind a trellis that leads from Jackson's back porch to the rows of chardonnay grapes that run for nearly a mile. I pretend I don't see the wiggles of blond backlit by the bright sun. Her slim body fits behind the trellis, but that hair can't be contained. Reminds me of my own crazy waves that are currently swept into a topknot, though a million rogue strands have sprung loose.

"What're you doing, Fi?" Jackson's voice booms from the porch.

I hold a finger to my lips and shake my head. He goes quiet and takes a step back. "I can't find her," I tell him in a dramatically loud voice.

"Oh, she outsmarted you, huh?"

We hear a giggle behind the trellis. Jackson's face lights up at the sound, and I light up watching him.

*Because I like him as a person.*

I smile, glad he's caught on. He walks right past Fiona and spins in a circle, intentionally looking everywhere except where she stands with her eyes squeezed shut as though that will make her invisible.

He stomps back over to the porch, slumping his shoulders in mock defeat. "I can't find her either. Wow, she's really good at this game."

"She has her daddy's brains, so I shouldn't be surprised," I tell him.

I'm not flirting. It's the truth. I've never met a kid as sharp as Fiona, and she gets the same intense look as her dad when she's trying to work something out. She's all Jackson.

His smile doesn't carry to his eyes, which are focused on something in the distance. I can't blame him—when I look out at the vineyards, I find myself lost in reverie as well, but in Jackson's case, I'm not sure that's all there is to it.

"Hey, where'd you go?"

He blinks and squares his shoulders. "Eh, just work stuff. Still thinking about it, I guess." His sigh tells the truth. He's more than thinking about it.

"Want to talk instead of just thinking? I'm more of a science gal, but if you feel like throwing some numbers at me, I'll try to keep up."

Even though he's been coming home from work earlier over the past week or so, I don't get a sense that he's any less stressed about his job.

He rubs the back of his neck, face set in grim resignation. "I have no doubt you could keep up." His voice lowers, barely above a whisper. "Trouble is I'm not sure I can explain it. Everything comes down to the numbers, and they're not adding up."

"Any new idea how to fix that?"

"No." A muscle in his cheek ticks. I wait to see if he'll explain more than the little he told me at the burger place, even though it's none of my business. Maybe the finances of the winery are proprietary information, and I'm just an employee in the tasting room. Even if I do have a college degree, it doesn't give me any special insight.

"Well, the answer is there, and I'm sure you'll find it. Or maybe someone on your team will come up with a lead."

"I'm not discussing it with my team," he admits, rubbing his neck again. "I don't really have much of a team, actually. Just my assistant and an accountant who works with the numbers I give him."

"So you're a lone wolf, basically."

"I guess you could call it that."

I nod. It makes sense. This is the man who was shouldering a job and being the sole caregiver for his daughter until a month ago.

"Ever consider working on that? Letting people help?" I elbow him gently in the ribs, and he catches my arm before I can pull it back. I feel the zing of electricity when his hand wraps around my elbow, then casually slides down the length of my forearm and squeezes my hand.

I stand frozen, unsure if I want to meet his eye and search for meaning where there might be none.

"You *guys*. I was hiding right there!" Fiona steps out from behind the vine, hands on her hips, bottom lip jutting out.

Jackson drops my hand like it stings and takes a step away from me.

The seriousness of the moment rides off on the breeze as he strides over to hug Fiona.

"You're a very good hider, what can I say?"

Fiona laps up his praise and tilts her head, looking from one of us to the other. "Who wants to play tag?" She doesn't wait for us to answer before poking each of us with a finger and spinning away. "You're both it! And you can't catch me."

Fiona has the spindly-legged gait of a colt as she races down a row of vines with her arms pumping. I watch her blond waves bounce and catch the sun as she runs carefree through the rows of twining plants. Her smile is so wide; I could count her teeth from here when she turns back to see if we're hot on her heels.

In the distant sky, a glider sails along, something I've gotten used to seeing over the vineyards. They fertilize the vines or drop pesticides on neighboring crops, just not at Buttercup because the vines here are organically grown.

I turn back to Jackson, who shoves his hand into the pocket of his jeans. "Thanks for offering to talk. Or listen. Maybe I'll take you up on it sometime." He inhales, and I think he might say more, but he clamps his lips shut.

"Anytime."

We turn our attention to Fiona, who's barely visible now that she's turned down a row of vines. A whisp of her pink dress is our only indication of where she is, and we take off jogging in her direction.

"I can't believe how much energy that girl has," he says, his stride so long it takes me two steps to every one of his to keep pace.

"She's a dynamo. Gotta tire her out before bed," I tell him. "I thought I had at least an extra hour before you came home."

"You want me to leave and come back?" He stops moving and takes a step away, testing me.

"Don't you dare. You're the only one with any hope of catching her."

"That the only reason you want me to stick around?" His eyes are teasing, and I suck in a breath, stammering for a response. What is he asking me?

He winks and takes off in Fiona's direction again, calling back to me, "I'll wrangle my daughter. You order us some takeout, and I'll meet you back at the house in an hour."

I start to yell that I'll cook dinner. He doesn't need to order food for me like I'm a guest. But as soon as he starts moving, he's quickly out of earshot, so I turn back toward the house. I'm grateful for the reprieve, but I feel a little bit guilty about sticking around and collecting an extra two hours of pay, plus dinner, when Jackson clearly doesn't need my help.

Walking slowly back to the house, I realize I'm more tired than I thought. Bodies in motion stay in motion, and I have a feeling that if I sit down, I won't want to get up.

And then I do exactly the opposite of what I should do. As soon as I've called the order in for tacos at a place down the road, I sit down on the couch. Stretching my legs out, I put my feet up on the table and enjoy the few minutes of inertia while I have them. Soon enough, I'll be back on my feet and shuttling Fiona up for her bath.

Might as well enjoy the quiet moment while I have it. That's the prevailing thought as my eyes slip shut. Just for a moment. Only a moment.

# CHAPTER
## Seventeen

JAX

I wasn't about to wake Ruby last night, not when I found her fast asleep on my couch after working late. Not wanting to disturb her or have her drive home that exhausted, I tucked a pillow beneath her head and put a blanket over her so she'd stay warm.

Now, I creep downstairs like I have cat paws for feet, half expecting to find an empty couch. I slept poorly, listening for signs that Ruby woke up on the couch and bolted out of my house in the middle of the night. Even though I didn't hear the front door close, I still worried she'd found another way to slip away.

And since I was busy not sleeping well, I took time to continue raking myself over the coals for my behavior the last time she stayed for dinner. I can't decide the reason I'm mad at myself—for putting us in a position where a kiss felt inevitable or for not kissing her when I had the chance.

When I hit the bottom step, the staircase creaks, groaning like it's upset for being used at five in the morning. Well, too damn bad. I need to get to my office and see if the loan payment I stumbled on yesterday is really what I think it is—evidence that my father borrowed nearly a billion dollars to buy grapes we shouldn't need because our production is efficient.

Unless it's not efficient…but Archer would have said something about that.

If I'm right about what I think I saw, it means one of two things: at best, it's a mistake, and the money may be sitting in an offshore account; at worst, it means my dad was borrowing money Buttercup can't repay and buying grapes that will taint our legacy vintages if they're used to make wine. With his mind slipping, it's anyone's guess what he was doing.

When I get to the living room, I see a cascade of copper hair splayed over the pillow on one end of the couch, bare feet propped on the sofa arm opposite. I feel like a voyeur as I creep closer and study her face, long lashes fanned out over the apples of her cheeks, lips a warm pink without a drop of lipstick. She looks peaceful in that way Fiona does when she's in a deep sleep and oblivious to the vagaries of the waking world. Only in Fiona's case, she's mostly oblivious when she's awake, too, and I hope she retains her youth for as long as possible.

Ruby hasn't budged from how she was splayed out last night when I came back to the house with Fiona, who begged me to let Ruby "keep dreaming." I covered her with a blanket, and she slept through our taco dinner. There was no way I was waking her and putting her on the road.

Now, I feel like an asshole for not realizing how damn tired she must be, despite her insistence that she's built for working two jobs and commuting back and forth. Doesn't matter how young and energetic a person is—there's a limit. She reached hers last night, and I was relieved it happened here on my couch instead of on the road.

I pull the blanket over her feet and mull an idea that's popped into my brain as I move to the kitchen to make us some coffee.

Turning on the dim light over the sink, I keep my movements small and quiet, aware that the sun will come blasting through my kitchen windows and into the living room in less than thirty minutes. Until then, I want to let her sleep.

I pop a pod into the Nespresso machine while a frothing jug whips the milk for a restaurant-grade latte. I know Ruby takes milk in her coffee because I watch her add it when she makes herself a cup each night before she drives home.

Do I know what my siblings take in their coffee? Nope. But they don't force my heart to run laps around my ribcage like her.

Glancing at her again, I realize that the sight of her bathes my normal workaday morning in a sweet glow I didn't know I was missing. Even when I was with Fiona's mom, I never woke up and felt grateful that she was there.

It's a jarring thought, made more so by the sudden loud grind of the coffee machine as it presses hot water through the pod.

"What? Hey. Hold on… Wait, did I…?" Ruby sits bolt upright on the couch and scrambles for her phone, which I've laid on the coffee table beside her.

"It's five in the morning. Relax. You're good."

"Five in the…?" She blinks and tries to open her eyes wider against the heavy strain of exhaustion.

"Morning. You fell asleep on the couch, and I didn't want to wake you."

She slaps a hand against her forehead. "I slept here all night? Oh, geez. I'm so sorry."

I swirl the steamed milk around in the frother and tap the container twice on the counter to get the foam to settle on top. Then I pour milk into the espresso and top it with a dollop of foam.

Ruby takes it from me wordlessly and sips it, a quiet groan of approval escaping her lips. I drop a second pod into the machine and make myself a matching cup. I watch the brown liquid pour into the cup because it keeps me from staring at her messy hair and imagining my hands combing through it.

"You don't need to apologize for being tired. You've been working yourself to the bone."

She tips the mug back for another sip, which leaves a faint mustache of foam on her lip. I'm dying to reach over and wipe it off, but I just stare, fantasizing about licking it off instead.

Apparently, I'm not at all subtle about where I'm staring because she licks her bottom lip and wipes her upper one with one finger. Then she licks the foam from that, either completely oblivious to the effect she has on me or completely aware. Is she toying with me?

"You okay?" she asks.

I grunt and clear my throat.

"Thank you for the coffee, by the way. Should have said that before, but I was too busy inhaling the whole cup." She shows me the now-drained ceramic cup.

"I can make you another."

"Nope, I'm good. But I…" Shucking off the sherpa blanket, she stares down at her black pants and lace-trimmed tank top. "I can't wear this to work again today, and I don't have time to go home. Showing up in yesterday's clothes isn't a good look for the nanny."

"I can ask one of my sisters for something to wear. You're a little smaller than them, but I'm sure one of them has something that will fit."

Her jaw drops open. "Yes, let's invite more people into this walk of shame."

My mind immediately goes to an image of Ruby walking out of my house wearing one of my button-up shirts like a dress and a pair of stilettos. Then my dick swells in my pants because I've truly lost my grip on reality.

"Sorry. You could run over to Duck Feather when it opens. I know they have a gift shop."

She laughs. "Yeah, that'll work. I hit that place up the day I showed up for my interview in a flimsy top and booty shorts. Your reaction was priceless, by the way."

I'd been meaning to talk about that. In the month since she's worked here, we've talked about so many things, but never that. "Can I apologize for that a month too late?"

Ruby folds up the blanket and lays it on a corner of the couch. "Never too late for an apology. But it's fine." She checks her phone for the time. "Actually, I can make a quick run home and back. All good."

Glancing around the room, she spots her sweater and pulls it on. My brain starts firing disjointed thoughts, all of them telling me to remove the sweater because she looks so damn good in the tank top.

But then...she works for me. And Fiona loves her. For the first time in two years, I'm getting enough sleep that I can actually see straight.

The last thing I should be doing is putting our nanny in the position of having to turn me down and report to work the next day. I've had enough sexual harassment training to know I should stay focused on my job and not on my employee.

Buttoning the sweater halfway, she stifles a yawn. "Thanks for letting me crash here, even if I didn't know I was planning to do it."

"Of course. It was the least I could do. Really, Ginger, you're the reason I'm not losing my shit every day of the week. You're keeping everything running around here, and I'm grateful."

She runs a hand through her hair, causing long pieces to fall in front of her face, but not before I catch sight of a shy smile. "You got it."

As she goes for the door, I debate whether to propose what I'm thinking. "Listen, I have an idea." I shift from one foot to the other, giving myself a last-ditch hope of coming up with something better. I fail.

"Yeah? What's that?"

"I-I think you should move onto the property. We have some cottages near the hotel for staff who work nights, and they're not all being used. At least, I don't think they are. I need to run to my office and look at the spreadsheets, but I believe we have space."

She looks confused. "You want me to live…here?"

I nod. I do want that. More than she knows. But I try to make it sound casual. "It just makes sense. It saves you more than two hours in the car each day, and you can use that time to poke around the wine cave and shadow our sommelier here if you want. Seems like a win-win."

"Only I'm the only one winning. I don't want to feel like you're just giving me money. I won't take your charity. What do you get out of it?"

*If she only knew.*

"I get an employee who isn't running on fumes. I get to sleep at night because I'm not worried about your car running off the road when you fall asleep at the wheel. And, best case, we get a trained sommelier who's come up through the ranks internally here."

She smiles, and I know that offering her a path to her dream job seals the deal. Best part is that it's a genuine offer. It just makes sense.

Ruby extends her hand. "If you're serious, I can't say no to that."

I don't want to shake her hand. Of all the things I want to do to her, this is dead bottom of the list. But it's all I'm being offered.

"I'm serious. Pack your bags."

# CHAPTER
*Eighteen*

RUBY

"I changed my mind. I'm moving out of the winery," I tell Ella, whose foot taps like she's keeping time with music on her headphones, only she's not wearing headphones.

The OB/GYN's waiting room is packed, and we've snagged the last two chairs. In front of us, a low square table has several magazines fanned out, each one at least a month old. Ella normally loves a good gossip rag, but today, she sits with her hands in her lap, eyes staring straight ahead.

"You're not. It's a great idea," she says, not looking at me.

"But—"

"But nothing. I'm not even at the dorm most of the time, so it's not like I'm lonely, and it saves you two hours of driving each day. It's a no-brainer." I regard her serious face and know she's being honest. "Really. Just do it."

"Okay. I feel guilty, but okay."

She turns her whole body in her seat to face me. "Why?"

I shrug. I've been trying to figure out the answer to this question ever since Jackson proposed it.

"I guess it's guilt over being given free lodging, guilt that I won't see you as much, guilt that I might not be able to help if you need something."

Ella waves a hand. "Stop it. You're lovely to worry about me, but get over it. I'm fine. It's not like you're leaving the country. And as to the free lodging, you were sponging off of me, so what's the big deal if you're sponging off someone else now?"

I get her point, but it doesn't make me feel much better. "I guess."

"Just take it, say thank you, and get some more sleep. I beg you."

"Fine. Bossy."

"Kettle."

The receptionist calls Ella's name, and a nurse leads us to an exam room with light wood floors and an open window shade, letting in some sun. The nurse hands Ella a gown with a light blue pattern and tells her to get undressed and put it on with the opening in front.

She leaves us, pulling the door closed with a quiet click.

"What if the doctor gets mad at me for being irresponsible?" Ella asks, more fearful of a woman she sees once a year than of a potential child she could have in nine months. She starts getting undressed, throwing her clothes into a pile on the chair. Then she puts her arms through the gown and hops onto the exam table.

I start folding her clothes and putting them back on the chair. "She won't get mad at you. That's not her job."

"I know. You're right." She bites her bottom lip and looks up at me through her dark lashes. Despite her nerves and the fact that she's barely slept since she took the pregnancy test, she's managed to put on mascara and blush. Her eyes are puffy from all the crying she did when she told her boyfriend about the positive test.

He held her hand, let her cry on his shoulder for an hour, and said he supports her whether she has the baby or not. He offered to come with her here, but she told him she'd rather call him when we're done.

Now, I'm the one holding her hand in the exam room, where she sits as far away from the stirrups as she can get.

"Tell me something to distract me," she says, looking around the room like a fairy tale prince might emerge from a cupboard and entertain her.

"Um, well, I'm going to get to do something different next week. I'm helping set up a wine tasting for three hundred people in the restaurant." I expect my excitement to become her excitement, so I wait for her to ask more about the wine, the restaurant, the guests.

Instead, she groans. "Ugh, I don't care about that."

"Thanks, El."

She leans back and drapes an arm over her forehead dramatically. "I don't mean that. I care. Obviously, I care. I just can't relate. That's your world. It would be like you getting all excited about the preservation of an eighteenth century kitchen with a woodburning oven." Historical preservation is her major, and no one gets more excited about arcane architecture than her.

"I would have found it interesting."

"Oh, I'm sure." Her voice drips with sarcasm as she shoots me a disbelieving look.

"I'd at least pretend," I admit.

"Exactly. Let's agree to disagree about each other's weird obsessions and talk about something we both find interesting—your boss."

She knows nearly nothing about Jackson, except that I have a boss. I've kept it that way intentionally. My sister has a tendency to make a bigger deal out of men in my life than they warrant. Mainly because these days, the only men in my life are online instructors, our mail carrier, and the guy who does my oil change.

"What about him?"

"I know he's hot. I looked him up."

Leave it to my sister to choose a major that allows her to be offline and on the ground, restoring buildings and visiting historic sites, only to become an internet Sherlock Holmes when I drop the name of the vineyard where I work. I'm curious about her methods.

"How do you even know which Corbett is my boss?"

"I know your type."

"I don't have a type." I totally have a type, and she's right that Jackson fits the bill one hundred percent. "Besides, even if I did have a type, there's no guarantee I'd be working for that particular individual."

I spin around on the small stool in the room because I don't want to meet her eye. Which tells her everything she needs to know. "Jackson Corbett. And now I know you have a thing for him because you called him an individual. You only do that when you're trying to deflect."

"I do not do that."

*Do I do that?* I'm going to have to think about it later.

It's the first time she looks slightly less miserable since we got here, so I reluctantly indulge the conversation. "Yes, he's my boss. Good guess."

"So tell me about him. I love that he asked you to move in. That's a good sign."

"He did not ask me to move in. He offered me an empty guest place, so I don't have to commute. Big difference."

"Zero difference."

I'm about to come up with a list of all the ways Jackson Corbett and I have no future together when there's a sharp knock, and the door swings open.

A serious woman with thick glasses and jowls for cheeks strides into the room; eyes focused on an iPad held in her palm. "Ella, nice to see you. I understand we may have had an 'oops?'"

I cringe at her reference to a potential pregnancy and the big deal it is for my sister, but Doctor Sanchez isn't my doctor, and Ella says she likes her.

"I tested positive," Ella says.

Doctor Sanchez rubs gel on an ultrasound wand and indicates that Ella should lie back with her feet in the stirrups. She scoots down, and I roll my stool closer to the ultrasound screen. "Yes. The blood test confirmed the same. Let's have a look."

Ella reaches for my hand and squeezes it harder than I expect. I put my other hand on top of our clenched palms and give her a reassuring smile, even though I'm freaking out too.

"Any nausea? Vomiting? Bleeding?" Doctor Sanchez asks. Her methodical, detached bedside manner makes it feel like Ella is a lab experiment, not a person.

Ella shakes her head. "No. I feel fine, but I missed a period and took a test." She presses her lips together. "Actually, I took three." She hasn't told me that, and she doesn't look at me when she admits it. I know Tim has been spending every night with her, but I still feel guilty about how much time I've been at the winery, especially now that I'm spending nights in the staff cottage.

"Stop it," Ella says.

"What?"

"Stop beating yourself up. You've been amazing. Just...stop."

Our conversation is put on hold when Doctor Sanchez inserts the ultrasound wand and moves it around, making the gray images on the screen move along with it. She rubs a hand on Ella's stomach. "Any tenderness here?"

Ella cringes and squirms on the table. "Yes, right there."

The doctor snaps a few images and continues moving the wand before holding it still. She points to a white dot amid the gray. "This is your fallopian tube. That's where the pregnancy is."

"Wait, what?" Ella drops my hand and pushes up onto her elbows to see the screen better. "Hang on. Is that even possible?" I peer at the small dot and feel a surge of emotion. That could be a baby. It could be family.

Ella stares at the dot, and I wonder if she's thinking it too.

"It's called an ectopic pregnancy. It happens sometimes when the egg gets fertilized and doesn't make it to the uterus. It's not viable."

"It's not--?" Ella looks defeated. "So I'm…not pregnant?"

Doctor Sanchez starts rattling off medical information about the two percent of pregnancies that are ectopic and the danger it can pose, especially if it goes untreated because the tube can rupture. "So we need to take care of this now."

"It's okay, sweetie. It'll be okay," I whisper, brushing a few strands of hair out of her eyes.

"Will it?"

I have no idea, but she's looking to me for support, and I want to give her everything I have. "Yes. Whatever you need. I'm here. Not going anywhere."

Nodding, Ella looks away, and I see her eyes fill with tears. "I mean, I wasn't trying to get pregnant. So…"

"I know…"

"It's just…I didn't even get the choice…"

I lean over her and hug her tight, wishing I could absorb all the stress and fear from her body and transfer it to mine. It's how I've always felt about her. I just want to protect her from the world.

"Um, gown's open in the front…" Ella makes a feeble attempt at a laugh, and I back away so she can pull the gown closed. She looks at me. "Maybe somehow…this is a good thing?"

I smooth her hair. "I think so, sweetie. Right?"

Nodding, she blinks back tears. "It's the right thing." She swallows hard, and I reach into my tote bag for a bottle of water. She takes a sip and exhales a long breath. "Okay. This is going to be okay."

The doctor is busy typing on her iPad. A moment later, a nurse in hot pink scrubs enters the room with a tray containing a syringe and several vials. Doctor Sanchez accepts the tray wordlessly in one hand while holding the iPad in the other.

"This is going to be fine." The doctor's tone sounds slightly more caring, and she smiles at Ella, who manages a half-hearted smile in return. "I'm going to inject a medication that will stop the cells from multiplying, and you'll come back in a couple days to see how well it's working."

Ella dries her eyes and sits up. It's the first time I've seen a glimmer of relief on her face since she first saw the little pink plus sign on the pregnancy test. I know she wants to have kids someday, but with two years of college left, it would be challenging.

"That's it?" Ella asks.

The doctor nods. "Fingers crossed. If the cells reduce, it could pass on its own. If that doesn't happen, you'll need surgery, which most likely we'll be able to do laparoscopically."

At my sister's confusion, she clarifies. "Through a tiny incision with a scope." My stomach seizes at the mention of surgery. I need my sister to be okay, and the thought of her undergoing surgery terrifies me.

Doctor Sanchez washes her hands at the metal sink and dries them. "Get something in your stomach after the injection, and I'll see you on Wednesday."

"Okay," Ella says. I simply nod because the lump in my throat won't budge, and I don't want to cry

The doctor gives Ella some instructions and sweeps from the room with her nurse in tow, leaving us alone.

"Things work out for a reason, I guess," she says.

I nod.

Ella crumples the hem of her paper gown and looks at me. "Distract me, please. Tell me about your boss."

Anyone else would want to talk about ectopic pregnancies, but not my sister.

"Fine," I tell her. "But first, we're getting some food in your stomach."

"I could eat a burger."

I reach over and hug her, which gives me a chance to dry my tears before she can see them. She's all the family I have.

# CHAPTER
## *Nineteen*

JAX

It's a lazy Sunday, and it's Ruby's first day off in weeks. I know this because I'm half the reason she hasn't had a break. On Friday night, when she left my house, she told me her sister is feeling better after her doctor's appointment and plans to spend today with her boyfriend at a volleyball tournament.

So Ruby is spending her day off here. And I know for a fact she hasn't seen the pool.

It's nestled at the base of the looming hill, whose peak gets shrouded in fog most mornings. The pool is near Archer's house, but it functions more as a common area where my various siblings sometimes entertain. There's a broad patio and outdoor kitchen under the shade of live oaks. The pool house has changing rooms, restrooms, steam showers, and a dry sauna. It's like a mini spa, which seems like the perfect place to spend a Sunday.

Trix hung the tiny lights between the trees, and I have to admit it was a good idea. The place is magic at night. Not too bad during the day either.

"It was all Fi's idea." I lean a forearm against the doorframe of

Ruby's guest cottage and explain our plan for the day—swimming and a picnic lunch.

Fiona pops out from behind me. "No, it was daddy's idea."

Betrayed by a seven-year-old. The truth is that I didn't want to wait until tomorrow to see Ruby.

My little traitor is practically jumping out of her skin with excitement, bouncing on her toes. Her hair flops around like a golden mop. "Actually, it was my idea too. I want to have a diving contest with you."

Ruby nods at me, cheeks pulling her mouth into a smile. "Well, I guess she's the boss," she agrees. I love that she has as hard a time resisting my daughter as I do.

"I'll wait in the car." Fiona darts back to the Jeep, leaving me to sort out the logistics of this poorly conceived plan.

"Do you have a swimsuit? I can ask one of my sisters about borrowing one." I realize I've made assumptions that might put her in a bind.

Ruby smooths the crease in my brow with a finger, and I feel my breath hitch. I try to follow her instructions to relax, but it's hard when she's just touched my skin.

"Don't worry. Pretty sure I have something. Give me a minute."

"Bring a book. The pool's a relaxing place to spend a Sunday." My voice sounds like gravel, the result of that small bit of contact with her.

The door closes, and a few minutes later, Ruby emerges in an oversized white shirt and flip-flops. She hops into the car, and we make the short drive to the pool.

The weather is perfect, not blazing hot but warm enough that the pool is the right place to be. When Ruby goes to the trunk to take out the bag of sandwiches I brought from Sweet Butter, I shoo her away. "You're not working today. Take a load off, Ginger."

She mock-sulks away, and I can't help but look at the shape of her legs as she goes. I tell myself that will be the last wolfish glance I give her today. We're just three people enjoying a swim and a picnic.

If only I could make myself believe it.

———

Ruby

"I'm ready," Fiona calls a few minutes later from the changing room next to mine.

I wrap a towel around my waist and look down at my black string bikini, the only one I grabbed when I moved some of my clothes from the dorm. I should probably be wearing a conservative one-piece like a lifeguard, but I can't worry about that now.

Every afternoon, we talk about swimming, which makes good sense in the Napa heat, but then we always get sidetracked with art projects and other things. I'm so glad to be able to do this with her today.

As soon as we settle ourselves at the pool, Jackson hunkers down on a lounge, claiming he'll only work for an hour or so. I want him to get a break the same way he's giving me a break today. I feel like he wants it, but he's having trouble allowing himself to have it.

"Ready too. Cannonball?" I challenge.

"Last one in is a rotten egg!" Fiona shouts, running ahead of me into the bright sunlight.

Fiona's small body hits the water with a small splash, and I follow with a bigger one, my cannonball turning into more of a belly flop with my forward momentum.

When I pop up from the water, I see Jackson fighting a smile, droplets of water clinging to the strands of hair that he pushes off his forehead, revealing the worry lines he seems to have permanently etched there. He hasn't taken out his laptop yet, so the only thing wet is him.

"Sorry, not sorry," Fiona shrieks, and I watch Jackson's face, the crinkles forming around his amused eyes as he debates whether to freak out that his daughter is growing up so fast.

"I'm a little sorry," I tell him, hauling myself over the side of the pool and grabbing a yellow striped towel from a stack on a lounge chair. He accepts the towel I hand him and runs it over his face. Looking down, he sees the water spots on his pale blue tee and shakes his head.

"Guess if I can't beat 'em…" Reaching behind his neck, Jackson pulls off his shirt in one swift motion, and I do my best not to stare at his chest.

I fail miserably.

Lightly dusted with chest hair, his pecs swell hard and lean above a set of abs that create their own shadows beneath each one. The sunlight dances off skin that manages a golden tan that belies a man who works in an office all day. His shoulders and biceps flex as he pushes himself up from the lounge chair and stalks toward me.

"You better move quick, Ruby." His growl is a warning, but his eyes are playful as I back away and he advances.

I manage a clumsy swan dive into the pool a second before his hands reach out to push me. A second splash next to mine tells me he's in the water.

Thank goodness, because I don't think I can pretend not to notice his bare chest for another minute.

"Who wants to play Marco Polo?" Fiona yells, delighted that she has both of us in the water. A captive audience at her bidding.

"Me!" Jackson says, swimming away from her.

"Me too." I swim in the same direction as Jackson while Fiona turns her back and counts to six.

"Marco," she calls, spinning around with her eyes closed and drifting atop the water.

"Polo," Jackson calls in a quiet voice that sounds like a parrot. I've never seen him so playful before, and it warms my heart.

Fiona swims off in his direction, and he gracefully pivots toward me, hand brushing against my leg as he positions himself farther from Fiona. I feel the electric zing of awareness at his touch. Water does conduct electricity, so it's probably magnified.

*Sure. Keep telling yourself that.*

"Marco," she calls, reaching around her without seeing.

"Polo," I squeak like a tiny mouse. She cracks up and lurches in my direction. I'm stuck between the wall and Jackson, with no hope of escaping if Fiona continues in my direction.

I dunk under the water and swim like crazy for the other side of the pool. Jackson takes the fall, and Fiona nabs him in the next round. I've never seen a man look more delighted to lose a game.

We spend another lazy few hours like this—Jackson accidentally brushing past me in the water, me trying not to feel anything each time he does. Fiona is delighted by every game until she realizes how hungry she is.

Sitting on a lounge with a towel around my waist, I notice Jackson's eyes dropping from my face to where my bikini top minimally covers my breasts—it's enough coverage for a South of France beach, but probably not for a G-rated day with my boss.

He shouldn't be looking, and I shouldn't be enjoying watching his Adam's apple bob each time he swallows hard and forces his gaze away. I'm no better, sneaking hungry looks at his chest and abs whenever I think he's distracted by Fiona.

"How'd you remember I like the Caprese sandwich?" I say, marveling at how this man's brain files away details mentioned in passing. I hadn't even gotten the job here yet, and he remembers something I said on my interview day.

Jackson shrugs, but I catch the trace of a smug smile on his lips. "I remember stuff that matters." And my heart melts.

And when he takes out a batch of misshapen cookies, which I know he and Fiona must have baked themselves, my heart might as well be a stick of butter in the Napa sun.

# CHAPTER
## *Twenty*

RUBY

After just a week of living in the staff cottages, I have to admit I have more energy.

And the place is beautiful.

If this is a staff cottage, I can't imagine what the guest cottages look like, and with my busy schedule, I don't have a moment of spare time to investigate them. There's no need. With my patio's sweeping view of the vineyards crawling up the hills beneath the warm sun, I don't need anything more.

My cottage has a tidy bedroom with a double bed under a fluffy white duvet, plantation shutters painted cornflower blue, a small kitchen, and a bathroom with a clawfoot tub. After living on a futon in the corner of Ella's dorm, this feels like five-star resort living. I guess it is.

At the same time, there's a rustic charm to everything at Buttercup Hill. The door hinges creak, frogs in the lily ponds croak, and the winds that blow across the vineyards sweep everything into a beautiful sort of chaos. Guests feel like they're part of the Corbett family while they're here.

Then there's the wine community itself. If anything functions like a small town, it's the small insider group of vintners who live up here, sharing gossip like it's their job and counting each other's grape arbors to make sure no one crosses property lines.

I've come to understand why Jackson keeps to himself. Any bit of information makes its way through the grapevine—literally —and he controls the most coveted information about Buttercup Hill. Any competitor would love to get a glimpse at the bottom line of the biggest winery in the country.

I wonder about that aspect of Jackson's life as I get dressed for work, luxuriating in the extra hour of time I had this morning to jog along the pathways within the property before showering and making coffee.

More and more, he seems frustrated by work. I know about the debts, but he's vague about everything else, saying things like, "if I can figure out what's going on," and "once I get a handle on a few things," but then I've gotten sidetracked by Fiona before I could push him for more.

Oh, I'm definitely planning to ask. It may not be any of my business, but then again, maybe it is. I'm not going to self-censor. If he doesn't want to tell me something, that's on him to say.

In fact, I decide to make it a point to ask about what's bugging him at work when I see him later. He has a work event tonight, but I'll find some time before he scoots out the door. I'll make a point of it.

As I'm walking along the path toward the restaurant, my phone pings with a text from my sister, right on schedule. I bought Ella a new alarm clock. It's a small blue ball that rings and vibrates and can be set remotely.

I set it each night.

When the alarm goes off, if Ella doesn't get up and go across the room to turn it off, it rolls off the dresser and starts moving around the room, getting louder and louder until she chases it down. It's been working like a charm. Every morning, I get an annoyed series of texts once she's turned the sneaky thing off, but at least she's awake.

Ella: Damn you

Me: Love you too, El

Ella: Remind me not to schedule an 8 a.m. class next semester

Me: How are you feeling?

Ella: Weirdly good. Just knowing what's up with my ovaries makes me feel better

Me: Technically it's your tubes

Ella: Why are you like this?

Me: You love me

Ella: I do. Talk tomorrow

Me: You'll see me tomorrow. Remember?

Ella: Yes. I'll see you. Annoying

I'll feel better once Ella gets an all-clear from her doctor about the ectopic and everything looks good. I don't want to think about the possibility of surgery. And her insurance will cover most of the cost, minus her deductible, which means I still need to scrounge together fifteen hundred dollars.

I didn't mention the deductible when I told Jackson about the ectopic because, knowing him, he'd find a way to double my salary somehow, and I don't want that kind of charity.

Running a quick calculation on the notepad in my kitchen, I add another month to the tally for how long it will take me to put away enough for my own apartment. One more month. Because surely, I can't live in staff housing at the winery forever. It's a temporary gift, and I don't want to outstay my welcome.

"We have a lot to do today. Thanks for coming early," Beatrix Corbett calls to me from the open front door of the restaurant, where I've been enjoying the respite from pouring glasses of wine for tourists. Not that I don't love that part of my job—talking to people and hearing where they're visiting from is part of what I love about the wine business. It's built into the culture of stopping, tasting, discussing, relaxing. And my log of tasting notes has grown to several dozen pages.

But the beauty of Buttercup is all the areas of wine and hospitality that the company handles on a daily basis. So I jumped at the chance to learn about how the restaurant makes a wine and cheese party interesting for three hundred people in the wine industry with refined palates.

"Same as yesterday?" I ask. Yesterday was spent putting together tasting notes for the wines that will be served at the event with Victor, the restaurant's sommelier. I tried to act casual when Beatrix told me what I'd be doing, but my brain was exploding.

I've been wanting to work with Victor since I arrived, but I knew I needed to pay my dues and wait for the right time.

Beatrix picks up her phone and swipes across a couple screens. Light jazz begins piping in through the speakers, and suddenly, the room feels like a speakeasy. All that's missing is the crowd.

"Yes," Beatrix says. I haven't spent much time with her, but I already like her a lot. She has a certain sophistication, always well-dressed in pantsuits with red lipstick and her blond hair wound into a chic chignon at the nape of her neck. Shaking her head, she consults a clipboard. "I can't believe Dashiell hired you and didn't think to let me know you're a trained sommelier. What the actual heck?"

"I don't have experience, just training."

She leans in and puts her arm around my shoulders, speaking

quietly. "Promise me I'm the last person you ever say that to. From now on, you're a trained sommelier. Period."

"O-okay."

"Exactly. You studied, you earned it. And if someone has a job opening, you put your foot right through that door and fake it til you make it."

I nod. "Okay. Thank you."

"You're welcome. I'm glad at least one of my brothers knows what's what. Jax told me you're making wine. That's amazing."

I tell her about my viniculture, which is still back in Berkeley because it needs to ferment, and Ella's dark closet is the perfect environment for it. "I haven't tasted them, but everything seems like it's on track, so come fall, I should have a pretty robust science experiment."

As I'm explaining my methods, I wonder what else Jackson told her. It seems clear now that he must have had a hand in getting me moved to the team that's planning this weekend's event, and he did it to give me more experience with the restaurant's sommelier.

I make a mental note to do something nice to thank him.

Beatrix hands me a Butter and Rosemary apron, and I tie it around my waist, noticing Victor walking toward us, wringing his hands. He's over six feet tall and often holds his hands behind his back, making him appear like he might topple forward. "We need to change the wine pairings. Is it too late?" His worry pulls his mouth down in a frown until he overcorrects, looking like a slightly menacing cartoon sloth.

Beatrix sucks through her teeth. "It's going to be tight, but I'll do you this one solid, Victor. Tell me what needs to be changed by end of day today, and I'll make it happen."

He nods and scurries off while she confides, "I never print the menus until the day of an event, but it's better to have people think I need everything sooner." She winks. "Tricks of the trade."

"Smart."

Her smile matches Jackson's and feels just as hard-earned. She works hard, running two restaurants, but unlike Jackson, she manages a large staff and farms out the day-to-day work to them. She has managers, bookkeepers, and executive chefs who manage their own teams and keep the restaurants running while she attends to bigger picture issues.

I get the feeling I could learn a lot from her about the restaurant side of the business. "Come. Victor will be a minute, and I could use another set of eyes on these." She signals me over to a velvet sofa in the foyer of the restaurant and takes out a stack of photos from a leather folder on a side table.

"Has he told you about her?" Beatrix separates the photos into one color stack and one of black and whites. She shuffles through the first stack, all photos of the property. She's so intensely focused that I almost think she's asking me something about the photos.

"I'm sorry?"

"Jax. Has he told you about his wife?" Folding her hands on top of the stack, she looks at me. "He doesn't like to talk about her —at least not with me—but since you work for him, I figured I should fill you in since he never will…"

"I-no, not really." I feel like I want to protect him, even though she's his sister. "He just said that she left two years ago."

"Well, that part is true, but he's definitely leaving out the juicy bits."

"Oh, yeah?" I feign nonchalance, but I'm dying to know more. "Want me to look at those?" I point to the photos.

Beatrix shuffles through them once more and smooths a hand over her hair, even though not a strand is out of place. "Right. Yes. I'm using one of these for the cover of the event menu, but I haven't decided. Does one of them scream 'world's best winery with understated elegance?'"

I look through the photos, mostly images of the farmhouse. Lower in the stack are some more casual ones of the vineyards. I have no idea if she's put them in order of preference.

"Annabelle was so wrong for Jax. She'd been following a

Grateful Dead cover band around the country for two years and selling macrame bracelets to support herself. Not that there's anything wrong with that, but Jax is in his head a lot, and she did nothing to wind him down. If anything, she made him more uptight because she was unreliable."

She continues, "Most of us thought he'd break up with her after a month. But she got pregnant, and he proposed. Our father insisted, not that it was any of his business. I told Jax that about a hundred times, but he's always cared way too much about what our dad thinks."

I stay focused on the photos in my lap, but I'm listening intently. "So they'd dated a month?"

"Maybe a couple of months. I don't remember exactly, but once she told him about the pregnancy, he started making plans for the two of them. It was like it almost didn't matter whether or not he was happy. He just wanted to do the right thing."

"Sounds like Jax."

She nods. "Yup. And when Fiona was born, it was done."

I look up, confused. "What was done?"

"He was all in. Loved that girl to pieces. Same as now. And Annabelle was just kind of there, part of the package. I don't think he ever considered divorce, even though they were completely incompatible. They didn't even share a bedroom."

My eyebrows go up. There have been moments over the past few weeks when I've felt almost jealous of his ex-wife, not knowing anything about her except that she was with him and Fiona.

"And then she left. Said she didn't plan to have kids, didn't want to be a parent, didn't love Fiona. That's what sealed the deal."

"I can't imagine anyone saying that after meeting Fiona."

"Exactly. My brother didn't exactly take that well. She left the next day." She pauses and looks searchingly at me like she's beginning to realize something.

I stop shuffling through the photos. "Wow."

Beatrix nods. "Yeah. Even though he knew who she was, I think he still hoped it could work out." She's still looking at me the same way, eyes wide, almost hopeful. "Some people are just good…and some aren't."

My chest aches at the thought of Jackson having that kind of hope despite all the signs. It confirms why he guards his life with Fiona so fiercely, not wanting anyone or anything to pierce the protective space he's created with her. It's a reminder to me that the little moments where a small electric charge flashes between us shouldn't happen.

Beatrix looks at the photo on top of the pile and holds it up. It's a black and white image of the vineyard behind Jax's house. "You like this one?" Her lips twist into a knowing smile.

Without realizing it, I've been staring at it for most of our conversation. "I do. Probably because I'm out there every day with Fi. It just feels free to me. The ones of the house are a little stodgy."

She considers the photo again and nods. "Yeah. I can see that. And this event is about the wine, not our farmhouse. Everyone knows they're at Buttercup when they're here. But it's our vines that set us apart. This could work."

Victor sweeps back into the room holding a piece of paper. "Okay, Beatrix, here is the new list. I appreciate you making the changes," he says, rubbing a hand over his beard and handing a scribbled sheet to Beatrix with a shy grin.

"Not a problem, Victor." She sweeps the page into her folder and stands from the couch with such nonchalance that no one would imagine we were just talking about Jackson's marriage. "So nice chatting, Ruby. I'll catch up with you later."

Victor extends a hand to pull me up from the couch. "Shall we?"

"Yes. Ready."

I follow him through the dining room and downstairs to the wine cave, where we worked all day yesterday. We pass tables being set for lunch with white linen cloths, sterling, and glass plates in varying shades of blue. Olive trees grow in pots beneath the large skylights, which cast the restaurant in different shades depending on the time of day.

The wine cave itself is divided into a workspace and a storage area. It's a much smaller version of the cave included in the vineyard tour, which stretches nearly a mile beneath the property and contains much of the wine that gets shipped to shops all over California.

"Have you dined in the restaurant?" Victor asks as we sit at a small table sitting by a wine barrel. Leaves from an ivy plant trail down the sides.

"Here? No."

"You must. It's world-class."

Of course it is, as I'm well aware. I just can't afford it. "It's on my list," I tell him, which is the truth.

He nods, running a hand over his graying beard. Victor looks to be in his late forties, and his beard has more gray in it than the full head of hair, which only shows a bit of salt amid the pepper. Even though we're not around winery guests, he's dressed in a gray suit with a white shirt open at the collar and an apron like mine tied around his waist.

"You're working for Jackson." It's not a question, but I feel compelled to answer.

"Yes. I take care of Fiona in the afternoons."

He nods, wiping down a bottle of Cabernet Franc, which wasn't on the menu he showed me yesterday. "How is it going? She's the test case, you know."

"What do you mean?"

"She's the first grandchild of Kingston Corbett, the first child to be raised on the grounds here. Surely, others will follow, and soon there will be a passel of kids running around." He's more relaxed when he's not around Beatrix, and his eyes flash with mischief. "That'll change the tenor of the place, don't you think?"

Unsure what he's implying, I tilt my head to the side. "I...guess?"

"Shenanigans. Kids are always good for some shenanigans." He grins and roots through a large wall of refrigerated bottles and comes back with three whites, which he places on a table. Turning, he bends down to the cases along the wall, pulls a few more reds, and begins polishing the bottles with a white cloth.

I shrug. "Change is good."

Victor wipes the condensation from the white wine bottles and arranges them in a line on the table. "You don't like to gossip, I see," he observes.

"I like my job."

"Fair enough." When the bottles are shiny enough to see Victor's reflection, he pushes them toward me and hands me a corkscrew. "You may do the honors."

"All of them?"

"Yes. They're just peaking, so I've added them to the tasting menu. None of our guests will have tried them. I want to get your take."

He sits back and waits, arms crossed. It suddenly feels less like a training session and more like a test. I know how to score wines on the Parker scale, and I know what I like. I just hope my knowledge is enough to hold my own with a professional sommelier.

"Sure." I set about opening the first bottle, careful to insert the corkscrew at an angle so it goes in smoothly and doesn't break the cork. My cheeks heat under the pressure of his attentive assessment. "I've been learning as much as I can and tasting the vintages from as many years as I can."

He nods. "Smart."

The cork slides from the bottle, and I hand it to Victor. While he taps the wet end, I surreptitiously wipe the beads of sweat from my brow with the back of my hand, reminding myself that I know what I'm doing. I've been studying wines for years now.

By the time I've opened the third bottle, I start to relax. A minute later, all the open bottles sit in a line on the table.

Victor extends a hand, indicating that I should pour. I twist each bottle to catch the drip after about an ounce has hit the bottom of each crystal clear glass.

"Do you mind if I make notes on these?" I ask. "I've been keeping a log." If these will be on the tasting menu eventually, it would be good to start a new page for each one and add my thoughts.

"Not at all."

Slipping my iPad from my purse, I type up new columns for each of the new vintages. Then we taste them.

"Plum, maybe even a little pepper," I note on the first one. Victor sips his and nods.

"Pepper for sure, but I'm getting more of a jammy taste, red fruit like a berry," he says, holding a glass of red up to the light. It's so dark and full-bodied that almost no light shines through. Unusual for a younger wine.

"What is this one?" I reach for the bottle and turn it to see the label.

"It's a blend. The vintners are doing more of those this year, supposedly." Victor shrugs like it's not of concern, but I'm curious.

"Are they experimenting with flavors, or is there some reason they're shifting that direction?"

Victor doesn't answer immediately, and I wonder if he didn't hear me. He bends down to retrieve a bottle from a case near the table where we're sitting. I'm about to repeat my question when he responds, "I don't know, but I'll admit it's a little bit strange. This vineyard has the terroir to grow some of the best grapes in the country. Blending them is a contradiction."

Which is exactly what I was thinking. I start to wonder whether it's related to Jackson's stress about the family business.

And what he plans to do about it.

# CHAPTER
## Twenty~One

JAX

"Why am I nervous?" I ask Dash, who's riding the elevator in our parents' home that looks like an East Hampton estate. Grandiose, even then.

"Because he didn't recognize you last week? And because you're always nervous?"

"I know, and it's dumb."

It's not dumb, but I don't want my brother to know the extent to which our company is underwater right now. Not when I still think I can move money around and fix the issue.

Who am I kidding? I've been reallocating funds from one line of the balance sheet to the other for weeks, trying to find ways to save so we can absorb the big losses my dad warned me about, and I still have a Grand Canyon-sized abyss between the totals.

I need to get my brain around the fact that I might not be able to fix this. Which means telling everyone—my siblings, investors, employees—that we may not survive to do business in a year.

I do not want to be the bearer of that kind of news, and the stubborn optimist in me still thinks I can find a solution. A new investor, a new source of funds, a giant bandaid when we've been bleeding money.

The elevator reaches the third floor, and the doors trundle open. I always wonder why the home elevator Dad purchased for his house is so much slower than any elevator I've ever ridden in. Maybe because he never planned to use it. Well, joke's on us because he never did use it, and we're only riding in it because someone thought it made sense to refinish the staircase today.

"Why is it dumb?"

"It's not like anything's changed the last few times we've come."

"But it could. That's why you're nervous."

We start down the long hallway, a parquet floor designed in an expensive herringbone pattern that I only know cost a fortune because my dad made a point of telling me. And anyone else who's ever visited the McMansion.

Dad's gone through a rough patch over the past couple weeks, ever since he asked me to come so he could harp on me about getting help with Fiona. I haven't even been able to let him know I succeeded on that front because he hasn't recognized me the past two times I've been here.

His blank stare chills me to my bones, and I prepare myself for a repeat today. Lately, if he does have glimmers of recognition, it's mostly thinking my sister is our mother or thinking I'm Dash or Archer.

Sometimes, I wonder if it confuses him more when we come in pairs because it's always a different combination of kids showing up. That would confuse anyone, dementia aside.

He repeats conversations he's already had with each of us long ago. It makes me think he doesn't regret the advice he gave at the time, which is something, I guess.

"This is the new pattern, maybe," Dash says. "One step forward, three back?"

"The new drug is supposed to slow the progression, or at least maintain where he is. The protocol was pretty successful in trials."

Dash huffs a laugh. "Well, Dad's never been a conformist."

"True." Dad's nurse called and said he was more lucid when he woke up this morning, so we hightailed it over here at the end of his morning nap, hopeful he'll wake up and recognize us. I've been hamstrung trying to balance the budget without knowing where Dad spent money last year without recording any of it.

Our accountants are having a fit because mysterious losses don't fly with the IRS. I still haven't told my siblings about it, and we're getting close to the deadline for telling shareholders that their investment may be a giant bust.

That shitshow just can't happen.

"I'm here to help. Just nudge me if you need me to step in more." Dash walks fast and talks faster. I have long legs, but I feel like I'm speed walking to keep up with him as our shoes clack on the hardwood floor.

I gave him the bare-bones description of what I need our dad to tell us without revealing our financial straits. I don't plan to push for details or clutter up the conversation with unimportant facts. I just need to know what happened to the money. And I need to know if my dad made these murky business decisions before he was diagnosed with Alzheimer's. Every detail matters.

We reach the left wing of the house, which opens into a large landing rimmed with an ornate railing and overlooking an indoor orchid garden that's tended to by a dedicated staff. Our parents were collectors of rare orchids, and even though my dad hasn't left his room in weeks, the blooms are regularly spritzed and fed.

It all seems ridiculous to me, and each time I visit the mansion, I vow never to let my life turn into something with this kind of excess. Then I wonder if it already has.

Seeing Ruby's wide-eyed glow every day despite having to support her sister makes me feel like I've been sheltered from real world problems for far too long. Maybe I've already lost touch.

Dad's nurse, Betsy, pokes her head out the doorway of Dad's room at the center of the sweeping landing. Rooms on either side are a home gym and an office. Other than the need to eat, our father never had reason to leave this wing of the house.

When he was working on a project, like building the first restaurant on the property and excavating one of the hills to house the wine cave, he'd stay up here for days and have his food brought in.

We all had eras of our childhoods when he wasn't around for months at a time. He was here but not around.

"He's been sleeping all morning." Her hushed voice matches her neat nurse's uniform, and she smooths her hands down the skirt. "I left him alone, so hopefully, he'll be more alert for you when I wake him now."

"Thanks, Betsy," Dash says, taking a step backward to lean on the railing. We wait outside, listening to the sounds of Betsy waking our dad with her lilting voice and encouraging words.

"Kingston, it's time to wake up…Good morning, Kingston."

We hear grumbles from our dad that don't translate into words. Then, movements and wrestling around as she helps him to the bathroom and gets him oriented.

A few minutes go by, and Dash and I stare at each other, hating this surreal experience of waiting for a man who has only really been able or willing to spend time with us because he doesn't know any better.

Betsy signals us into the room, and I tell myself not to react to how my dad looks, but to my relief, he looks the same as he did last week. Still dressed in a short-sleeved button-up shirt and one of the hundreds of bowties from his collection. He doesn't recognize his own kids, but he knows enough to insist on a bowtie each day.

Perched on a settee at the end of the bed, he raises a hand in greeting. It's been his signature for so long that it's not surprising his fading memory hasn't eliminated the gesture. It's built-in.

"Hi dad," I say. Dash stays behind me, silent, not wanting to confuse him.

He squints at me like he always does, his brain trying to do calculations it's too compromised for most of the time. I'm expecting him to call me Archer, and even then, I'm going to ask him what I came to ask.

But he surprises me. "Jackson." He nods. "And Dashiell back there." I hear Dash suck in a breath behind me. This feels momentous. It feels like a breakthrough. A part of me is dying to ask Betsy if she thinks the new protocol he's on is working, but there will be time for that later. If he's lucid, I need to ask my questions now.

"Good to see you. I was hoping we could chat," I begin, sliding a chair over from the desk so it faces him. I intentionally move it so close that he has to look at me, and so he won't be distracted by anything else in the room. I know that if he's uncomfortable or nervous, he'll ask me to back away. But he doesn't.

"Of course. Happy to chat with a friend."

*Friend?*

He nods at me and raises his hand again as though he didn't just do that exact thing. And by calling me a friend, he doesn't really know who I am, even if he knows my name. Maybe it works to my advantage.

Betsy unobtrusively sets a tray on a small table and wheels it over next to my dad. He ignores the glass of water there and the single orchid in a vase.

"Can we talk about the loan and how you spent the money?" I watch his face for a glimmer of recognition. I get nothing. He stares straight ahead in the way he often does. I'm waiting for him to go off on a tangent, which also sometimes happens.

Preparing myself. Expecting the worst. It's been a series of progressions over time from hope to hopelessness.

"Yes." His response gets my attention, and my eyes shoot to his. He's looking directly at me, something he rarely does anymore.

"Okay. How did we lose that money? Was it a payoff for a

lawsuit?" If he had to settle a suit, I can handle that. I can explain it. I just need an answer.

"Lawsuits get settled. That's the beauty of money."

My spirits plummet. He's confused. Wrong. And now I think I'm losing him.

"We—"

He cuts me off. "Our grapes were garbage. Hayden Lanes sold me what we needed. 'Course it cost money. Everything costs money."

Wait, *what*? Our grapes are world-renowned. My pulse ticks up, flitting like a snare drum.

"Dad, we have the best vines. Why would you buy grapes from someone else?" I've never heard of Hayden Lanes, but there are so many new wineries popping up in the area all the time. It might not even be in Napa.

He waves a hand, dismissing the idea. "I did what I had to do."

"Why isn't there anything in the books about buying from Hayden Lanes?"

"The books?" Dad looks at a built-in bookshelf that lines one wall of his room. He scans the rows of books.

I see the confusion in his eyes and have a bad feeling about what's coming next. The same thing happened last week after only five minutes with him. But this is important, and I need to pull anything I can from his ailing brain.

"Yes. Who's suing us? Why are we buying from Hayden Lanes?" I ask quietly. Like I'm trying not to frighten a squirrel perched an inch from a nut I'm holding.

If Dad is buying grapes from another vineyard, there must be a reason. Maybe he got confused, or someone convinced him to gamble. Maybe I can fix this. I feel my brother's hand at my back, urging me to keep going.

"I did what I had to do," he repeats. "It was what I had to do to save us." He starts coughing as soon as he says it, and Betsy rushes over with a glass of water. My father drinks it, wipes his face, and lifts his hand to wave at me again.

The blank stare has returned to his eyes, but I have to take one more stab at getting information. "Dad, can you just—"

He lurches back on the settee like I've just punched him. "Who said you could come in here?"

"Dad…"

"Who is this?" he asks his nurse.

I feel Dash step closer to me. He whispers, "We should go. He'll only get more agitated."

But I can't go, not when I'm finally close to a piece of information that might make sense of why we're bleeding money.

"I'm Jackson. Your son."

My dad starts shaking his head. He looks afraid and lost. I don't want to stress him, but I need his help. Just for another minute. It's impossible for me to give in and walk away when I'm this close.

He plucks the orchid from the vase, plucks off a petal and bites into it.

I look at Betsy, who shakes her head. "They're safe to eat. It's okay. But you're probably not going to get him back."

I know she's right, but I feel defeated coming away with a shred of information only to be confounded by something else.

"That was impressive, actually, that he focused as long as he did," the nurse says quietly before turning her full attention to my dad. I watch her move the orchid plant out of reach and push his water glass closer to his hand. He lifts it and drinks. Then he opens his newspaper and pretends to read.

"What was that about?" Dash asks as we descend the stairs. I feel sucker punched. Each time I get another dribble of information, it digs me deeper into a hole I can't get out of, and the hole just turned into a gaping chasm today.

"Nothing. He's not making sense," I tell Dash, unwilling to let him into my problems. I'll solve them somehow and protect the business from whatever Dad has done.

Dash casts a suspicious look. "Dude, you can tell me. Maybe I can help."

"You can't. But it's all good. Don't worry."

He nods slowly. "Yeah, sure, okay. Tell you what—I'll ask you again in a week. That gives you a week to decide whether you want to keep lying to me or let me try to help."

"It's a financial issue. I'll handle it."

"Sounds like something bigger. It's okay to ask for help, you know." He's walking faster now, and I tell myself that's why my pulse has kicked up a notch. Apparently, I'm lying to myself about shit now too. "I'm giving you a week."

"Fine. Whatever."

One week. A new deadline for figuring out why Dad spent half a million dollars on grapes we shouldn't need. Or on paying off lawsuits he won't explain. Not nearly enough time, but it's what I have.

# CHAPTER
## Twenty-Two

RUBY

"Can I please stay up late? Please!" Fiona isn't subtle. When she wraps her arms around Jackson's leg and presses the side of her face to his stomach, she knows he's putty in her hands.

"Fine. But you have to do whatever Ruby says. She's the boss, and when she tells you it's time for bed, no arguing."

It's the first time Jackson has asked me to stay late, but since it's Friday night and I have tomorrow off from working in the tasting room, I don't mind. I became so accustomed to slugging down an espresso before hitting the road each evening that I still do it even now that I live on the property.

I'm addicted. And not just to the caffeine.

Watching Jackson read *Harry Potter and the Half-Blood Prince* to Fiona, my heart melts. He's so good with her, and for the life of me, I can't understand why her mother would leave either one of them. I don't understand how she *could* leave.

I have trouble leaving sometimes at the end of the day because being with the two of them resembles the kind of family I'll want someday, and it takes an extra effort to remind myself to focus on my priorities—earning money, establishing myself in the career I want. My hopes and dreams for my romantic life and the family I want can wait.

Besides, it's not like the scene in front of me will ever be mine. Jackson told me he'd never risk getting into a relationship again. I don't need to get my heart broken by fantasizing about things that will never happen.

I'm an employee, nothing more.

Fiona sits at the kitchen table, which we've turned into an art lab. Yellow cylinders of Playdough sit next to brightly colored modeling clay, markers, paper, feathers, Styrofoam balls of different sizes, and pipe cleaners.

I spent some time at an art supply store after work yesterday in anticipation of our big night together while Jackson goes to a corporate dinner he seems to be dreading. Fiona treated me to her jack-o-lantern grin when I spread everything out on the table, but the glee turned to a pout when I told her we needed to take a break for dinner. "Lentils tonight."

"Ugh, not lentils."

Fiona has surprised me by being game for almost every vegetable I throw her way, but she's having some trouble with any type of bean.

Tonight, I'm betting I can get her to eat the lentils, especially if an extra few stories or a TV show is on the table as a reward. "Remember, your dad said it's okay if you do what I'm asking."

I wink at Jackson. Two against one. Fiona doesn't stand a chance, even if she doesn't realize it. He chimes in, "Try them, Fi."

She rolls her eyes.

"I think you'll like the lentils this time. I made them into a sort of salad. We're going to eat it on crackers. No forks tonight," I say.

That piques her interest, and she creeps over to the bowl where I've combined feta cheese, a bruschetta-like mix of tomatoes and garlic, and some greens thrown in for color and texture. Mixed together, the lentils are partially disguised by the tomatoes and everything else. "Hmm. Okay, I'll try."

Jackson stands off to the side, leaning against the counter with his feet crossed at the ankles. He often does this when I cook for Fiona—observes from a corner of the kitchen. Most days, he insists I stay for dinner with the two of them, or he creeps upstairs to his home office to get a bit more work done, claiming to have forgotten the last few items on his to-do list.

I know he's aware that money is tight for me, and I have a feeling he goes out of his way to let me clock a few extra hours here and there since it makes no difference to his wallet. He never brings up the difference between our financial situations, and neither do I, but I know he's aware of it. I am too. All the time.

"Okay, you two. Don't burn the place down. I've gotta go get ready."

Jackson's eyes drift from my face down to my bare legs under the shorts I'm still wearing from when Fiona and I went to the lake earlier. He seems to do that a lot, and I wonder if he's aware he's doing it. When his eyes trail down my legs, I swear I can feel it like a melting stick of butter.

Without another word, he leaves us to make messes with art and eat dinner while he showers and gets dressed for the "business thing" he's been complaining about all week long. He makes it sound like an annual torture ritual.

The evening breeze filters through the open windows of the kitchen, carrying with it all the summer smells I love—lavender, star jasmine—mingling with the pervasive earthy smell of the vines.

"Can we work on our art a little longer before we eat?" Fiona asks.

"Sure. Should I keep working on the Playdough?" I ask, pointing to my artless attempt to make a family of gnomes. They look more like Smurfs. Or blobs.

I expect Fiona to dismantle them and put their pieces back into the appropriately-colored containers like we usually do, but she gleefully tells me she's keeping them. "They're a family. They'll live in my room."

"Sounds good to me," I say, rolling a small piece into a ball to make one more.

Her chatter fills the room for the next half hour, and I almost forget I'm supposed to be feeding her dinner. Being with her never feels like a job.

Fiona concentrates hard on cutting out red paper hearts she plans to paste into a book she's decided to write. "It's going to be a pop-up book," she announces, dabbing the corner of a heart with a fat glue stick. She bends the heart so it lays flat against the page and unfolds it to show how it "pops up."

"I love it. What's your story going to be about?"

She looks at the ceiling and purses her mouth before nodding her head decisively. "A princess. And a handsome prince. Like you and Daddy."

My heart lurches in my chest, and I get ready to dispel that thought from her head. I have to because it's the kind of story that won't have the happy ending she imagines.

Before I can form the words, her head twists to the side and she beams at her dad, who rests one hand on the counter. I wonder how long he's been standing there. Did he hear what she said?

"Daddy, you smell weird." Fiona waves a hand in front of her nose.

I couldn't disagree more. The pine and citrus scent that normally soothes my nerves comes in stronger post-shower. But that's not what knocks my senses for a loop.

The sheer sight of Jackson Corbett in a navy blue suit, crisp white shirt, and lavender tie is the most decadent dessert I didn't know I was craving. I'd blow every diet rule to take a bite.

With his wet hair slicked back and the way his frame fills out the suit, I'm speechless. And staring with my jaw hanging open, imagining myself on his arm tonight as his date.

Just as quickly, that bubble bursts when I realize how he's dressed. How he smells. How fresh and clean-shaven he looks. My stomach pitches because Jax is dressed for a date, all right.

It just isn't with me.

A knock at the door startles me out of my fantasy. It seems like it startles Jackson too, because his smile immediately arches down into a wince. His eyes locked on mine as soon as he entered the room, and I find myself wishing he'll ignore the knock and hang with us instead.

Reluctantly, he pushes away from the counter, and I see his shoulders flex beneath his suit. My gaze follows him as he walks to the door. His broad shoulders emphasize his trim waist and a muscular ass I could reach out and squeeze…if he wasn't opening the door to the most gorgeous woman I've seen since I started working at the winery.

Dressed in a glittery knee-length navy cocktail dress with a boat neck and tiny straps over her tanned shoulders, she smiles a red lipstick smile that looks like it took time to perfect in a magnifying mirror. Her lips glisten like they've just been kissed, and my mind wastes no time picturing Jackson doing just that.

She leans in and kisses him on the cheek, then uses her thumb to rub the lipstick remnants from his skin. Wrapping a long, thin arm around his neck, she tips her head to whisper something into his ear before laughing like they've shared an intimate joke. The sound of her laughter cuts through me like a sharp blade.

I try to erase the vision of him standing across from me earlier, when I thought he was staring at my legs and watching my lips as I spoke.

That must have felt like child's play. A cheap roadhouse appetizer of buffalo wings before his four-course caviar and champagne dinner. The moment the door opened, I gained a new perspective on Jackson, an image I've tried to deny.

The worst part is that I've succeeded. I've actually allowed myself to believe someone like him might be interested in someone like me. I've allowed myself to think that his gestures mean more than simple charity for the employee in tough straights. The naïve girl falling for her boss like a scullery maid in a fairy tale.

How did I allow myself to think like that for even one moment?

Of course this is the kind of woman he'd like. She fits right in with the wealthy family social circles he grew up in—as much as he's been telling me he feels like he's not a good fit for that life, standing next to this woman, he certainly looks the part.

His chest pulls at the crisp white cotton of his dress shirt. Under a suit that fits him like a glove, made for him by a tailor. His tie is expertly knotted at his throat, where his Adam's apple works as he regards his stunning date.

Her perfume swirls through the room, hitting my nose with a sickening pang that overwhelms my senses.

"Should we go? Did you ask the car to wait? If not, I can drive us." I hear Jackson's deep voice orchestrating their night, and a nauseated surge of bile hits my throat as I try to calm my pounding heart.

*I have a business thing down at the restaurant.*

He made it sound like a boring shareholder meeting. Instead, he's going to the very gala event I've spent a week working on with his sister. And because I'm clueless, I didn't realize the two were one and the same. But of course they are, and of course he'll be there. He's CFO of the company, for heaven's sake.

He could have just said he was going on a date. Or bringing a date to his fancy winery event. It's not like I have any claim on him, so why would he bother trying to downplay his night out or the fact that he has a date?

"In a minute," the woman's silky voice intones as she glides into the room. Jackson follows her, and his eyes flit to mine, bottomless and smoldering. That's the effect she has on him, and it makes me sick.

I want to hold his gaze and smile like I'm an enthusiastic supporter of him and his dating choices, but I can't, so I look away. I notice an uncomfortable stiffness in his movements as he follows her, but he's probably just nervous. He hasn't dated since his wife left. He told me that. I'm just the dimwit who assumed he was resigned to that fate, and somehow, in my wildest moments of insane fantasy, I conjured up a scenario where I might be the one he'd want.

I look up when a hand grazes my forearm. Like a cat reaching out to paw the mouse she intends to torture slowly.

"Hello. You're the babysitter?" She doesn't wait for me to answer, which is just as well because her sudden proximity has me tongue-tied.

Moving past me, she reaches over to ruffle Fiona's hair, something I know she hates. "You must be Fiona." Fiona lifts her shoulders as if to shoo the irritant away.

"Yes. Who are you?" Fiona asks.

"Fi, manners." The growl of Jackson's voice shouldn't affect me, but a chill rolls down my spine, and goosebumps prickle the back of my neck. The sight of his date is all but human birth control for my brain, and yet my body still hums in his presence.

It's not lost on me that he hasn't yet brought her to meet his daughter, but she's here now, staking her claim in his life.

I hope he can't see how he affects me. It's so mortifying that I've read him wrong and allowed myself the tiny glimmer of hope that he could feel something for me. He almost kissed me once, but there's been zero evidence he intended to try again, and yet…I let myself wish. So stupid.

I steady myself and walk to the fridge. I need a sip of club soda or something to calm my stomach, even if the thought of swallowing anything makes me want to retch.

The high titter of the woman's laugh sends a chill down my spine, making me fight to avoid cringing in her presence. Fortunately, I have my back to her as I root around in the fridge, but I can feel Jackson's eyes on me. When I turn, his eyes lock on mine with just as much heat as they contained earlier, but now I know the fire is being fed by the woman to my right.

"I'm Mallory. A *friend* of your dad's." The way she emphasizes "friend" is almost like she's winking, making it clear that they are anything but friends. Or rather, *everything* that friends never are.

"We should go." The deep rasp of Jackson's voice leaves no room for arguing.

"Such a bore." The tinkle of Mallory's voice reminds me of urine hitting the toilet bowl, and that thought steels me enough to look up just as Jackson's hand goes to the small of her back as he ushers her toward the door.

That tiny gesture I allowed myself to believe he reserved just for me…

I push down the urge to puke all over Mallory's shimmery dress.

"Fi, whatever Ruby says goes," Jackson says.

"Bye, Daddy." Fiona jumps up and goes over to the art table, disinterested in anything else happening around her. Wish I could say the same.

"We won't be out late," Jackson says. I nod without looking at him.

When the door closes, I feel an equal-sized door in my heart slam shut. Joy, optimism, frivolous hope—they're all gone. For good.

# CHAPTER
## Twenty-Three

JAX

I can't expel the image from my head of Ruby standing in my kitchen and looking gutted at the sight of Mallory flouncing through my house like she owns the place.

For the past month, I've done a pretty good job of convincing myself that any brief moments of connection between Ruby and me were figments of my imagination. Wishful thinking that fueled too many sessions of jerking off in the shower after waking to blindingly hot sex dreams involving Ruby. Cold showers each night as soon as she left my house. I'm the cleanest guy in three fucking counties.

Now, I'm toying with the idea that at least a few of those appreciative glances I thought I imagined may have been real. It's enough to have me completely distracted from everything that's happening around me tonight, most notably Mallory, who hasn't left my side and keeps rubbing herself against me at every turn.

"Babe, can you grab me another glass of prosecco while I run to the ladies' room?" she purrs in my ear while running a finger down my arm and squeezing my hand at the bottom. I wrest my hand from hers and look around to see if anyone noticed.

Not like anyone here is likely to make a big deal about Mallory and me together because she's stoked rumors about us ever since Annabelle left. And that one night. It's old news, even though it's not actually news.

Still, the thought of Ruby hearing someone tell tales out of school about me makes me acutely uncomfortable.

"Babe?" she asks again, making me shudder at the endearment. Only Mallory Rutherford would come to an event at a California winery and ask for a drink from Italy. We have a renowned sparkling cava, and I plan to bring her a glass of that. See if she knows the difference.

"Sure." The extent of our conversation for the past hour has been her oblivious chattering and my one-word answers. It doesn't seem to bother her. She's stuck close by my side and made sure to flip her hair so it cascades over one shoulder each time a photographer takes a photo of us together. It's normal industry insider stuff, photos that won't be seen outside of the glossy Napa magazines that adorn hotel room tables. At least, that's how it was until my sister invited the *Times* here to take photos for their society page.

Now, each time the shutter clicks, I feel the nauseous tick of my blood pressure rising. Each photo with Mallory makes me think about Ruby, wondering what she and Fiona are up to, remembering how upset she looked when Mallory showed up at my house.

All I want is to go home and see if I'm right about what I'm imagining. If there's a chance she's thinking of me the way I haven't been able to stop thinking about her, I need to know.

And yet, I'm like a handcuffed prisoner tonight, miles from freedom.

I've never been attracted to Mallory's brand of beauty—overly perfumed, hair and makeup done by a professional, every decision about who she talks to and how she walks through a room premeditated. She's good at playing her role, and she'll probably get what she wants because she knows how to play the game.

But I have no fucking interest in playing.

I'm laser focused on the attributes of only one woman. Sassy and smart, unafraid of bugs, able to wrangle my daughter and enchant her in the same moment. Can't stop thinking about Ruby, how she'd look in a silk slip of a dress with a slit halfway up her gorgeous thigh. She's everything I've never experienced in a woman.

Only kissed her in my dreams, but it doesn't matter. I'm gone for her.

I have to rearrange my dick in my pants, so I don't advertise my interest to every person in the room.

Various people intercept me as I make my way to the bar, which is packed three deep, even though waiters move through the crowd with glasses of wine and appetizers, so there's little need to line up for a drink.

"I was hoping you'd give the keynote again this year." Ken Dupont slaps me on the back and clasps my hand in his meaty paw. The mountain of a man inherited a swath of property on the north end of Napa from a relative, and he's a regular attendee at these events. He likes to know the industry scoop, though I'd lay good money on him never selling an acre of his land, even though he talks a good game.

"Nah, no one wants to hear from me these days."

"Are you kidding? You're the only one with a sense of humor."

Used to be. I used to have a sense of humor, but after my marriage imploded, I don't find the world so funny.

Not to mention that I feel our business teetering on the edge of something that could tank us. It bothers me that I haven't been able to find funds to prop us up, and despite my dad's cryptic reference to Hayden Lanes, I haven't been able to track down a vineyard with that name. Or any company, for that matter.

Fortunately, the owner of Magpie Vineyards catches Mallory's eye when she comes back from the restroom. He's been rumored to be interested in her property, so she'll let him talk her ear off for as long as he wants, which grants me a few extra minutes without her by my side while I scan the room.

My strategy at these things is always to get in, talk to the necessary people, and get out.

Regardless of having Mallory on my arm, I have the same plan tonight. The only problem is that I'm not sure who the necessary people are anymore.

"You looked miserable in every one of those shots," My sister's voice tsks over my shoulder as she hands me the glass of scotch I desperately need.

"I am miserable. That woman is a nightmare."

PJ laughs. "I know. I'm sorry."

I look at her, face alight with mischievous glee. "You're so not sorry. This is your jam, all this social media crap, and honestly, I don't know how you can stand it."

"You're lucky it's my jam because otherwise you might have to do it."

I hold up my glass in a toast. "Amen to that. Just tell me I've done my penance for the night, and I can send Mallory off to harass some other billionaire."

"Crabby face aside, yes. You've done what I need."

"Excellent."

We're silent a moment, taking in the several hundred people mingling through the room, munching on caviar blinis, ahi tuna on wontons, and sparkling wine. We're sizing up the crowd for different reasons. PJ is judging the success of the event while I look around and wonder if anyone in the room is from a vineyard named Hayden Lanes.

"Have you ever heard of the vineyard around here called Hayden Lanes?" I ask.

"Is it new?"

"I'm guessing. Or it's a shell company. But it's screwing with our business. Dad said the name to me in a moment of sort-of clarity."

"Yeah, Trix told me the nurse is optimistic about the new meds."

I shrug and take a sip of my drink. "Cautiously optimistic. It's still in trial phase, but yeah, if he has more moments of sort-of clarity, it'll be a great thing."

PJ pulls out her phone and scans a couple screens. "Not a single vintner from Napa, Sonoma, or even Paso Robles named Hayden Lanes. But you already knew that."

I nod. "I already knew that. Checked the business database as soon as Dad said it. But that doesn't mean there isn't someone here from that place, if it exists. Half these people I've never seen before."

PJ scans the crowd again. I watch her eyes dart from face to face as she registers recognition, but then she grimaces. "A lot are plus-ones, and people don't tell me who they're bringing. We've never required it. There was never a need."

"I know." It's always been a handshake and a smile business up here. "But I think things may be changing. At least where Dad's business deals were concerned."

"How worried are you?" she asks in a hushed voice.

I look around again. The couple dozen people in our immediate vicinity talk and laugh in groups, drinking sparkling wine from flutes and nibbling artichoke croquettes and Wagyu sliders from cocktail napkins with the Buttercup logo emblazoned in gold leaf. "Enough that I want the photographer to take pictures of everyone here and hand them off to me tomorrow with names attached. Can you make that happen?"

"For sure." She voice texts instructions to the photographer and slips the phone into her pocket. "Hope it gets you what you need."

"Probably won't come to anything, but at least I'll have the information."

Nodding, she claps me on the arm and flashes a smile at a

silver-haired man in a gray suit. "Calvin, the man of the hour!" My sister fawns over the keynote speaker who runs a winery in Sonoma, and I half-listen to his story about brush fires and the information he plans to tell the room once everyone's seated for dinner.

Then I go through the motions for the rest of the night, looking at each unfamiliar face and wondering if it's someone from Hayden Lanes. But even the potential to come face-to-face with someone who may lead me to the money trail I've been chasing for months doesn't really hold my attention.

Every time there's a lull in a conversation or a moment when no one is pumping my arm and telling me how great the restaurant's food tastes, my thoughts drift back to Ruby. That look on her face. That sucker punch in my gut.

She tried to act indifferent, hiding her face from me, but there was no hiding the hurt in her eyes before she managed to look away. I never wanted to hurt her—ever—but at least now I have the evidence I need that she wants me.

I just have to hope she still does after the shit show of this evening.

Finally, after four long hours, I've air-kissed enough cheeks, gladhanded enough fellow winemakers, and tried unsuccessfully to find an answer to my questions, I get the go-ahead from PJ to get the hell out.

The misty air hits my face as I stride toward the exit.

I have no idea what I'm going to do when I get home, but I'm not planning to sit on my fucking hands anymore, telling myself this woman is off-limits.

No.

Not anymore.

# CHAPTER
## Twenty-Four

RUBY

"But I'm not tired." Fiona yawns, barely able to get the words out before her exhaustion takes over. Her eyes are at half-mast, and she's fighting against gravity with every fiber of her being.

"Okay," I tell her. "You can stay up later if you want." I dim the lights in her room so that everything looks gray, with a pale blue cast coming through the half-open blinds.

Her lips widen into a half grin, but she doesn't have the energy to smile fully. Her cheek rests on the pillow, blond hair splashed over her Hello Kitty pink pillowcase, limbs starfished on the mattress. "Yes, please."

Even tired, she's polite. We've made a forest's worth of clay animals and a diorama to display them. Brown clay tree trunks have real green leaves on them, plucked from the ferns growing outside in the shade. We used blue permanent marker on a tiny tin foil brook running beneath the trees. Then we ate lentils, made a couch fort, and filled half a notebook with doodles and designs.

Her eyes are closed tight, her body heavy on the bed. Fast asleep, despite herself.

I should be as tired as Fiona, except that my adrenaline is running high, every torturous scenario playing in my head on a loop, wondering how Jackson's date with Mallory is going.

I don't want to be thinking about him, or her, but I can't stop my mind from replaying the scene in the house earlier, his hand on the small of her back… It still makes me nauseous, and it shouldn't. It can't.

He's probably kissing her. Probably fucking her in a bathroom. Or maybe they have special rooms at the fancy restaurant just for that.

*Shit!* What if he brings her back to the house? What should I do, other than die of embarrassment? Me, the hired help, sneaking out the back door as he invites this classy, rich date back to share his wine…and his bed.

*God, why did I have to fall for my boss? So. Stupid.*

"Out like a light." The voice makes me jump. Its deep tenor sends a jolt of electricity through my chest, part nervousness, part dread. I don't want to look at him, lest he see exactly how much he still affects me, despite an entire evening of talking myself down and telling myself to build a wall around my feelings.

I still feel the disappointment dragging down the muscles in my face.

"Yeah, not a minute ago, she insisted she was wide awake," I choke out, hoping my voice sounds normal, knowing it sounds higher than it should. I need some water.

It's dark in the room, so I can probably make a run for it, dashing past Jackson and heading downstairs. I'll call out a quick goodbye, grab my things, and race out before he can get a solid look at me. Then, I'll get a good night's sleep and reset my expectations in the morning.

Or maybe I'll call in sick.

I turn to go, but Jackson has moved closer, a wall of man in my path. Instead of the cloying smell of Mallory's perfume, I inhale a deep breath that's all Jackson—his manly pine and citrus scent that brings a shot of awareness to my core.

Stepping to the side, I plan to go around him. Even in the dimly lit room, I can see a path to the door.

His hand catches mine, stopping my progress. He tugs gently, and I turn, still unwilling to look at him. I look down.

"Hey." His deep voice rolls through my veins like lava. One finger tilts my chin up to look at him. His eyes burn like dark infernos that tell me nothing about what he's thinking.

"Hey," I say. "Is everything okay?"

"No."

I feel a momentary surge of panic. I know it's not Fiona since she's right here, but maybe it's something with another one of his family members?

"Did something happen at the gala?"

He doesn't answer. Not with words, anyway.

Tracing a finger down the side of my face, he looks mesmerized, like he's seeing me for the first time. His hand pushes into my hair, and his fingers tangle in the strands. My pulse rushes with the heat of his touch.

"I've been wanting to do this since the day you showed up here." His eyes are lazy, and I wonder if he's a little drunk. Probably. It was a winery event, after all.

"And?"

He speaks slowly, each word hitting me like a dart. "It was… worth…the wait."

His eyes stay locked on mine, daring me to look away, but I can't. I want to know what this is.

Guiding me the last few steps out of Fiona's bedroom, Jackson says nothing. He closes the door quietly, and I feel a slight relief because the air out here in the hallway is cooler. Still, I'm burning up, starting at the connection point of our hands and racing up my arm and through my veins like a fever.

I don't remember turning the hallway lights off, but Jackson must've done after he came up the stairs. He's also removed his jacket.

A beam of light from downstairs creeps up the far staircase, but we're in near darkness. He turns me so my back hits the wall and leans toward me, framing my face with his forearms.

I know what these forearms look like, and a part of me wants to take in the up-close view of his roped muscles. But I can't take my eyes off his face.

His eyes search mine, then drop to my lips and stay there. My tongue darts out to lick my lips because I feel like he might kiss me. But that's crazy. This is crazy.

"Jax." My voice sounds breathy, and I search my mind for what to say next. "Are you okay?"

When he speaks, he's so close that I feel his words more than I hear them. "I am now." He doesn't move, doesn't give me space, not that I want it. I'm so overcome by the proximity of him that I can barely form words.

"Okay," I manage, my mind still spinning out of control, trying to figure out what changed since he left the house with a stunning woman who looked like his perfect match.

*Did he have a fight with her? Am I his backup booty call?*

I'm not sure what my role is supposed to be here, but I also know that I don't want to move. I want to be right here, even if I'm the backup booty call, because I've wondered how his hands would feel on me since the day we met, but I didn't have the temerity to game out a scenario for how it might happen.

This. I would never have imagined this.

I'm caught between the sense of wanting him and needing to know what he's thinking.

"If you tell me to stop, I'll stop."

He hasn't done anything I'd want him to stop. On the contrary, I want to see what happens when he doesn't stop.

"Okay," I say.

"Tell me to stop."

I shake my head. In my late-night fantasies of how this would go down, I've never asked Jackson Corbett to stop.

"Last chance." His voice sounds strained, as though he hates saying the words, but he knows he should. I'm not sure if he's telling me or himself.

Jackson closes his eyes for a long beat, and when he opens them, he looks determined. There's a fire burning within the darkness that I haven't seen before.

Moving one arm from the wall, he caresses my cheek again, leaving goosebumps in his hand's wake. Cupping my jaw, Jackson leans closer until I can't focus on his face anymore, and my eyes drift shut.

His lips are soft as they brush over mine. He takes my face in both hands this time and kisses me, tilting my head to the side so our mouths match up, and I feel his lips more fully. Then I stop thinking and wondering what we're doing, and time stops moving.

My hands hang limp at my sides because I'm in a hypnotic state. I think my lips part because I feel Jackson's tongue work over mine, delicately at first. Then, with abandon, plundering and taking what he wants. I'm doing the same, drinking in the taste of him and finally letting my hands roam up his muscular chest.

I'm losing track of my senses, idle messages pressing through my brain.

*What if you lose your job?*

*This feels too good to stop.*

*Just quit thinking for once and enjoy this.*

*You've worked too hard to throw it all away over a guy.*

It's the record scratch that sends sensibility careening back. So I break the kiss.

Jackson blinks a couple times, as if willing himself to reenter reality. He takes a deep breath and half a step back, which allows me to focus on his face.

He has a dreamy look that mirrors how I feel, but that's not good. We need to stop. "That…we should probably stop," I say, wriggling from between him and the wall.

"If that's what you really want."

Standing in the dark hallway, I feel around on the wall for a light switch, but I can't find one. So I glare at him in the dark. "I don't want to be your booty call."

I can't escape the truth. I need this job—both jobs. And as much as I want him, I want my career more, and I have responsibilities. I can't throw it away over a guy.

He takes a step closer to me. "Yeah?" His voice is gruff, sexy, dripping with everything that makes my skin heat. And I think he knows it. "That's what you think this is?"

"Um, yeah. Isn't it?"

Jackson growls out a harsh "Fuck," and looks off to the side like he's replaying previous moments between us in his head. He shakes his head.

Despite the growl, his expression is soft and loving as he takes in my confusion. His thumb reaches up, smoothing away the worried frown from my forehead and tipping his head against mine. His nose sweeps along mine, eyes closed in a silent reprimand. "Fuck, no. That's not what this is."

When he looks back at me, his eyes are ablaze again, but I can't let myself fall for him. "You're not thinking clearly."

I make my way down the hallway toward the light. If I can get some distance between us, we can both come to our senses. But Jackson follows, hot on my heels.

"Ruby…" His voice comes with an ache I haven't heard before, so I turn. He reaches for my hand and intertwines our fingers. Then he brings my hand to his lips and kisses my knuckles, but he doesn't let go. Holding my hand against his lips, he feathers my skin with the barest breath of a kiss, and all the air leaves my lungs. "I promise you I'm thinking clearly."

"Prove it." I can barely form words.

"How?"

I shrug. "Are you drunk?"

"No." He pulls me closer, wedging our hands between our chests. In my bare feet, he towers over me, tipping his head down to study my face.

"I just…this doesn't make sense."

Slowly, he nods. "Watching you leave every day when I want you here…that makes no sense. I can't sleep, Ginger. All I do is think about you. I tried to stop, but I can't. I can't fucking stop."

"Don't stop," I whisper. I feel like I'm in a dream.

His lips are on mine, and this time, there's no gentle prelude. His kiss is demanding and rough, taking what he wants from me, but I'm just as demanding because my body wants this, even if it's fatal.

Never breaking the kiss, he walks us down the hallway toward his room, at the opposite end from where Fiona sleeps. When we reach the doorway, he scoops me up and carries me to his bed. My arms wrap around his neck and hold on while he lowers me to a soft blue quilt.

"You have no idea how often I've thought about doing this." He holds himself above me and lets his eyes roam my face, my body. "I can't fucking think about anything else. I try, but all I do is think about you."

"I think about you too," I gasp, breathless with anticipation. Watching him watching me is a new kind of turn-on. I've seen his sharp focus on problem solving at work and the way he looks at Fiona with adulation and wonder, but the way he's looking at me right now trumps everything.

Eyes consuming me with intensity and focus. Sharp jaw soft as his Adam's apple works to swallow. I see reverence. And desire. And a kind of desperation I've never witnessed in a man before. It's almost overwhelming.

Reaching for his shirt, I undo one button at a time. He loosens his tie and pulls it over his head. When I reach the bottom button, I yank the shirt from his pants, and he shrugs it off his shoulders.

I shouldn't be so overwhelmed at the sight of him. I've seen him shirtless before in the pool with Fiona, and granted, I had to keep myself from drooling then. Seeing him now has me panting like I've lived a year in a desert.

A smirk settles on his face as I drink him in. He knows what he does to me, and I don't even care that I've just shown my hand.

Running one palm from his belt buckle up the ripples of his abs, I swallow hard. One hand isn't enough, so I let my other one roam his abs and chest while he leans forward and meets my lips.

Our kisses aren't hasty or frantic, maybe because neither one of us is trying to convince the other of anything. I still could lose my job, and I'm just as aware of that fact as I was earlier, but I feel like I can trust Jackson. I may live to regret it, but right now, the gamble feels worth it.

Jackson works my shirt up over my head until I'm free of the annoying fabric, and he tosses it on the floor where I not so delicately threw his shirt a few minutes earlier. His mouth goes to my breast, licking and sucking through the thin silk and making me arch my back to get closer to his hot mouth.

He pushes the fabric aside and nips at my skin, which is riddled with goosebumps. He's setting me on fire with each lap of his tongue and each sharp bite, which he soothes right afterward with his mouth.

I moan as his tongue circles the taut peak, and he undoes my bra clasp so he can give my other breast equal attention.

My hands are at the waist of his pants, moving us right along to where my mind has been since he took my hand in Fiona's room. No. It's been there since he came sauntering out of the farmhouse that first day when I showed up for an interview twelve hours too soon.

I've wanted him since then, even as I told myself we were impossible. Maybe we are, but I'm not backing out now.

Jackson works his way down my body, covering me with tiny kisses and licking my skin like it's a cool dessert in an inferno. And I'm letting myself have this moment. I'm allowing myself this one indulgence in the weeks and months of working multiple jobs, keeping my focus on my career goals, taking care of my family, and never letting my foot off the gas pedal.

I'm not going to regret a single moment with hot-as-sin Jackson Corbett because I need this.

And I want him.

# CHAPTER
## Twenty~Five

JAX

Maybe I should stop and have a nice long conversation with myself about jeopardizing every part of my life, but I have no fucking interest in doing that. Every day, I do what I'm supposed to do in the name of the family business.

Right now, in this moment, I'm doing what I want.

I have a woman on my bed who I find so goddamn attractive that I can't see straight, and that's where the conversation with myself ends.

Pulling her shorts down an inch at a time reveals the legs I've obsessed over since she showed up at my front door, all sass and fiery copper hair, asking me if I was nuts.

The answer to that question is easy now.

Yes, I am. One hundred percent nuts for her.

"Damn, Ruby," I groan as she kicks off the shorts. I crouch near her feet and get a good look at her tanned yoga legs leading up to a tiny triangle of fabric I'm desperate to remove. But first, I want to taste her skin, starting at the sexy curve where her heel meets her calf.

Her head falls back on my pillow, and I've never appreciated my midnight blue sheets as much as right now because they light up her copper hair in new, stunning ways. And I'm dying to pull down those panties to see if there's more gorgeous copper for me underneath.

"Jax, you're wearing too much clothing." She points a finger at me as her eyes travel over my chest and down my abs, resting on my belt buckle. "Feels unfair."

Before I can decide if it feels unfair to me, she sits up and unbuckles my belt. Pulling it through the loops with a quick tug, she rolls it into a coil before tossing it into the growing clothing pile. Then she gets to work on my pants, popping the button and unzipping them with nimble fingers.

I slide them down my legs, and they go on the floor as well. "Am I ruining your nice suit? Do you need to fold it?" she asks with a teasing smile.

"First of all, I've got a closet full of useless suits. And second, I don't give a shit what you're ruining. I'm not letting you off this bed."

The ring of her laughter is a balm that soothes my soul. I'd do just about anything to hear it forever, and the realization hits me like a wrecking ball. I'm at risk of falling so far, so fast for this woman, and there's not a goddamn thing I can do about it. I'll enjoy the entire way down, even if I land on my face.

With my hand against her chest, I push her back onto the bed and settle again between her legs.

"These are pretty, but they need to go." I grab the silky fabric of her thong with my teeth and drag it down her legs, stopping every few inches to nip at her skin on the way down and on the way back, ending at the soft skin of her inner thighs.

Glancing up, I confirm what I hoped I'd see beneath her panties, and it makes my cock swell even more.

She sucks in a breath when my tongue makes circles along the sensitive flesh, teasing her the closer I get to her center and backing away just enough to make her chest heave with frustrated breath.

"You can torture me, but best you believe I will get you back."

"I'm counting on it, Ruby."

Keeping a hand on the skin of her inner thigh, I move up her body for a kiss that consumes us both. Our mouths fuse in a molten dance that goes on and on for so long that I almost forget about the part of her gorgeous body that I just left behind, the part I'm dying to taste more than anything. Almost.

Rolling us over so I'm beneath her, I break the kiss and stare at her, hair all mussed from my pillow, lips pink and swollen. Pure beauty. She looks down at me with a guilty grin and rubs against me shamelessly. I love that she's as into this as I am. I wouldn't be here if she wasn't.

"C'mere, sweetheart," I tell her, taking her face in my hands and kissing her chin, each cheek, her lips. Then I flip her over again, a little rougher, and her eyes flame.

Kneeling over her, I move down her body, kissing her breasts, her stomach, the swell of her hip. Then I part her legs and work my way along the flesh at the top of one thigh until I reach her gorgeous folds and tug her closer to my mouth.

Her knees bend, giving me just the angle I want. "There we go, sweetheart," I breathe against her flesh, feeling her hips shudder beneath my hands.

Her response is a quiet hum of agreement that turns into a sultry moan when I run my tongue straight up her center.

"So wet, so sweet."

She doesn't respond with words, but there's no mistaking how she feels. Her ragged breathing and the way her head lolls on the pillow only fuels my own building orgasm. But she's getting hers first.

I have to grab my cock to relieve some of the building pressure. My fingers dig into the flesh of her hip as I pull her flush against my mouth. When my lips close around her clit, I suck hard until she gasps. I watch her head sink deeper into the pillow, and her features go slack.

Yeah, I'm going to enjoy myself as much as she does.

# CHAPTER
## Twenty-Six

RUBY

Holy shit.

Jackson Corbett's tongue is doing things to my body that have me gasping like I'm running out of air.

Swirling around my clit, sucking hard, working me into a frenzy of sensation like nothing I've ever felt. There was a reason it was easy to give up hookups and relationships—none of them ever made me feel like this. And now…there's no going back.

"Jax," I sigh, watching him watch me. I want to tell him how good this feels, but I don't have enough words. I don't have any words.

My legs are quivering, my chest heaving. If I were wearing a bodice, I'd be voluptuously spilling out of it with all the heaving I'm doing.

And yet, there's more. He slides two fingers inside me while his tongue works expertly to draw out the orgasm I've always denied I could have like this. It's building, and I lose the battle against every last bit of inhibition. There's something so hot about letting him see me at my most vulnerable.

He's magic. I want to write poems about just how magical he is.

"Come for me, Ginger." His deep growl is a command.

I nod, my head tipping back, eyes closing so the only sensation I feel is where his mouth clamps down on my clit and sucks hard. "Jax, oh god."

That's the beginning and end of my poetic words because I'm lost, careening down an icy mountain on a flaming sled, melting everything in its path.

I need a moment to recover from this. Only, I don't think I'll ever recover from this.

And Jackson doesn't give me the option of recovering from this. He works his way back up my body, lavishing kisses as he goes.

"Tell me what you want, Ruby."

When he gets close enough, I put my hands on both cheeks and pull his mouth to mine, tasting myself on his lips, fueling me to ask for what I want. "More of you."

"Hmm, that's not very descriptive."

"Because you've made me orgasmic and dumb."

That earns me a smug smile. "I like you this way. Makes me want to keep you orgasmic, though not dumb. You'll never be dumb."

I could really fall for this man. I could fall for his whole stern-financial-guy-with-the-cinnamon-roll-dad thing, and it wouldn't even take a second orgasm. But I want that too. Oh, I want it.

Reaching down, I wrap my hand around his hard cock, which pulses under my grip. I watch his throat work as he swallows and tries to steady his breathing, but he can't. I love watching his control slip.

Reaching for the drawer of the bedside table, he grabs a condom and shreds the wrapper with his teeth. I take it from him and roll it on, squeezing him a little tighter as I go until he growls, "Ruby…"

"Yes?" I bat my eyelashes and look at him with innocence.

"You should've been my date tonight." He sucks in a breath as I continue to run my hand over his length.

"It might not have ended like this if I hadn't been jealous of your date."

"No, Ginger. It would have fucking ended like this. But I'd have driven myself crazy watching every man in the room want you as much as I do." He flips us over so he's beneath me, and I grind down on him, watching his eyelids drop as his control slides farther from his grasp.

Grabbing my hips, he positions me above his cock, but he doesn't lower me down. His biceps and shoulders flex as he holds me where he wants me, lowering me an inch, two inches, then lifting me away until I moan in desperation.

Then he does it again. I just want to sink down and take him in completely, but he won't let me. And with each inch he gives me, he takes it back moments later until I'm writhing over him, desperate, hot, and ready to orgasm again, and he's not even inside me.

"Dammit, Jax."

He smiles again, so smug, so good at every damn thing he does.

And with one beautiful thrust, he fills me, and this time, he doesn't push me away. "Ride me, sweetheart. Take what you want."

So I do. Moving over him and pushing us both higher.

Until he's growling, "Fuck, Ruby." And I'm orgasmic and dumb again, saying nothing that qualifies as words.

His hands are on my breasts, massaging my nipples as he moves beneath me, and that's all it takes for me to come tumbling over the ice hill again. Only this time, he's with me, and careening out of control feels even better. So much better.

It's everything.

————

"Shh, Fiona's a light sleeper," Jackson tells me as we creep down the hallway toward the creaky stairs. I'm certain he's walking me back to my car so I can zip back over to the staff quarters before morning.

Wearing one of his soft tees and nothing else, I'm aware that I've left my clothes upstairs, but the awareness of Fiona's proximity has my brains scattered, and I'm prepared to make a quick getaway.

I grab my sweater from where I left it on the kitchen chair and head for the door. As I'm reaching for the knob, Jackson's hand wraps around my waist, and he tugs me back into him. "Where do you think you're going?"

"Um, home? Or really, my home away from home over there in the staff area." I point in the direction of the bungalows even though we both know where they are. He wraps his arms around me and holds me against him, nuzzling kisses into my neck.

"Yeah, you're not leaving."

"You just said Fiona's a light sleeper."

Swiveling me around, he kisses me softly. Then deeper. Insatiable, as we melt into each other.

When we break the kiss, he smooths the messy strands of hair off my forehead and kisses my temple. "I meant that we should be quiet in the kitchen. I want to cook you breakfast."

I can't see a clock, but it's pitch black outside the windows, and I'm fairly certain it's the middle of the night.

I start to explain this, but Jackson places a finger over my lips. "I know. It's like four in the morning. But if she sees you at the normal breakfast hour, there will be questions. Lots of questions."

Gazing up at Jackson, who's tangling his fingers in my waves of hair like he can't stand not to be touching me somewhere, I try to come up with a reason to say no. "Gorgeous. This color."

"It was darker when I was born. It's why my parents named me Ruby. They thought the name would match my hair."

"I wouldn't change a thing, Ginger." The low, gruff tones of his voice stir up everything inside me again. This is crazy. It's the middle of the night, and we both have to work in the morning. I should go home, and we should each get some sleep.

But I don't say any of those things because Jackson is beautiful and sweet with his puppy dog eyes, beckoning me to his kitchen.

He leads me to one of the stools on his granite countertop and lifts me onto it before padding over to the family room sofa, grabbing a soft white throw blanket, and draping it over my shoulders. He plants one more kiss on my lips before flipping on the light above the stove and getting to work.

"I feel useless," I say, crossing my legs and hunkering under the blanket.

Jackson laughs quietly. "Good. I like seeing you take a load off for once."

He quietly takes a pan down from a hanging rack above the stove, which is backed by a wall of pale green tile that offsets the countertops and rustic wood cabinets. Turning on the flame, he sets the pan down and lets it heat.

"Not gonna lie, it's not the easiest thing for me to take a break."

"Ha. I know, Ginger. I know." His voice is low, and with all the kitchen lights off except the one above the stove, the space feels intimate in the early morning.

"Thank you for not holding it against me. You wouldn't be the first to get annoyed."

"Nothing about you annoys me, except how far away you are," he says, returning to me for another kiss.

*I could get used to this...*

Jackson retrieves a carton of eggs, a stick of butter, milk, and a block of pale yellow cheese from the refrigerator. Just as quietly, he takes out a blue ceramic bowl and cracks six eggs into it. Stirring in some milk, he starts beating the eggs.

Once they're a frothy pale yellow, he reaches for a fresh loaf of bread from Sweet Butter, which is part bakery, part café. He slices the baguette into two-inch hunks while I watch, mesmerized like I'm watching my own personal cooking show. Only no cooking show host I've ever seen looked like Jackson, delectable in his plaid pajama bottoms and sexy bare chest.

I don't realize I'm gaping at him until he laughs, walks over, and uses his knuckle to close my mouth. He knows I like what I see, and I don't mind showing my hand.

"You okay?"

"Mm-hmm."

He smiles. "I like seeing you take a break, especially when half the reason you're busy is because of me."

"Well, Fiona, technically." He dumps the eggs into the pan where butter sizzles and begins whisking them. He turns down the heat and lets the eggs sit.

"True. It's the kid's fault."

"But we love her." His eyes shoot to mine, and for a moment, I worry I've made him uncomfortable. She's his kid. I have no claim on her. "I don't mean—"

"No. Don't take it back."

I shift on the stool and debate hopping down and going over to him, but I feel frozen. "If I'm overstepping, tell me."

Jackson puts down the whisk and walks over to me without a word. He comes up behind me, encircling me with his arms. His lips brush my cheek, and he nuzzles my neck.

"You are not overstepping," he whispers against my skin. "I love that you love my daughter."

My heart twists in my chest, and I inhale a shaky breath. Who is this man, and what has he done with the stand-offish guy who didn't want to hire me a month ago? The one who has me wrapped tight bears almost no resemblance to him. And yet, I think I knew who he was all along.

Not wanting Jackson to let go of me, I slip off the stool, and we move back toward the stove. He stands behind me, one arm around my waist, while I shred the block of cheese and he finishes up the eggs with one hand. We sprinkle in the cheese and let the eggs set.

Jackson leans to the left and grabs a plate. I lean to the right and pick up a few chunks of bread. I put them on the plate while Jackson spoons out the eggs and grabs a single fork.

"Bon appetite," he says, scooping up a forkful and turning me to face him. He slides a bite of eggs into my mouth and kisses my lips as I chew.

"How are these so good?" I ask once I swallow.

"A tablespoon of butter per egg. The French way."

My eyes go wide. "Six tablespoons of butter? That's more butter than I eat in a week."

He takes a bite and chews, nodding. "Worth it, right?"

"Totally worth it," I agree, leaning my head against his chest. "And I'm not just talking about the eggs."

# CHAPTER
## Twenty~Seven

JAX

"You're like a Doberman with a chew toy when you get an idea stuck in your head." Beatrix rolls her eyes, and it occurs to me I ought to apologize to Ruby for accusing her of teaching that to Fiona. Turns out nearly every one of the women I know could have taught it to her.

Trix turns her back on me and goes upstairs to her office without another word, leaving me at the hostess stand where she was clipping today's menus onto rectangular boards made from wine crates.

With no choice but to wait for her, I sit on one of the worn velvet couches that flank the restaurant's entrance and serve as a cocktail area when tables aren't ready. Taking in the rough-hewn beams that make the place look like it could easily be a Fourteenth Century apartment in France, I wonder what Ruby thought when she first saw it.

My untrained eye sees a rustic farmhouse dressed up with white linen. It's supposed to give off the vibe of being homey but high-end.

To my sister's credit, she did a first-rate job of designing the space. By far the most artistic of all of us, she really ought to be working in a creative field like design or graphics. And like all of us, whatever dreams she may have had to paint in an atelier were subsumed by the family business.

The restaurant is one of the most profitable arms of our property, so Trix is in the planning stages of opening a smaller bistro and market that will create custom picnic baskets for wine tasters to buy and take with them for the day.

"Okay, I'm back." Holding a worn leather binder in her hands, Trix bounds down the wide staircase. "I'm debating redoing the upstairs bathrooms with wallpaper. Can I show you?" At least this part of the restaurant business allows her to be a little creative.

"Sure, if you think I know anything about wallpaper. I don't spend a lot of time looking at restroom walls."

She flips open the binder to show me page after page of wallpaper samples, most of which have large leaves on them. Different colored leaves, different species of leaves, but all leaves. I shrug.

"Doesn't matter. I just want an opinion."

Trix flips through the pages again as though I might react differently this time around. I shake my head and throw up my hands. "They all have leaves. Therefore, they all seem great."

Shaking her head, she closes the book.

"So, can we do it?" I ask, antsy to get back to my office and finish my work. I have a surprise planned for Ruby tonight, dinner at the restaurant, provided my sister cooperates. She's a stickler about reservations, and the place is always full. Even family members need to book tables—it's a rule.

I can see Trix's brow crease. Her fingers tap on the leather binder, and I know I have to weigh in on bathroom leaves if I have any prayer of getting her to focus on what I need.

"The purple and red leaves seem nice. I think they're best."

She shakes her head. "No. Not those. Why do I even bother asking you?"

"You've got me." I shift from one foot to the other, knowing if I push my sister, she'll find some other inane task for me to do before she arranges what I need.

"Calm down, little brother. We're good to go tonight. But only because I really like Ruby, and I love how she's making you take yourself less seriously. PJ is still all about keeping up appearances, but I'll talk to her. I'm Team Ruby. So get to work on your own end of things." I must look confused because she laughs and points me out the door. "Figure out how you're going to surprise her, what you're going to do to make it romantic."

Now I really am confused because I thought that dinner at a great restaurant where she's never eaten qualifies as romantic. "Um, such as?"

"I dunno. Tell her you have something else planned to throw her off, show up when she thinks she has to work late tonight, and whisk her away. Plan something even I haven't thought of. Sheesh, dude, you need some moves."

Maybe she's right. In the time since Annabelle left, I've pretty much given up on romance, but Ruby deserves my A-game.

I need some moves.

# CHAPTER
## Twenty-Eight

RUBY

My long red dress whips around my ankles in the light evening breeze while I wait outside my bungalow for Jackson to pick me up. I told him it was ridiculous for him to drive over and fetch me when I have my own car, but he just scowled and shook his head.

"It's a date. I'm picking you up."

"You're being bossy," I complain, not really complaining.

"You like it." He could get a woman pregnant with his smirk.

"I do."

All I know is that Fiona is sleeping at Auntie PJ's house, and we're going out to dinner. He won't tell me where we're going, just that I shouldn't wear shorts. "You look great in shorts, Ginger, but they won't let you in where we're going."

Before work this morning, I raced down to Berkeley, added some more sugar to my viniculture, and grabbed a dress. For once, I didn't have to make an emergency run to the Duck Feather gift shop.

Jackson's tires crunch on the gravel when he pulls his SUV

around, followed by a catcall that makes me blush. He puts the car in park a few feet from where I'm waiting and hops out.

The way his shoulders fill out his navy sports coat nearly makes me drool. Slicked back hair, crisp white dress shirt, dangerous smile. "Beautiful," he says, reaching for my hand and grazing my knuckles with a kiss.

I feel more heat rise in my cheeks, but the wind does me a solid by whipping my hair around to obscure it. "Looking good, yourself." Such an understatement.

He looks like a decadent meal wrapped in a navy suit. Useless clothing obscuring the hot skin and hard lines underneath, and I'll spend all of dinner fantasizing about what I can't see.

Leading me to the car, Jackson drapes an arm over my shoulders, bare under the spaghetti straps of my dress. I'm not wearing a bra under the sheet of red silk, and I catch Jackson angling for a view down the front of my dress. "Manners," I tease.

"Impossible when you're wearing that, Ginger." Opening my car door, he leans closer, his breath brushing my neck. "And you should always be wearing that."

My first clue to our destination is that we don't leave the Buttercup property, instead taking a back road I know about after my stint at Butter and Rosemary restaurant. It was weeks ago that I mentioned in passing that I'd never eaten there, and he tucked that piece of information away.

The drive is short, less than half a mile. The evening air is warm and fragrant, perfect for a walk, but in my three-inch sandals, I'm glad for once to be in a car instead of hoofing it up the gravel road.

Jackson grabs my hand, interlacing our fingers. It feels so casual, like we're always this way with each other. More than that, it feels like we've been this way from the first day we met, even if neither of us felt brave enough to acknowledge it until now.

I still feel like I'm leading a double life, acting like a professional at work and around Fiona, even though I catch myself standing a little too close to him or wanting to put a hand on him someplace. I notice him doing the same—our eyes meet, and a secret conversation passes between us in a look. My resistance feels stretched to the limit, ready to snap.

It feels light and perfectly casual, a scoop of vanilla with whipped cream in relationship form. New affection, hot sex. I tell myself it's okay to feel drawn to him the way I am. But the day I find my mind slipping into a fairy tale life, pretending we're a family, is the day I need to leave.

That's not what this is.

*But it could be.*

No. It can't. I have obligations to my sister and big career goals. There's no room in that equation for a relationship right now. And I can't think beyond that just because I'm infatuated.

The restaurant looks different to me now that I'm going to be a guest here. The twinkling lights that dot the ivy-covered walls in front sparkle a little more brightly tonight.

When the valet opens my door, Jackson is there in a heartbeat, asking him to step aside so he can reach for my hand. His eyes snap to my bare calf as I extend my leg and step on the small ledge of the Jeep as I exit. It's exhilarating to feel his eyes drink me in with wolfish thirst.

Jackson's arm drapes casually over my shoulders, and I prepare myself for glances from the maître d' and staff who know Jackson and might be gossiping as soon as we're out of sight, but Beatrix intercepts us as soon as we walk in the door.

"Your table is ready." She escorts us up a set of stairs I noticed during the week I worked there, setting up for the tasting event, but I never knew where they led. The dimly lit staircase sits off to the side in the foyer of the restaurant and looks like it leads to a restroom or office.

When we reach the top, and Beatrix sweeps open a small door, I gasp. This is no restroom or office. "Enjoy, you two," Beatrix says, already heading back down the staircase.

Jackson leads me out the door, which has opened to a rooftop terrace with pathways winding among trellises of flowers. The scene is lit by tiny bulbs that twinkle gently, almost like they're moved by the breeze. With his arm still over my bare shoulder, Jackson leads us down one winding pathway to another that's abloom with wide pink blossoms that bounce on their stems.

"These were always my favorite." He plucks one of the blooms by the stem and hands it to me. I'm still processing the fact that he has a favorite flower when he turns me to face him and brushes his hand down my bare arm.

"Are they not anymore?"

He shakes his head, mesmerizing me with the sight of his beautiful face. "Now you're my favorite."

His kiss sucks the air from my lungs. I'm instantly dizzy, drunk on the taste of his lips and confounded by the crazy twist of fate that brought me here. I could have shown up at the correct time and never met Jackson Corbett. I could have left the winery when I was supposed to and never met Fiona, never offered to be Jackson's nanny.

Instead, I'm here, and I don't want to leave.

I stare at the flower grasped between my fingers. "Don't give up on the flower. She's a beauty."

"She is." He tips my chin up and kisses me again, sweetly, gently. Unhurried. Because this isn't a stolen kiss while Fiona isn't looking. His fingers trail down the length of my arm, ending at my hand, where he intertwines them with mine.

Leading me down the winding pathway again, Jackson directs me to where the flowers and potted olive trees give way to a private nook overlooking the acres of vineyards. The sun has dropped, and the vines wind around their stakes under a periwinkle sky, which outlines their shadows. The moon hasn't risen yet.

One table on the terrace is set with small votive candles and the same blue glass dishware from the restaurant. Enough flatware for a multi-course dinner. Several wine glasses stand sentry by each plate. But it's not the beauty of the table setting that gets me. It's the way Jackson is looking at me when I turn to thank him for setting this up.

His eyes are soft, searching, almost…disbelieving. Like he's just as gobsmacked by the moment as me, even though he's the one who arranged it.

"I'm going to enjoy everything about tonight," he says, winking against a wolfish gleam that says he'd like to have me for a pre-dinner snack. My nerves flood with jitters. This isn't just lust at an opportune time. This is a date. It feels…loaded.

I bite down on my bottom lip, suddenly nervous, but Jackson leans closer. With his teeth, he wrests my lip away and sucks it into his mouth, making me forget my jangled nerves for the moment with a kiss that brings me back to sanity.

When he breaks the kiss, he tugs me close, whispering against my lips. "You're all I think about." Lust drags through my bones.

I spend so much time holding myself to a strict line, staying focused on all the moving parts in my life, making sure everything is covered before allowing myself a moment of relaxation.

*Relax. Everything is covered.*

Jackson guides us to the table, where I notice a bottle of the wine I tasted and loved when I worked with Victor. He's done his homework.

He pulls out my chair, and I'm struck with a revelation—I don't think anyone has ever pulled out a chair for me. The feminist in me doesn't need the gesture, but it's so kind and sweet that I fall for him a little harder.

Sitting across from me, Jackson pours wine into each of our glasses and holds his up for a toast. "To a red dress on the floor of my bedroom."

"Ha. Getting ahead of ourselves, aren't we?"

He shakes his head slowly, eyes never leaving mine. "Anticipating. It's all I'm going to think about until I get you home."

*Home.*

I love the sound of it. For someone who's bounced between a tiny rental to her sister's dorm to a borrowed bungalow, home is an elusive concept. I love the idea of it, but he's talking about his home, not mine. I need to be careful. Rein in my heart.

His hand covers mine on the table, and two small plates arrive. "Amuse bouche. Tuna with mustard seed and plum coulis," our waiter tells us before disappearing.

We nibble on the tiny bite, and I nod my approval. "This is already the best meal I've ever had."

Jackson laughs. "After one bite?"

"Yup."

Leaning back in his chair, he rubs his hands together. "Looks like my work is done. Guess we can move right onto the stage where that pretty dress hits the floor."

I hold up a hand. "No way, mister. This dress is staying on until I've eaten every last morsel of food from this fancy place."

The waiters have been expertly trained at their jobs, knowing how to slip in when we're momentarily distracted and clear plates of food, bring new ones, refill wine glasses

It's a carefully orchestrated dance, and each dish is more spectacular than the next. After experiencing it as a guest, I have no doubt as to why this restaurant earned its Michelin star. No one says it out loud for fear of jinxing it, but there's a good chance it will earn a second star this year.

Another course appears, along with an explanation about heirloom tomatoes and wild-caught salmon in honey butter, and it's clear we're nowhere close to dessert.

He groans in mock horror. "What have I done? I was trying to seduce you, and I've just shot myself in the foot with a ninety-course meal that won't end til I'm sixty."

"You'd look cute at sixty. Same smoking hot body and face, but with a little gray at the temples."

His grin shows me he'll never be anything but smoking hot at any age. "Come," he says, pushing his chair back. "Dance with me."

It isn't until then that I realize there's quiet music playing, and

I laugh when I realize it's a danceable ballad by Taylor Swift. "Did you know I'm a Swiftie?"

He shakes his head. "Lucky guess." He pulls me toward him and leads us to a space amid the empty tables on the terrace where we can dance. He's light on his feet, leading me in his arms.

"Hey, you're a good dancer. Who knew the tightly wound Jackson Corbett had moves?"

"You've said that before, that I'm tightly wound. What do I do that makes you think that?"

I toss my head back to get out from under his gaze, which melts me to jelly if I don't look away. "I dunno. Maybe it was the way you flipped out when I taught Fiona to catch bugs? Or your strict bedtime routine? Or the fact that you hold everything in unless I drag it out of you?"

When I meet his gaze, he looks a little sad. "Yeah, guilty, I guess. Probably left over from when Annabelle took off. Hard to trust people, so I just keep control over everything because I'll always be the last man standing. I have to be, for Fi."

"I know. But you can trust me," I tell him. He should know it already, but I want to make sure he does.

His answer is a kiss, and I'm not surprised it's all he's willing to give me. I can tell him to trust me, but he won't until he feels it.

"I'm still dealing with the death of my parents. Maybe always will be. When people leave, there's damage. I find it hard to get close to anyone, and when I do, I cling. Abandonment issues mixed with some unhealthy coping mechanisms," I admit.

"There is…" He takes a breath, and I wait. I don't want to push, but I sense he might want to talk, and I don't want to crowd the moment with more of my own thoughts. So I just…dance with him. And wait.

He leads me around the small space, drawing me in close and nuzzling my neck. The song changes to something by Bruno Mars, and Jackson starts talking. At first, he's so quiet I almost think he's talking to himself. He keeps his face close to mine. Maybe it's easier not to make eye contact.

"Everything about our relationship was backwards. We started with the marriage and the kid and then tried to get to know each other after that," he says. "No wonder it didn't work. And yet…"

I slide a hand up his back, ending behind his neck. I just want to reassure him. I want him to trust me.

"It would be one thing if she left right after Fi was born, before she knew what an awesome human being our daughter had become. Maybe then I could forgive it because I could chalk it up to ignorance. And regretful mistakes. But—" He closes his eyes against the pain of remembering.

I reach for his hand. As soon as my fingers wrap around his, he opens his eyes. There's vulnerability but also appreciation in them. I don't have to say anything, but I want to make sure he knows.

"I know. I wouldn't be able to leave her either."

He inhales and looks at the sky, which holds a near-perfect crescent moon against the darkness. Uncomprehending sky.

"I know it makes her sound heartless." His eyes fall to mine. Vulnerable. Hurt, two years later. "Don't know why I feel the need to defend her."

I shrug. "She's Fiona's mom. She gave you an amazing girl, even if she left."

He nods. "True. I try to be satisfied by that, but sometimes, I want to show her what she's missing."

I'm struck by an inappropriate pang of jealousy, not wanting her to come back and lay claim to this girl I've come to love. And this man…I'm not sure I could bear to watch him go back to her. And he would. He'd have to. For Fi.

The mounting anger makes no sense. I certainly have no right to feel possessive of him. We're just two people filling emptiness with each other. Maybe it's slightly more, but it can't take the place of five years together and parenthood.

I don't know why I'm getting so far ahead of myself. No one is suggesting Annabelle is on her way back to ask for Jackson's forgiveness. She's given no indication she wants to reunite this family. And I don't even factor into the equation.

All the more reason for me to take a giant step back when I can feel my heart pulling me toward Jackson in ways I can't fully control.

Control is important. It's the only thing tethering me to reality, where I have a sister who depends on me and two jobs that keep everything afloat. And I have goals, career goals I've worked toward, and the around Jackson can't make me forget about all of it.

But it does. All I want to do when I'm around him is abandon all my responsibilities and run away, lose myself in him. It's dangerous. I know better.

We walk farther down the path to where a square of plum trees still blossom even though it's long past spring. I'm about to ask Jackson if they have some special trick for fertilizing them or otherwise tricking them into thinking it's still spring, so they'll put on a show for the guests.

But his hand on my shoulder halts my brain from holding any rational thought.

I stop walking and turn toward him, half thinking I'll tell him about how torn I feel. Now is the time to explain why nights like this feel too frivolous in my life right now. He'll understand. We're both weighed down by family commitments that are bigger than our momentary lust. Even if the momentary lust feels better than anything I've experienced.

"Jax, I—"

He doesn't give me time to articulate anything. His finger traces the shape of my lips, and he watches it, mesmerized.

My worried thoughts vanish. I'm equally mesmerized.

The fraction of a moment when I had the power to fight this has vanished.

"Mostly, I'm just so fucking happy she set me free, so I had the chance to end up right here." His finger continues its slow perusal of my face, as though he's memorizing every curve. He smiles when his knuckle brushes across my cheek. He shakes his head. "I look at you and I forget to breathe. I forget everything. And it's the one time in a day when I'm not bogged down by all the business shit, and I just feel…weightless."

I feel weightless.

He kisses me, and my resistance crumbles. We've passed the point where we need words. It's new. It feels different from any of my other sort-of relationships, and my heart pronounces it a point of no return, even as my useless brain tries to protest.

I'm falling for Jackson Corbett. Best-laid plans for only sleeping with the guy and walking away with my heart intact have failed miserably. And I'm not sure I mind.

# CHAPTER
## Twenty-Nine

JAX

"Wait, *what*?" Hand on her forehead, Ruby sits up in bed. The covers are everywhere, and I take in the view of her smooth back with those long copper waves hanging over one shoulder.

She sounds upset or confused, so I reach up and lay a hand on her other shoulder, the bare one, and the sight of her lightly freckled skin makes me want to kiss each golden dot.

But she holds up a hand, stopping me. Which is unlike her.

Since we left the restaurant and tumbled through my front door last night, there's been no stopping. No pausing. That red dress hit the floor faster than I could shut the front door, and we had the orgasms to prove it.

And I didn't have regret after talking about Annabelle, even though the few things I shared probably don't qualify as opening up for most people. For me, they do.

She understood that.

Now, the sight of her hand concerns me a little bit, but I give her space while she's on the phone. I can tell it's her sister, and I know how much she relies on Ruby.

I also know this is the first time that Ruby can spend the entire night at my house without creeping around in the early morning hours and driving home. Fiona has a sleepover with Trix, who's taking tomorrow off to go to Stinson Beach.

Best laid plans. I'm worried about what's happening with Ella, but I'm more worried about the toll it takes on Ruby, who never seems to get a break from people relying on her.

Sometimes, I'm tempted to find another nanny, so Fiona and I won't be yet another pair who need something from Ruby. But Fiona loves her so much, and both of our lives have been so much better with Ruby in them that I don't have the heart to change it up.

"Okay, no, of course you shouldn't feel bad. I'm the one who feels bad. Why didn't you let me know?" She hunches over, pulling farther away from me. I don't like it, but I let her be. For now.

"I'll come right now."

My heart rate kicks up a notch. I can't read between the lines, but something must be very wrong if Ruby's going to race down to Berkeley. And selfishly, I want us to have this night together. I don't know when we'll get another chance.

"Stop arguing with me." The volume of her voice notches up. "Do you really want to do this right now?"

I move to the side so I can see her face. Ruby has her eyes shut and her fingers pinching her temples. We didn't get much sleep last night, and ordinarily, we'd both relish the exhaustion, casting each other secret glances and comparing whose dark circles were most unbecoming.

Mine, always mine. She couldn't do a damn thing to make herself unbecoming.

Except that right now, the anguish on her face dims her usual exuberance, and it pinches deep within my chest. Her pain is my pain.

It's what makes me certain I've never been in love before. And now that I know what it feels like, I'm floored by how deeply I'm in love with her.

"Fine. Text me in an hour, and if it's not any better, I'm getting in the car."

My relief at hearing that she's not speeding away is tempered by the tortured look on her face when she hangs up. She looks... defeated. And that's not something I ever thought I'd see in Ruby. She doesn't get defeated. She fights.

As soon as she hangs up, she starts scrolling through her phone. "Oh my god, she called me four times last night, and I didn't hear the phone."

I remember her phone buzzing a few times while I was going down on her, and there was no way she was answering.

I can't let her feel guilty about it without offering my support, so I reach for her, gently putting my hand on her bare shoulder to remind her I'm here and see if she'll let me in. She responds by folding her entire body into my chest, and I'm relieved.

It's not rational, but I feel like if I can hold her like this, she'll realize everything is okay.

"What happened?"

She turns so I can see her face. Her eyes are dry, but bloodshot. She needs sleep.

Arms still encircling her body, I tilt her to the side to lay her on the bed. She doesn't fight me, and without loosening my hold on her, I face her. If she drifts off to sleep like Fiona does every night while protesting her exhaustion, I'll consider it a victory.

She stares into my eyes, blinking against fatigue but unwilling to yield to it. I admire her toughness, even when it means I can't do anything for her.

"Talk to me, sweetheart."

"She was feeling pain, and she had a little bleeding, so her boyfriend took her to the doctor yesterday." The words sound choked.

"And? What happened?"

Ruby shakes her head. "She's going to be fine. The doctor said it was smart that she came in and did some scans to make sure everything's okay. She doesn't need surgery."

"That's a good thing."

Ruby slumps against my shoulder like a rag doll. I smooth her hair and wrap an arm around her. "I should've been there for her. I should have been the one to take her to the doctor."

I want to be supportive, and I know I'm straddling a fine line between doing that and saying the wrong thing, but I can't keep my mouth shut when I can see how she's torturing herself needlessly.

"You *were* there for her. Right now, when she called, you were there. That's what she was asking you for. She didn't ask you to go with her to the doctor."

I feel her stiffen, but I keep holding her tight. Maybe a part of me thinks she'll bolt if I don't prevent it. It's an irrational fear, but I can feel how unsettled she is.

"It's like I took my eye off the ball to be selfish for one second, and everything fell apart."

"You know that's not true, though, right? Even if it feels like that, you are always there for her. She knows that. You don't have to save everyone all the time."

I don't mean for it to sound insensitive, but I can tell from the way she pulls away from me that she doesn't like it. "She's my only family. I'm all she has." Her voice cracks at the end, and I feel guilty about my extended family and all the times I've groused about them, even if it's all in good fun. We're tightly knit, and I can't imagine how it would feel to have only one blood relative who has my back.

"I know, sweetie. And I can't imagine anyone luckier than her."

Her wan smile doesn't make me feel like she agrees. Neither does her monotone. "Thanks."

I feel like I'm losing her.

With each inhale and exhale, she's pulling away, curling into herself and retreating.

"And you're an amazing sister to her, but maybe she's telling you she wants to stand on her own two feet. She just proved she's capable of it."

Ruby nods and moves farther away from me. I want to give her the space she needs, but this isn't what I need. Another relationship where I'm chasing a woman down and begging her to stay when she doesn't want to be here.

I know I'm overreacting, picturing the last days with Annabelle and unfairly projecting them onto Ruby, but it's hard to be rational when it feels exactly the same way.

All the memories I've pushed away for two years come barreling back, and I'm powerless against them. I feel suddenly hopeless. Now, I'm the one backing away from her.

"Hey," Ruby says, leaning toward me and nudging me so I'm forced to look at her. "I'm sorry. I know you're trying to help. I'll work this out."

I nod, feeling oddly numb, considering she's telling me what I want to hear. "Yeah. Okay."

She kisses my forehead, my cheek, my chin. I feel myself come back to life at her touch, and I start to calm back down.

She's not Annabelle. Her issues are not the same. And I'm not the same guy I was two years ago. I'm better. We're better together. I just need to calm the fuck down.

With a hand on my chest, Ruby pushes me down on the bed. Then she straddles my lap and leans down to kiss me. The minute her lips touch mine, my doubts and fears burn off like the morning dew on the grapevines when the sun begins to blaze. No match against something stronger.

Ruby kisses me slowly, and the heaviness I felt moments ago is replaced by contentment. I'm back in the present, letting regrets about the past slip away and not worrying for once about the future.

This is where I need to stay. If I can manage it. Not sure I can manage it.

Wordlessly, she convinces me I can. Tracing the shape of her lips with my tongue, I stop thinking and let my senses take over. Her lips part and our tongues meet.

The kiss deepens until I can't distinguish her from me, and even if this one kiss lasts forever, it will never be enough.

I roll us over and grind against her, loving her instant response. Her arms wrap around my back and she pulls me closer. Our kiss never breaks as I slide inside her.

And everything in the world is okay.

# CHAPTER
## *Thirty*

RUBY

"I have an idea," Jackson calls from the bathroom, where he's turned on the shower. I can feel the steam creeping into the bedroom.

I'm not sure how I feel about ideas when I'm trying to figure out how I feel about Jackson. Scratch that. I know how I feel—I'm falling hard and fast for the guy, and I still can't read him all the time. Something felt off last night. At least, I think it did.

I know I pushed him away when I was worrying about Ella, and he pulled back too. But maybe that was just a reaction to me. Ugh, I should stop reading so much into everything.

"I hope it doesn't entail me getting out of bed because I think I'm dead." I lost count of the orgasms after three. Or ten.

Sunlight edges through the cracks in the blinds, letting me know it's well past sunrise. Even though it's expected to top a hundred degrees today, it's cool in Jackson's bedroom, and I take advantage of my alone time here to stretch my body like a starfish and take over the bed.

Jackson peeks through the bathroom door, looking all tanned

and gorgeous as sin without a stitch of clothing. "Come on, lazybones."

"Hardly lazy. I stayed up with you all night, didn't I?"

He nods, beckoning me with a finger. "And now I want more."

Rolling off the bed, I groan because all of my various body parts are exhausted, but I'm not about to pass up a hot, steamy shower with Jackson. Sleep can wait.

"What's your idea?" I ask, stepping onto the river rock floor. It's like a day spa in here, with multiple jets shooting out of the walls and an overhead rain shower. Jackson already has a washcloth lathered with soap, and he rolls it over my breasts. "You better tell me quickly before all my brain cells melt away."

"Let's go wine tasting."

I bark out a laugh. "Seriously? You work at a winery. I thought you wanted to get away today."

"I do. I don't taste wine for a living, and you ought to be checking out the competition. Call it professional development."

"In other words, you want to day drink."

"It's a Saturday, and we're in the wine country. It's what people do."

Jackson turns me toward one of the jets to rinse off the soap. "Fine," I pant. "I'll do whatever you want today."

He pulls me close, pressing his cheek to mine, lips whispering dirty things into my ear. "Tell me how badly you want me to fuck you," he growls.

My body hums with desire, and I'm instantly dumb and orgasmic. No coherent phrases, just words. "Jax. Like that," I gasp as he moves the washcloth down my stomach and rubs circles against my clit. I suck air through my teeth, brain cells melting.

Water cascades over us. I'm wet, slippery, soapy, and about to combust, thanks to Jax's lips and hands everywhere.

All I can think is that I'd like to wake up like this every day. With him. And it's getting harder and harder to keep my emotions in check. I want him all the time like this.

"That's my girl," he says, rubbing languidly until I'm on the brink of coming apart in his hands. With my back pressed against his chest, Jax leans forward and nips at my neck. I arch into his hard cock and press my hands against the cold tiles of the shower wall, the only thing holding me up.

"Jax…god…"

One more sweep of the washcloth, and I slump against him like a ragdoll.

He holds me up as my ragged breathing returns to normal. And when I've regained a fraction of sensibility, I turn around and train my fingers down his abs, relishing in the taut, wet planes.

My hand slides between us, and I work his length, which is already rock-hard and ready. I kiss his chest, lapping my tongue over his pecs in the rain shower, using my other hand to appreciate every single one of his six-pack abs.

I work my way down, dropping to my knees. Water drips down my hair and into my eyes, as I sweep the tip of his cock into my mouth and lick off the water droplets. I want to taste him. I want to show him the same pleasure he just gave me.

Grasping his length in my hands, I revel in his hard thickness, the weight of him in my palms as they slide along the shaft. Water drips down my cheeks as I bend to kiss and nibble the length of him, listening to his groans and curses as I make my way over every inch. I suck the tip softly into my mouth, watching his face and waiting for him to open his eyes.

The fierce heat in his eyes turns them a deeper blue, and I hold his gaze, wanting him to focus on me, wanting him to watch. Only then do I take him fully into my mouth, sucking down the length of him and feeling the groan as he thrusts against the back of my throat.

Then, I release him. His eyes snap to mine with the realization that I intend to torture him with this delicious game, bringing him closer and closer to the brink of madness before I cave.

"Fuck, Ginger," he growls when I've released him for the third time. He's shaking beneath my hands, and I take him deep once more, barely able to breathe.

He groans louder, his hands coming into my hair and piling it on top of my head.

He puts a hand behind my head, coaxing me to take him faster. I hum my approval, and his head falls back. He thrusts harder, and I suck every last drop from him, loving the feeling of watching him lose control.

And then wine tasting is the last thing on my mind.

————

Now, wine tasting is the main thing on my mind. I've called my sister, who's feeling much better, so I'm trying to let myself have this day off.

Somehow, Jackson's "idea" turned into him calling in some favors at wineries where he has good friends, and they're letting us into tasting rooms and cellars that aren't open to the public.

We show up at Cherry Forest Cellars in sweats, me wearing a baseball cap and braids, and the winery owner shows us to a private patio that overlooks a koi pond. The only sound I hear is birds twittering in the nearby olive trees.

"Okay, show me your sommelier stuff," he says, leaning back in an Adirondack chair on the patio, where an outdoor tasting counter has been set up for us with ten different vintages of wine.

My little wine nerd heart beats faster upon seeing the bottles set out next to a corkscrew, cloth napkin, spittoon bucket, and foil cutter.

Jackson looks very relaxed, tipped back in his chair, sun dancing over his features. "Taking a day off agrees with you," I say, pouring wine tastes into glasses and lining up the bottles behind each one to identify them.

Eyes closed, he smiles. The sun paints his cheeks with light, and I take in the sight of him, arms splayed over the arms of the chair, legs stretched out in front of him. He's as tired as I am, but I love that he'd rather spend the day giving me sommelier practice than catching up on sleep.

And despite myself, I think I might be in love with him.

It's inconvenient because I'm here to work my two jobs and make money. I'm not here to fall in love, and the last thing in the world I want to do is hurt Fiona. I know that's top of mind for Jackson, too, which is why we're super careful to keep our affection for each other under wraps.

"It agrees with you, too." He still has one eye closed, but he's peeking at me through the other.

We stopped at the grocery store for cheese and baguettes, which I've sliced up and displayed on a platter next to four different kinds of hard and soft cheeses. I opened all the bottles except for one, which I'm saving to open in front of Jackson. A little demonstration of the sommelier magic.

"I'm all ready, but you look so content sitting there, I don't want to make you move."

Head tipped back, he gives me a closed-mouthed smile before unfolding his large frame from the chair and walking over to the bar counter, which is equipped with four stools. He perches on the one in front of where I stand, and I lean across and kiss him.

He holds up a hand. "If you plan to do that with all the customers, I'll warn Trix never to let you fill in at the restaurant."

For emphasis, I give him another quick kiss. "Only you." He picks up my hand off the bar and pulls me in, kissing me back. Longer. Deeper.

"Deal." He settles himself on his stool and leans against the wrought iron back, tucking his hands behind his head and looking so damn relaxed. "What've we got going here?" He tips his head toward the bottles and glasses of wine.

I slide a glass of ruby red toward him. "This is a pinot noir that comes from a strain of French grapes. It's been growing in Napa for sixty years, and the minerals in the soil have changed it from the original vines."

He lifts his glass up to let the sunlight stream through the liquid, casting a rosy glow on the beaten wood countertop. I hold mine up, examining the clarity of the wine. "Looks good to me.

Does it offend you that I'm a third-generation winery owner and I don't have more to say than that?"

Laughing, I lean on the bar counter and take a sip from my glass, which barely contains more than a large mouthful. We have a lot of bottles ahead of us, and we'll be smashed inside of an hour if I pour too much. "It doesn't offend me at all because you work on the business side."

"I know what I like from what we grow, the cab specifically."

"Do you like this one?"

He sips and rolls the liquid over his tongue before swallowing. I stand there mesmerized by the light stain of red on his lips and the way his throat works when he swallows. He's wine porn in the flesh.

"Not sure. It's a little sour. Do you taste that?"

I smile, grateful that he wants to share this with me. "I like how light it is, and yeah, a bit sour. Pinots can definitely taste like that if your go-to is a fuller-bodied cab."

"Like I said, I know what I like."

I pour from the next bottle, a ten-year-old cabernet sauvignon that's won several awards. "I think this'll be more your speed."

He swirls it in his glass and holds it up to the light. "See how much darker it is? That's from the grape skin, which gives it that bigger taste you like."

Jackson nods. "Yup, this is my kind of wine. Get me a steak and some scalloped potatoes and I'm in heaven."

"Ooh, you like scalloped potatoes? I have a great recipe."

He lights up like I've just surprised him with Christmas in June. "Tonight. Let's have that for dinner. I'll have Trix set aside some steaks from the restaurant, and we can pick up potatoes on the way home."

My heart skips a beat like it always does at the mention of "home." When I'm there, it feels like home. It almost feels like I'm part of their family, which makes me blurt out a question I hadn't planned to ask yet. If at all.

"Should we, maybe, tell Fiona? About us?" The words falter

awkwardly as they start tripping from my lips. My eyes go wide as though I've shocked myself. It's the wrong question, the wrong timing, just…wrong in all ways.

Jackson has just popped a piece of cheese into his mouth, and I feel like he's chewing extra slowly as I fan the air around us, trying to dismiss the words before he can answer.

His hand comes up to still my own, and he swallows. I don't give him time to answer before I start amending what I've just said.

"That was too much. We're good how we are, and she's impressionable. Would only make things awkward when it ends. More awkward than this conversation, even. We don't even know how we feel about each other, so just forget I said it, please."

Jackson cups my cheeks in his hands and kisses the blather from my lips.

"Ruby, stop. I know how I feel about you. I love you," he says, setting my heart free to bump around in my chest. "I'm in love with you."

I'm not breathing. I will need paddles or CPR in a second because I'm aware that no air has come or gone from my lungs, but I can't jumpstart them. My heart floods with so much emotion that a gasp finally charges from my lungs. And I smile.

I want to tell him I love him, too. I want to articulate just how much I love him, but he's not finished talking.

"But she's my daughter, and I need to be really careful about her feelings. So if that means waiting to make sure we're really good before I say anything to her, I…think we need to wait."

It's everything and none of the things I want to hear. I focus on the love part.

And my heart goes careening off a cliff.

# CHAPTER
*Thirty~One*

JAX

For the first time in a month, I feel like I may have a chance at turning our losses around. Even if I don't know why my dad did what he did, my siblings and I can pitch in with our personal assets and shore up the company's losses. Temporarily. Long enough to buy us time to figure out what's going on.

At least, that's my last-ditch idea before Dash's random deadline to tell him what's going on. I've researched every business database in the country, and there's no winery, no business, no person named Hayden Lanes.

And despite the new protocol, my dad's cognizance hasn't improved this week. I haven't been able to get any information from him, and time is running out. Our shareholder meeting is approaching, and I'll either need to answer for why their investment has tanked or I'll need to find money to replace what my dad spent.

My last-ditch solution is to borrow against our assets and put the money back into the company. It could work. I've run through the numbers and figured out how much it will cost the company in interest—a metric shit ton.

And I'll need my siblings to sign off on the plan, which will force me to admit we have a big problem. I don't want to do it, but I feel better knowing I have a potential, worst-case solution.

The result is that I can exhale for the first time in months. I celebrate with an almond croissant and a latte from the café.

I'm brushing the crumbs from my desk when both of my sisters ambush me in my office. "You're the worst." PJ perches on the edge of my sofa, finger pointed at me accusingly.

"What did I do now?"

She doesn't know I might be using her money for collateral, so it can't be that. But honestly, it could be just about anything else.

Trix laughs and picks lint from her navy blue suit. The only difference in her appearance from day to day is whether she wears her hair in a pony or a bun. Today, it's a bun.

"You're dating Ruby and I had to hear about it from Trix."

Oh. That. "I'm not required to share my dating life with you, am I?"

"You most certainly are. I share with you." The way she juts her lip out reminds me of Fiona, who gave me that exact look when I told her she couldn't wear cowboy boots to camp this morning.

"Sharing that you haven't gotten laid in three months isn't the same thing. And frankly, I'd just as soon not know about it."

"Not true anymore," she sings. In a pair of white cashmere sweatpants and a striped shirt, she looks like an upscale sailor.

"TMI, Peej. Seriously."

PJ presents me with a bakery bag, and I wonder why all my siblings seem to think they can bribe me with food. I'm not too proud to peek inside, however, and I spot another almond croissant. I'm in a good enough mood today that I might eat a second one.

Before I can make that decision, we're joined by Archer and

Dash. "Did someone call a family meeting I didn't know about?" I joke. That's how relieved I am today—I actually joke.

"Yup," Archer says. No sense of humor to be found. He's still wearing his running clothes, so I get the impression this meeting was very impromptu.

"That so?" I'm starting to feel less excited about the second croissant, and that's a sign I should walk out of my own office. But my siblings have other ideas.

"What were you talking about with Dad?" Archer asks.

I shoot a look at Dash, who shrugs. "Come on. It seems relevant if we're losing a bunch of money and the rest of us aren't in the loop. So get us up to speed."

With four of them staring me down, I have two options. I can deflect, make up a lie about what our dad meant, or I can tell them what's going on. If I want to borrow against our personal assets, I'll need them to sign off, so door number two quickly becomes the best choice.

"Dad spent a lot of money buying grapes we don't need or paying to settle lawsuits he won't talk about. I have no idea why, but now I have to account for a big loss on the books for what he spent. That's the gist." Maybe they'll be satisfied and leave me alone.

Nope.

There are questions, so many questions. Why did I wait so long to tell them? Why would Dad do that? What do I mean, the company doesn't exist? How much money are we talking about?

I answer them all. "I was hoping to resolve it without involving you. I'm the financial guy; it's my problem...Dad has dementia—he does a lot of things that don't make sense...There's no record of a winery or a person named Hayden Lanes, but he mentioned them...It's a half a billion dollars."

The cacophony of voices ensues again, and I can't make out a single train of thought until Archer's voice booms above the rest. "Hang on."

Everyone stops and looks at him.

"We did have a bad batch of grapes. Like, a lot of grapes. They're our proprietary cabernets, but a while back, Dad told me we couldn't sell them under our normal label because they won't pass organic certification. He wasn't making sense, talking about trademarks. But they're our proprietary grape variety, our biggest seller."

"What if they're not?" I ask. Four pairs of eyes lock on me.

"Meaning?" Archer asks, head cocked. Curious, hesitant.

"What if someone convinced Dad they own the trademark rights to the grape variety we're producing? What if we're being sued for it, and Dad has been quietly paying people off? Explains the losses."

"Anyone try getting our lawyers on the phone?" Dash says.

"I did that weeks ago. They don't know about it. This was just between Dad and whoever he was paying into an offshore account."

"But we're good, right? Our organic practices are still in place. Our grapes are good? We do have a proprietary cabernet that we own, right?" PJ asks.

I know what she's asking—*how much of what our father built is real?*

Archer looks down and swallows. "As far as I know, but… Wind could carry seeds from another farm. It's the risk we run when we grow organic, and other farmers are doing it differently. It always happens to some degree. This year, apparently, it hit a big part of our crop."

I exhale an aggravated breath. "Were you planning on saying anything?"

"Were *you*?" he asks pointedly.

"Stop it, you two," PJ says. "This isn't about pointing fingers. The reason we're here now is to get consensus. If Dad's condition doesn't improve, we need to communicate. I know we're all in charge of separate domains, but they're related. We need to work together."

"She's right," Dashiell says. "I'll share everything I know on the peopling end. There's no way to know what's relevant unless we talk."

There aren't enough pastries to go around, and my stomach feels like it might reject the one I've already eaten. I don't like sharing information. I don't like talking. There's a reason I sit up here alone doing my job.

But…this organic grape thing is interesting. Maybe it could explain a few things our dad can't. So I grudgingly sign on to the sibling plan to talk more often. Even if it gives me an ulcer.

"Okay, okay, as long as you're all singing kumbaya in my office, I might as well get your permission on something." I outline the plan to borrow money based on all of our assets to cover the company losses until we can right the ship and pay back the loan.

I expect questions. I expect pushback.

Instead, my four siblings agree, "For the good of the company."

Each of them says yes.

# CHAPTER
*Thirty-Two*

RUBY

"Fi!" Jackson shouts as soon as he walks in the door.

We're up in her room working on a Lego Harry Potter castle, and the pieces fly as she gets up and races toward his voice.

I follow as Fiona goes bounding down the stairs so fast I'm worried she'll trip, and she does, flying off the bottom step and into Jackson's waiting arms. He swings her in a circle, and she giggles.

"Put me down, Daddy."

"No way. You're the one who came crashing into me. That earns me one more circle." He swings her around again, and I feel the corners of my mouth pull into an undeniable grin. Impossible not to fall for him. Impossible not to look at him and see a future, even if we can't define what it is.

Fiona races into the kitchen, Harry Potter Lego all but forgotten because earlier this afternoon, we baked cookies. "Daddy, I made cookies in the shape of a heart for you."

"I'm going to eat them all before dinner. Okay, Fi?"

"Nooo. Not before. After dinner," she instructs. He pouts and she decides he can have one now. Same ritual every time.

The door to the yard flies open, and Fiona is out like a flash. Jackson slips his hand into mine, and we're about to chase after her when my phone rings. My sister's face fills the screen, making me frown. Normally, she texts unless it's urgent. I don't like the idea of urgent.

"Hey," I say. "How's it going?" The ectopic pregnancy is behind her, so I hope she's not having any more residual effects. Jackson waits, watching me expectantly, his face mirroring my concern the longer I listen.

Ella explains what just happened, and I feel my blood pressure plummeting by the second, making me feel light-headed. I drop onto Jackson's sofa and fight the urge to cry.

"Okay. We're gonna figure this out. I'm so sorry, El," I tell her, clearing my throat to keep the fear and concern from my voice.

She tells me it's okay, but it's not. By the time I hang up the phone, Jackson is sitting next to me with his hand on my thigh.

"What happened?" The concern on his face breaks my heart. Breaks it because I know how he's going to react to what I'm about to say.

"I need to go back to Berkeley."

"O-kay…" He waits for me to explain, but the wheels in my head are turning, sorting through what I need to do in the next twenty-four hours. I don't want to drag him into my problems. "Can I help?"

I don't see how he can. I inhale deeply and let my breath out slowly, trying to calm my nerves to no avail. "I screwed up." It's the understatement of the century.

"Talk to me, Ruby. What happened?" He lifts my hand and wraps it in his. The warmth of him soothes me, but I don't want to be soothed. This is all my fault.

"The resident advisor found my viniculture in Ella's closet because it exploded. The kids in the room next door smelled it, and Ella wasn't there, so they opened the door. Glass and wine was everywhere."

He nods with the dawning of recognition—this is not good anywhere, let alone in a university dorm that I'm not supposed to be sharing with a student. "Let me guess—there actually *are* rules against making wine in a student dorm."

"Yes, and Ella is under age twenty-one, so there's that, but I still don't know what I did wrong. Why did it explode?"

It takes me a moment to recognize the sound coming from the man next to me. Then I realize it's quiet laughter. "Do you know how much I love you right now? You've got the university up your ass, and your nerd brain is still thinking about exploding grapes."

My attempt at a laugh sounds hollow, even though I appreciate that he appreciates me. I decide I'll think much better after I eat one of the cookies we baked, so I go back to the kitchen and grab two. I take a bite of one and hand the other to Jackson. As soon as the sugar hits my tongue, the gears in my brain click into place.

I smack a hand against my forehead when I realize what I did wrong. "It was the sugar. I think I added it without potassium sorbate to stabilize it, and the fermentation started all over again. Too much CO2 and the pressure blew the glass apart. I was rushing. I can't believe I forgot the stabilizer."

I'm mainly talking to myself, but Jackson is gamely nodding. He's already told me he only knows the business side of wine making, but he's just being polite. I'm so mad at myself that I can barely see straight.

He puts an arm around my shoulders, and I want to get lost in the feel of him. It's the one thing that blunts all the stresses in my life that exist outside of this house.

But maybe that's the problem. I've been escaping here and neglecting my outside life, and my sister is suffering for it.

"Ella's going to lose her housing. It's all my fault."

He nods on a long blink, understanding registering in his sober features. "I'm sure you didn't intentionally flout the rules."

"No, I didn't even think. Of *course* it wouldn't be allowed in a student dorm. So stupid." I slip out from under Jackson's arm and start pacing in the kitchen, mind whirling as I decide what to do first. Apologize on behalf of Ella? Try to lobby for her to keep her housing?

"Could you tell them it's yours? Maybe they'll understand, and she can stay on campus."

I shake my head. "It's already been decided. She has a week to pack up and find another place to live. Which is impossible in Berkeley. Not enough housing, and part of her scholarship was a partial payment for the dorms."

He opens his mouth and then presses his lips together. "I-I want to help you…"

"No, please don't offer to pay for an apartment for her. I need to figure this out on my own."

"I didn't say a word."

"You wanted to," I warn.

"And would that be so bad? If I have the means and I want to help, why wouldn't you accept that? It's out of love, not obligation."

Hearing the word *love* pierces my heart. I love him too—I feel it in the depths of my soul—and it's overwhelming. I put my hands over my face, blotting out the daylight so I can figure out what to do next.

"I just…can't."

I stand with my back against the refrigerator, letting the cool metal hold me up. I'm choosing an appliance for support instead of Jackson. It feels safer, less likely to cloud my decisions. He stays on his side of the kitchen, and I meet his eyes, needing him to understand what I'm about to do.

"I've been neglecting my responsibilities, running away to play house at a winery. I should've been there," I say.

He walks over to face me, crossing his arms. "Really? What

could you have done? Wouldn't it have been even worse if they'd figured out you were living there?"

He's right, but I don't want to let myself off the hook. I'm too overwrought with guilt. All I can think is that I need to get in my car and drive to Berkeley. It may not be a solution, but it's the right thing to do.

"I don't know." It's a cop-out answer, but I can't come up with anything better.

Jackson reaches for my hand. Without realizing it, I've had my hand wrapped around the refrigerator door, white-knuckling it. I let go and allow myself to be comforted by what he's offering me —strength, reason, kindness.

He smooths the strands of hair from my forehead and tips his head against mine. "You're overwhelmed. I get it. You've lost people important to you, and you don't want to lose your sister. I get that too."

"She's my person," I whisper because I feel too choked up thinking about losing her to talk.

He nods against my forehead. "I know. Fiona is mine. But… maybe we can have more than one person."

I don't need to ask for clarification about who the second person would be. I want him to be it for me, but I can't find my way there right now. "Maybe," is all I can muster.

He's right. I'm overwhelmed. And terrified that loving him means losing my sister. All I've done is let her down since I took this job. "I'm stretched too thin. I need to go home."

He starts to answer when Fiona bounds in the door. "Hey. Why didn't you come?" She looks so hopeful, open to whatever the world has in store for her. I wish I could see the same in her dad. I know he loves me, but I'm only getting a shadow of him. It's not enough for me.

"I need to go back to Berkeley, sweetie. My sister needs my help."

"Okay, I'll see you tomorrow, then."

Jackson touches my shoulder. "Take the time you need. I'll talk to Dash about having someone fill in."

I don't want to leave without a more definitive plan, but I can't think straight. I need to get back to my sister and help her figure out the next move. I need to run numbers, see how much I can afford for an apartment, find an impossible vacancy in a jam-packed college town.

"Probably not, Fi. It may take me a bit to get her squared away, but I'll be back to see you, I promise."

I know Fiona is disappointed. I can see it on her face.

But it's nothing compared to how Jackson is looking at me, eyes soft, mouth set in a grim line. I want to tell him I'm not Annabelle, that my heart breaks at the idea of leaving him and Fiona. But I can't say that in front of her. It's too much, and she just wants to play in the vineyard. Can't say I blame her.

Holding Fiona's hand, Jackson walks me to the door and kisses me on the cheek. I can't look at either of them because I know it will make me cry, but Jackson doesn't let me off the hook that easily.

"Hey," he says, tipping up my chin. "This is going to work out. Take the time you need. And also…I'm sorry you lost your viniculture."

My heart squeezes in my chest, and my throat feels tight with a surge of tears that I try to blink back. He understands me. It makes it even harder to walk away.

# CHAPTER
## Thirty-Three

JAX

It's been nearly a week, and I haven't heard from Ruby. I don't know what I expected—texts and phone calls telling me she's okay and she realizes she loves me?

Even one text or phone call to keep my heart from tumbling off a cliff, feeling Annabelle leaving all over again?

I told her to take the time she needs, but maybe I didn't really mean it. I wanted her to need *me,* and I saw glimmers of Annabelle leaving to pursue her own goals and desires. I thought that if I gave her space, she'd find her way back here. But she hasn't, and now I'm losing faith.

In myself, in her. In us.

The sun may be shining its bright damn self over the vines and giving all the grape peepers the perfect damn selfie opportunities, but I don't want any of it. They can have their views.

I walk quickly down the winding path past the lake because I'm a masochist. Following the path that's now permanently imprinted with memories of Ruby and I wandering, talking, kissing…it just makes me miss her more.

This is what I get for taking my eye off the ball and allowing my heart out of its iron cage for once in the last two years.

Stupid. I knew this, and yet I allowed it to happen.

*You didn't have a choice.*

No, Ruby was right. I always have a choice, and this time, I made the wrong one. Chose the beautiful copper hair instead of logic. Chose her fiery sass over knowledge of what she'd do to my heart.

There's a reason I don't walk around the property like this. It's oppressively beautiful. The landscapers and groundskeepers have made sure of it. They've pruned every plum tree just so, fertilized them so they bloom late into spring and early summer. They've ensured that the lavender looks like it's growing wild when every plant has been trained into submission and has its place.

It's no place for a bruised ego or a smashed heart.

I have both, and I want neither.

And yet, I am a masochist, I guess, because the first place I want to come today is the path where I felt something shift. I felt Ruby's resistance give way. I felt her give up on her excuses and careful tending of her emotions. I felt her falling for me.

It was unmistakable because it mirrored the exact way I felt for her. Different from how I'd ever felt for a woman. The kind of inkling that this could be the permanent kind of love.

Fuck my stupid inklings.

"Slow down."

At first, I think it's my brain talking to me because I've actually lost it, and it needs to yell in real time in order for me to do the right thing.

But it's Archer, jogging up the path behind me. I'm not blocking his way, so he can easily pass me, but instead, he drops his pace to match the power walking I'm doing. "Why'd you stop?" I ask, surprised that I'm out of breath from walking.

"Because you're chewing up the path like you're doing everything possible not to run, and it's painful to watch."

I snort a non-laugh. "I'm not a runner."

"You might want to take it up. Would be easier on your body than this weird race walk you've got going."

I expect him to resume jogging now that he's done criticizing me, but he slows his walking pace even more. Apparently, he's not going away, so I slow down too.

"What's up, Archer?" Truthfully, I'm glad to slow down. I hadn't realized how fast I was moving until now. I'm sweating. The heat prickles my skin.

"Was about to ask you the same. First time I've seen you out here since…ever. You finally giving the cardio a try?"

"Not intentionally."

He huffs a laugh, and I shoot him a look, annoyed that he can find something funny when I'm miserable.

"Ruby? I noticed she hasn't been here this week."

"Shit, Archer. Does it really seem like I'm out here on a walk because I want to chitchat about it?" I pick up my pace, which is dumb because he can keep up with me no matter how fast or slow I go.

He shrugs and strides alongside me. It's not lost on me that he's not out of breath at all after however many miles he's already run. Meanwhile, I'm regretting my lack of cardio lately. "I gotta get back on my bike. Start doing hills again," I mutter.

"Yup."

"Okay, then. Message received, cardio boy. You can go now."

He doesn't. "Not why I stopped."

Without realizing it, I've managed to let him steer me off the path and toward the kitchen behind the tasting room. Where there's coffee brewing. My heart may be shriveling inside my chest, but the timer on the coffee machine is alive and well.

"Yeah, good call," I tell him, grabbing two cups. "You done running for the day?"

"I am now." He pulls out a stool at the bar counter and sits, waiting for me to pour his coffee how he likes it. Milk and sugar.

"At your service." I place two mugs on the bar and hunker down on my elbows across from where he sits.

"Good man. So, tell me. What happened?"

I shoot him my most irritated look, and he squints as though preventing it from penetrating. Slapping a hand against the back of my neck, I sip my coffee. It's too hot, but the burn feels good on my throat. It's freezing in here, a sharp contrast to the warming day.

"She had to deal with some family stuff in Berkeley. I thought she'd be back, but it's been radio silence. Now, I don't fucking know."

He sips his coffee thoughtfully. "Well, that must drive you nuts."

"Meaning?" Of course it drives me nuts, but I gather there's more to his observation.

"You like to control everything. Not like this is news."

No, it's not.

"Your point?"

"I fucking hate these shoes," he says, unlacing the Hokas and pulling them off his heels. They drop to the floor. "I'm going back to my old shoes. Shouldn't have tried to fix something that wasn't broke." His voice loses some of the gruffness as he admits his misstep, and it's so unfamiliar I'm not sure how to respond.

"But I think the opposite is true for you."

"I'm not following."

He nods. "Don't go back to your old habits. You're good with her, easier to be around, that's for sure. In your case, she's a fix for something that really was broken. Hang on to her."

I huff a laugh at his too-little-too-late advice. "Thanks, but she's not here to hang onto."

"That's just today. Have some faith in people."

He swivels on his stool and kicks his feet like Fiona does, and for a moment, I forget he's my stoic older brother, and I see a guy who's just trying to make sense of the world like I am. Maybe it's part of what I've always gotten wrong about him—seeing him one way when there's more to it.

"She's not Annabelle," he says.

"I know that."

"I'm saying, don't be so worried things will end the same way that you sabotage things in order to make sure you're right."

"Wow, therapist much?"

"Tell me I'm wrong." He waits. I don't tell him a damn thing. "I've been watching you ever since you took over the financial mess we inherited from Dad. It's changed you."

I shrug. "People change."

"Nah, they don't. You're still you, but you're sinking under the weight of something you can't control. When Ruby came along, I saw the weight lift, and it was a beautiful thing. And now the weight is back."

I drain the last of my coffee, and the caffeine boosts my mood. Or maybe it's the feeling that someone understands what's been plaguing me without my having to articulate it. Yeah, maybe it's that.

"I don't want the weight back. I want her. But I can't risk loving her if she has one foot out the door. I'd never do that to Fi. She's been through enough."

"She has." He nods thoughtfully. "So have you. I think you can allow yourself to risk a little bit, give up control a little bit. Maybe you'll surprise yourself."

"How'd you get so damn wise all of a sudden?"

"Running. I told you. Invest in some shoes. Asics are the best." He slid off the stool and took his coffee with him, calling out behind him, "Better yet, I'll buy you a pair. I know your size."

# CHAPTER
*Thirty-Four*

RUBY

Ella and I sit at Café Strada, each of us cupping our hands around tall mugs of café au lait on the outdoor patio. Students chatting in small groups surround us, and to our left, a man with a white mustache and a beret does the Sunday crossword puzzle.

"This is still my favorite coffee," I tell Ella. I'm treating us to four-dollar cups of café au lait because we deserve it after days of combing apartment listings, cleaning up red wine spatter in her closet, and washing fermentation smell from all of her clothes. Twice.

"More expensive than making it at home, though. You taught me to be frugal."

"I know. Sometimes it's worth a little splurge." I've always loved it at this café, with its tall trees and proximity to campus. Watching students walk to and from their classes gives me an optimistic feeling. Learning happening. Life abounding.

I take a large swallow of coffee, willing the caffeine to give me energy I don't have.

"You didn't sleep." Ella isn't asking. She's right. I haven't slept well in the five nights since I've been back from Buttercup. I haven't talked to Jackson at all, and I feel guilty about that. Instead, I've just spent most of my waking hours thinking about him, last night included.

A hundred different times, I thought about messaging him or calling, but I didn't want to say the wrong thing. With each day that went by, I felt pressure mounting to say the right thing, or the best thing, and then I told myself to focus on my sister. She's my priority.

But every day, I miss Jax and Fiona so much it hurts. And I feel so guilty for leaving.

"Did I keep you up?" I ask Ella.

"Nah. I fall back asleep easily."

I take a sip of coffee and wonder why it doesn't taste as magical as I remember. "You okay?" Ella asks.

"Yeah. I'm fine."

"Liar." Her directness and sharp stare get my attention. "Have you called Jackson?"

"Not yet. It's complicated."

"Is it?" Another pointed look. And an actual pointed finger. "You love him. And that little girl. How could you run out on them after you said you wouldn't?"

She's not wrong about any of it, but I stare at her like the answer is obvious. "You're my family."

"I'm part of it. Maybe they're the rest of it."

It's the last thing in the world I'm expecting her to say, which is why I don't have a ready answer. As I stammer and try to come up with a response, my window of opportunity slams shut.

"Hey, sorry I'm late." Ella's boyfriend Tim bounds across the street in his navy sweats, hair wet from water polo practice. Feet clad in white socks and slide sandals. He's dressed identically to the two guys beside him, who he fist bumps before coming into the café.

They head up Bancroft Avenue to their fraternity house, and he grabs the seat next to Ella, dropping a kiss on her lips.

She ruffles his wet, dark hair and leans into him. I recognize the look of bliss on her face. It's the same one I've been wearing for weeks now. She's in love, and from the way Tim looks back at her, it's completely mutual. I'm happy about that for my sister.

He snags the untouched coffee on the table, the only one without milk in it. "Thanks, ladies. Appreciate the cup."

His arm drapes over Ella's shoulders, and the morning light paints her features in pinks and oranges. I take out my phone and scroll through some apartment listings I've scrounged up over the past three days of looking.

Today is the first time Ella doesn't have a packed day full of architecture studio classes, which take up hours and hours of her time. "So, there isn't a lot on Southside, unless you're willing to ride a bike to class every day," I begin, already knowing it's a non-starter for Ella, who can barely get up in time to walk the ten minutes from the dorms.

She looks at Tim, who nods. "Ruby, we want to talk to you."

"We?" I look between the two of them.

"Yes." Ella clears her throat and takes a sip of her coffee. Then another. She squares her shoulders and turns to me. "I don't want you to find me an apartment."

A bus roars down Bancroft, temporarily blocking out the chatter from the people surrounding us but doing nothing to blunt what I've just heard.

"Are you serious? Where are you planning to live?"

She looks at Tim again. "Tim's friend has a spare room in her rental on the other side of campus. She didn't think she'd be able to fill it until summer, so she and her roommates were all just paying extra."

"Oh." I don't know why the thought of Ella and Tim handling this on their own has me suddenly feeling weepy. It takes me several sips of coffee before I can remove the lump from my throat and speak without my voice cracking.

"Well, great. You've seen the place?" I want her to tell me she hasn't seen it so I can offer to look at it with her. And find it rat-infested or too tiny or way too expensive.

Ella nods. "It's perfect."

I don't want to be the voice of doom, but my sister hasn't mentioned anything about cost, and there's no way it will be as cheap as a partially subsidized dorm. "How much is it?"

Tim clears his throat. "Eight hundred plus utilities."

He might as well have said eight thousand for as likely as it is for me to be able to afford that. Even with the scholarship, I still have to cover most of Ella's living expenses and some of her tuition, plus my student loan payments.

She looks so delighted with her potential new place that I almost don't have the heart to tell her I can't afford it. "El, I don't think—"

She cuts me off. "I'm getting a part-time job. We looked at the numbers and the time in my schedule, and I can make it work."

There it is again. That "we" that doesn't refer to her and me. It reminds me of Tim taking her to the doctor and solving problems without me. I'm not used to it, and it feels like chewing on gravel. Little bits choke me up and land hard in my gut.

"And being on Northside, it'll force me to get up a little earlier."

I cling to the remaining scrap of need. "Oh, well, I can make sure I call you in the mornings to be sure you're up…"

She shakes her head. "No. Don't do that. And don't send me any more alarm clocks." Ella lets out a long exhale and looks away like she's preparing to drop a guillotine across my unsuspecting neck. "I hate that thing," she mutters.

"El, what's up?"

Her hand wanders across the table to where Tim's hand rests next to his cup. He turns it over and wraps it around hers. "Nothing. I'm good. You should go back to Napa."

"But I'm here. I want to help you."

A friend of Tim's rides up on his bike, and he excuses himself and walks over to chat with him. "Dude, you shouldn't have left so early last night. It was lit," I hear him say.

Ella lets out an exhale. "I love the guy, but he's a little overprotective. He wanted to be here for me when I talked to you."

"What? Why?"

"I was nervous."

I feel like I've been slapped. Hearing that talking to me requires a chaperone makes tears prick at the corners of my eyes. "To talk to me?"

Ella grips her coffee with both hands and stares at the brown liquid. "I want to do this without your help. It's time, and even if I mess it up, you have to let me fall sometimes. Tim is a really good guy. He didn't freak out and run when I had the ectopic. He doubled down, and now he's helping me find housing."

I feel like a jerk when I admit to myself that I don't want Tim to be all of those things for her—because I want to be the one she comes to for help. And that's my issue, not hers.

"I'm sorry, El. I only wanted to be the best sister to you that I could."

"Oh my god, Ruby, are you kidding? You've done that a hundredfold. Which is why I want to pay it back a little bit." Another bus goes by. She has to wait to be heard, and we both watch the swirl of leaves whip into the air in the bus's wake.

"You should go back."

"We have a couple more nights until you have to vacate. Let's make sure this housing thing comes through."

Ella holds up a hand. "I've got this. Go back to him. Go back to your job. Start making wine again in your own closet. Be happy, sis."

I know she's trying to lift a burden from my shoulders, but I'm not quick to let it go. It's been mine for so long that it's part of my identity, and I'm not entirely sure who I am without it. But I know it's time to find out.

I look at my sister, leaning back calmly against a bench, the guy she loves laughing with his friends a few feet away. He's one of the good ones. So is she. "You got me to where I am. Be proud of it. I know I am."

And that does it. The tears spring from my eyes as Ella reaches out and pulls me into a hug. "I love you. Always will. Go. Be happy."

I nod, unwilling to let go of her. Yet. "Okay. I'll try."

She lets out a loud sigh, and I release her just as Tim ambles back over and plops down on the bench. "You two good?"

"We're good," Ella says, leaning into him.

But the gears in my brain are clunking into place. "Actually, I could be better. El, do you have access to the ceramics studio?"

"Sure. Anytime. You want to throw some pots?"

I drain the remains of my coffee and nod. "I think I want to try."

# CHAPTER
## Thirty-Five

JAX

Fiona sees it first—the candy-apple-red Fiat that gleams in the afternoon sun like a freshly picked berry. We've just returned from camp, and Fiona has just finished telling me how tired she is, but now she's bouncing in the backseat like a kangaroo.

"She's back!" my daughter shouts upon sighting Ruby's car parked in front of our house. Nerves seize my chest. But they're overwhelmed by the warm rush of feelings—hope, gratitude, love.

Ruby sits on our front porch with a bag and a box at her feet. Fiona doesn't care about any of that as she jumps into Ruby's waiting arms as soon as I open the door and pop her seatbelt. "I missed you!"

"I missed you too, sweetie." Ruby sweeps Fiona into her arms, squeezing her tight. Ruby's hands cup Fiona's little head to her chest, eyes closed, just breathing my daughter in.

The picture of the two of them together looks like a different kind of family portrait from the one hanging in my dad's house.

This is the kind of family that has my eyes welling, and I'm going to hang onto it with everything I've got.

Fiona doesn't wait for me to unlock the front door of the house, so happy to see Ruby that she drags her by the hand around to the vineyard in back.

Ruby dashes with her but casts me a look over her shoulder. A smile, a wink. It's enough to give me faith that she's not here to collect her final paycheck and take off again. I reel my heart back from the precipice it's been perched on for five days straight.

I bring Ruby's bag and a very heavy box into the house and walk out the back door to find Ruby hiding and Fiona pretending not to see her behind a very small grapevine.

"Hey, Fi. Can you go upstairs and pick out three of your favorite books for us to read together later?"

"Now, Daddy?"

"Yes, please."

"Okay, fine, but Ruby, I *see* you."

She harumphs into the house to complete the task I know will take her at least a half hour. She has so many favorite books that it's always a big decision to choose only three. "Actually, Daddy, I have a better idea. I'm going to work on my pop-up book."

"Sounds good." I have no idea what she even means, but Ruby is nodding like she does. And I'm desperate to get Ruby alone.

Ruby comes out from behind the vine and approaches me slowly. "Hi," she says.

"Hi."

I want to dispense with these niceties and kiss her for hours, but the tentative way she's standing apart from me makes me cautious.

"I'm Ruby. I'm here to interview for the nanny job," she says.

"Are we back to that? Because you already have the job. You don't need to convince me of a damn thing."

She tips her head toward the house, indicating I should follow her. "I want to show you something first. Come."

Noticing the bag and the box on the kitchen table, she nods. "Thanks. Did you peek?"

"I would never."

I don't know how long Fiona will stay occupied upstairs, and I'm desperate to pull this woman as close to me as I can get her, but I show what little restraint I possess and wait for what she wants to show me.

She opens the bag and starts removing takeout containers of burgers and fries from the roadside stand we stopped at two months ago. I notice packets of ketchup and mustard—plenty of both—and a large bag of peaches and plums because she's always trying to get Fi to eat more fruit.

"Figured I'd bring you dinner for a change."

"You didn't have to do that. But thank you."

I look at the brown box sitting on the table, expecting Ruby to open it next or offer an explanation, but she waits, chewing on her bottom lip.

We hear Fiona's feet shuffling on the floor above us, and it's probably a matter of minutes before she comes tearing down the stairs. Ruby opens the flaps of the box and takes out a single plate made of raw gray clay.

It's unglazed and a little imperfect around the edges. When she hands it to me, I run my hands over the cool surface, feeling the weight of it. But I still don't understand.

"My sister is an architecture major, but she's minoring in ceramics," Ruby says.

"Did she make this?"

"I did. She helped." Then she laughs. "A lot."

Ruby reaches over and smooths the furrows from my brow with a finger. And it's like she can't help it—she traces a line straight down between my eyes, down my nose, and over my lips. After standing here itching to kiss her since she got out of the car, I can't take it any longer. Clamping my hand over hers, I run my tongue over the tip of her finger and suck gently on it.

Her breath hitches, and I watch the fabric of her pink tank top flutter as her chest swells. "We can talk about ceramics later. I need to kiss you." My voice sounds as raw as I feel.

She nods, and I don't waste another second. Her mouth melts against mine as I push my hands over her cheeks and tangle them in her hair. It's a kiss that defies the laws of science. Hot, wet, desperate, and…over way too soon because Ruby pulls away.

"Hang on. I want to talk about ceramics."

Her words make no sense because I'm dizzy with desire for her, but I try to rein in a few brain cells. "Um, okay."

Wrapping my hand in hers, she goes back to the box and removes a series of plates, much like the first one she showed me. By the time she's taken out eight, I see that they're a matched set. "I didn't have time to glaze them, but this way, you and Fi can decide what color you like first."

My eyes widen as I realize what this is. "You made me a set of dishes? Why?"

"Because I love you, and I want you to believe I'll stick around to eat on these dishes for a long time."

She tells me about wanting to give her sister space to spread her wings and her immense pride that Ella found a place to live and got a job. I tell her about my fears about our finances, the meeting I had with my siblings, the A plans and B plans, and even a C plan I came up with in case we still need more money to cover the company's debts.

"It's risky, and we could all lose every penny we have, but it will keep the business afloat and the investors happy until we can figure out why my father spent half a billion dollars on grapes from a winery that doesn't seem to exist."

I spare her my theories about shell companies and offshore accounts, but she asks about that stuff anyhow because she's smart. She even wants the name of the mysterious winery I'm starting to believe my dad made up. "Hayden Lanes. Another outfit with a name ending in Lanes or Fields or Pines." I roll my eyes, feeling like the name of our winery isn't much better.

I expect her to roll hers back at me, but instead, her eyes go wide. "Hang on."

Ruby rifles through her purse and pulls out an iPad. She scrolls through several screens and types into the search engine, which returns a result. "Hayden Lanes was on a sign. I saw it when I was at Duck Feather." She shows me a photo she took of some signage pointing to several faux "lanes" running between the vineyards, each labeled with a different name—Swallow Circle, Hayden Lanes, Rose Way.

"Wait, *what?*" I can't believe what I'm seeing. I've been searching for Hayden Lanes, and Ruby took these photos weeks ago?

"I'm so sorry. I had no idea there was any connection."

"There's no way you would, but I don't get it. The small winery next door just happens to have a sign on its property with the same name my dad mentioned when he was explaining our losses and need to buy grapes?"

"Seems like more than a coincidence," she says.

"I'd say so. At least we have a financial solution for now that will pull us through the shareholder meeting. But this is...I don't even know what to think. But I'll get into that tomorrow." I'm talked out. Happy to be with her, exhausted from talking, and lighter than I've felt in a year.

But there's more. I tip my forehead against hers, helpless against the urge to be connected, finding more points of contact.

"I have a confession to make," I breathe against her cheek, pulling her off her stool so I can hold her closer.

"Spill it."

"I don't want you to be my nanny."

She laughs. It's a full belly laugh that forces her away from me as she tosses her head back. "Jax, that's no confession. You told me that the day we met."

"Okay, well, let me say it differently. I don't want you to be my nanny anymore."

I don't give her a chance to wriggle out of my arms, even though I feel her body stiffen. I get a side-eye and a frown.

"Nice. Way to fire a person when her defenses are down."

My hand slides into her hair, and I caress the back of her neck. Her head tips back into my hand, even as she continues to scowl at me. So I continue massaging her neck and willing her body into submission. I feel her relent despite herself.

"What I mean is that I want you to be in my life—and my daughter's life—because you belong there, not because I'm paying you. So yeah, I guess I'm firing you."

My other hand comes to her jaw, and I angle her face so I can kiss her the way I've been dying to since she walked out of my house nearly a week ago. There's no fight left in her. The woman I've been dreaming about for days is limp in my arms.

"Huh. This may be the first time in my life I don't mind being fired."

"Yeah?"

She smiles and leads me back to the box on the table. Reaching in, she takes out a stack of eight smaller plates, all made from raw clay, unglazed. "Here's the rest of the set. Salad plates. Fiona needs to eat green things."

"Ew," Fiona says, back without the usual stomping that lets us know she's here. "What kind of green things?"

Ruby flinches and starts to drop my hand, but I grab it more fiercely. "Not letting you go," I whisper against her ear. It only takes Fiona about two seconds to notice. Her smile takes over her face, and she starts dancing in the kitchen, holding a wad of pages over her head. A few cut-out red hearts fall to the floor.

"It's my pop-up book. It's my story." She opens the "book" to a page that shows carefully-drawn figures wearing crowns. One has long orange hair. Between them is a smaller figure with yellow hair. Also wearing a crown.

"No, lovebug," I tell her. "It's *our* story."

# Epilogue

RUBY

THREE MONTHS LATER

My alarm rings at half past five, and I wake up with a smile on my face. It's not because I read the weather report and know it's going to be a pretty fall day with clear skies and warm temperatures. It's not because I've been able to increase the scale of my viniculture and try new things. It's not because I love Jackson Corbett a little more each day that I know him.

It's all of those things. And so much more. For the first time, my goals feel within my reach.

Who cares that I stayed at Jackson's house until midnight last night, enjoying the private time after Fiona went to sleep? Who cares that I'll need an extra cup of coffee to get me through the day? The past three months have been the best of my life, and sleep is overrated anyway.

It helps, of course, that Ella is happy. She's more than happy, actually. Her new roommate situation has turned out to be so much better than living in the dorms. Her campus job in the engineering library pays better than minimum wage, so she's able to pay for her living expenses and have a little left over for the occasional splurge.

She has two sweet roommates, who've become real friends who stay up late and laugh with her and get up early to nudge her awake with the scent of coffee. She supplied them with a French press, and each of them has stashed four dollars into a jar each time they brew coffee at home instead of buying it. After only a month, they took themselves to a celebratory steak dinner with the savings.

She and Tim are still going strong, and he's been a huge support to her through the move and daily life.

As a nagging older sister, I feel like my job is done. Well, not totally done. I'll always find excuses to teach Ella those older sister lessons that she's probably already learned on her own, and so far, she still humors me.

Knowing she's doing well puts my mind at ease and makes it much easier to sink into the life I've been building in Napa.

I still come to Jackson's house every day to hang with Fiona, but it's become more of an unofficial agreement between Fiona and me than any kind of actual job. Even though Jax relieved me of my official duties, there was no turning down Fiona when she asked me to pick her up and spend afternoons with her.

Fortunately, the pay raise I received when Victor brought me on as assistant sommelier a month ago has bridged the gap, and… excuse me…assistant sommelier! I'm officially on my way to my dream job—not to mention that I have a bit more time in my day to work on making wine. And what better place to do it?

In my nearly six months working here, I've met a lot of the winemakers, so I've been learning so much more about aging my wine in the drier weather. With less humidity and using an oak barrel, there's less evaporation, which produces wine with lower alcohol concentrations. I'm experimenting with sauvignon blanc grapes.

For one batch, I'm trying a no-aging technique where the wine could be ready in a matter of months. I'm also trying for a more complex wine that will age for over a year. Only time will tell which I like better.

Which brings me to why I'm up so early. I've started fresh with new viniculture, and today is the day I need to test the sugar levels. I intend to do it right. No distractions. No mistakes.

I pull the containers from the darkest corner of my closet, where they've been working quietly for weeks. I'm about to run a test when there's a knock at my door.

Six sharp. Odd hour for a visitor. The guest cottage where I've been staying is barely more than a bedroom with a bathroom and kitchen, so there's no mistaking the light rapping of knuckles on wood. I can't imagine who's coming to see me this early, but several other employees live in the neighboring cottages, so it could be anyone.

Glancing down at the oversized tee I slept in, I grab a pair of shorts from a chair next to my bed and wriggle into them on my way to the door.

Jackson's smile greets me when I swing the door open, and I reflexively mirror it because it's impossible to look at his beautiful face and do anything other than smile and tip my head up to kiss his lips. Especially when they're mine to kiss.

"Hey," he says softly after a good morning kiss that practically takes us into afternoon.

"Hi." Staring up at him, I notice that he hasn't shaven, and the ruddy shadow on his face only makes him look more handsome. His blue eyes sparkle like Fiona's do when she's dying to tell me a secret. "You good?"

"Better now." He smiles but I know him well enough now to see there's something troubling him, and at this hour, I can't imagine what it could be.

"What's going on? Your dad?" His health has been in a holding pattern—no better, no worse—but I always worry.

"Indirectly…" He closes his eyes for a moment. "I just got

word that some New York journalist is sniffing around. Knows about the financial discrepancies somehow. This is all going to blow up."

He looks pained, shaking his head.

"Yuck. You'll get ahead of it—I know you will. Just one more challenge."

Jackson reaches for my hand and pulls me one step forward. Now I can see the faintest warm light coloring the vineyards behind him. "I know, and that's why I needed to see you." His eyes haven't left mine, and I know how much he loves to look at the vineyards. "I just feel better when I'm with you. Which is why I want to be with you all the time."

My heart squeezes, just as his hand squeezes mine. "Just so we're clear…" He drops to one knee.

The breath leaves my lungs in a whoosh. I'd be lying if I said I didn't imagine this day or hope for this day, but we told each other we'd take things slowly. For Fiona's sake. For our sake. Just to be sure.

"Jax…" My hand comes to my chest like I'm holding back my heart from jumping free.

"I can't take it slow anymore, Ruby. I tried. But you're all I want." He takes a deep breath and presses his lips together as though he's trying once more to stop himself. But his smile takes over, warming his face and heating my bones.

"Just like I couldn't stop thinking about you from the day you stormed into my life in a gorgeous cloud of fiery hair and sass at six in the morning, I haven't been able to stop thinking about *this* morning ever since."

He holds up his wrist, where his watch shows the six o'clock hour. "This will always be our hour of the day. The coincidence of me oversleeping and you thinking a normal person would interview you at six in the morning."

I can't help but shake my head and laugh at the recollection. Ridiculous in hindsight. "But it brought us here," he says. "Where

I want all of my six o'clocks to include you. If you'll marry me and hand over your calendar."

I nod, and Jackson opens a blue velvet ring box, where a square-cut solitaire sparkles in the sun. Slipping it on my finger, he tells me the only thing I really need to know in order for my life to feel complete. "I love you."

Holding both of my hands, Jackson stands and pulls me close, our hands sandwiched between us. His kiss pulls the breath from my lungs, and I was already unsteady to begin with. The ring effect, the Jackson effect, all of it.

"Love you more," I say when I can come up with a clear thought. My arms loop around his neck, and he tips our foreheads together.

"Not possible."

"And yet, true."

"We could do this all day long," he says, eyes soft, willing.

He cups my cheek with his hand. His lips brush against mine, and my nerve endings flare to life. I doubt that will ever change when he touches me.

"I'd rather do this all day long." His voice rumbles against my mouth.

"Works for me," I tell him.

In the distance, I see movement, and Jackson follows my eye to where Archer is rounding the backside of the lake. "Always out on his damn run," he mumbles, but the smile on his face softens the grump of his words.

"Only the best people are up at this hour," I remind him, arms around his neck.

He returns his gaze to me, and he nods. "Only the best." He kisses the tip of my nose, my forehead, my lips.

I love that six in the morning will always be our time.

Always.

―――

Thank you so much for reading Jax and Ruby's vineyard romance! Craving a few more juicy details about their happily ever after? Join my mailing list to have a BONUS EPILOGUE delivered right to your inbox. I'll only send you the best stuff—new release info, exclusive sales, and a monthly free romance from one of my author friends.

And...there's more to the mystery of Hayden Lanes and the missing money—much more! The small town wine country saga continues with LOVE YOU ANYWAY, a brother's best friend billionaire romance. Available for PREORDER now!

# *Bonus Epilogue*

Ruby

Three Years Later

"Dad, Dad, come quick!" Hudson's high-pitched voice always makes it sound like either the most exciting or the most dire thing is happening just outside of view. And Jackson never wastes a moment of time before dashing over to our toddler son.

Wanting our kids to be as close in age to Fiona as possible, we hadn't wasted any time trying to have children.

That meant that by the time we'd planned our wedding at the Inn—or rather, by the time Beatrix expertly helped us plan it—I was seven months pregnant. It made for a wedding dress that had to be altered—again—a week before the ceremony, even though I'd chosen a style that had some give.

The empire-waisted silk dress had an embroidered strapless bodice and a flowing long skirt. My flowers were a simple collection of blooms that grew on the property—buttercups, lilies, and sprigs of lavender—tied together with a white silk ribbon.

At first, we planned to have a small wedding. "Just immediate family," we told Beatrix, who nodded, willing to do whatever we wanted and already brimming with ideas for an intimate affair in a garden. But once plans were underway, I kept thinking about friends from college, and Jax came up with his own list of people he wanted to be there. By the time we said our vows, we had over a hundred guests sitting in the flower garden behind the barn, every single one of them having touched a part of our lives.

We danced long into the night, even though my feet were swollen and my eyelids were drooping. "I don't care," I told Jackson. "We'll only have one wedding. I'm not going to miss a minute of it."

Knowing he'd have no luck trying to convince me to take it easy, Jax swept me into his arms for every slow dance and kissed me until I melted against him. We were the last ones to leave, and he carried me back to our room at the Inn.

It's hard to believe two years have passed since then, mainly because I've been busy releasing the first vintage of my cabernet blend this year, chasing around a toddler, and waddling around under an increasingly large belly. In other words, I'm happier than I've ever been.

Today, sitting on a lounge chair behind our house and staring over my eight-months-pregnant belly, I have no hope of matching Jax's speed when he races over to Hudson. Besides, he called for his dad, not me. Just as well because nothing makes me happier than watching the two of them race through the vineyards.

Hudson is a tiny dark-haired version of Jackson, complete with a furrow between his brows that he's had since birth. He always seems to be contemplating the ways of the world, gazing with a serious expression that twists into a grin the second he sees Jackson—every day, at any hour.

If I thought Jackson was the perfect girl dad, I've now had to revise my view to simply say that Jackson is the perfect dad. Period.

He and Hudson disappear for a few seconds as they race down a row of grapes, our toddler wobbling along on short legs and Jackson barely jogging to keep pace. I have an idea where they're headed. The rows of cabernet grapes have tiny bluebird houses perched on the tops of some of the grape stakes, and I'm betting Hudson spotted a bird.

The small, wooden houses dot the acres of cabernet vines because bluebirds control the pests that might feast on grape leaves and harm the crop. The holes drilled into the square houses are just big enough for bluebirds to flit in and out but not so big that starlings can get inside. We don't want starlings anywhere near the vines.

I feel a rolling kick in my belly, probably an elbow or a foot, and give it a pat. "I know, girl, you're gonna be a soccer player."

Jackson comes jogging into view with Hudson on his shoulders. The sight of the two of them unleashes a flood of warmth in my heart, just like it does every time I see them together.

"Hey, what was the big emergency?" I ask Hudson as Jackson bends to let him dismount over his head. He scrambles toward me and launches himself into my outstretched arms as though he didn't just see me five minutes earlier.

Like father, like son.

"The bluebirds had babies. They're in the box! Come see!" Hudson only has one volume level—loud—unless he's exhausted. But exhausting a two-year-old is harder than I realized, even with acres where he can run.

"Really?"

"A couple have their head popped out through the hole. It's pretty adorable," Jackson says, extending his hand to help me out of the Adirondack chair. Arm around my shoulder, he leads me over to where Hudson has already disappeared.

When we turn down a row of vines, sure enough, the quiet chirp of baby birds catches my attention. "Oh, they're adorable."

"Shh," Hudson admonishes, clearly mimicking how Jackson told him the same. "Don't scare them."

"They're so sweet," I whisper, gazing at the tiny beaks and tufts of blue pushing out through the hole. I love that the organic way Buttercup farms allows for all kinds of bird species—the correct ones that don't harm the crops—to flourish in the vineyards.

Dropping Jackson's hand, I turn back for the house. I don't want to worry him, but I feel a sudden need to sit back down. But the guy doesn't miss a thing.

"What's wrong?" he whispers, catching up to me. Hudson trails behind, pulling the lowest-hanging grapes from the vines and humming a song I don't recognize.

"Braxton Hicks." I've been having more early contractions with this pregnancy than I did with the first one, but I'm not too concerned. "It's no big deal. I just need to sit until they calm down."

"You sure?" Jackson kisses my temple and rubs my lower back, which has been aching a bit more every day as the baby grows.

"Yeah, I'm just giant and tired."

He laughs. "I love all those versions of you." The best thing about Jackson is that he really means it.

Fiona greets us at the back door with her hands on her hips. "What took so long? I wanted to bake with Hud." She's been trying to teach him math through baking, but as just shy of two years old, her pupil isn't keeping up. The result is a new batch of cookies every week while she coaxes him to add and subtract balls of dough on the baking sheet. I have no doubt she'll get him there before he's three.

"Bluebird babies," Jackson says, plucking a ball of dough from a baking sheet and popping it into his mouth.

"Hey," Fiona protests. "Now I have to take a little bit from the other cookies to make a new one."

Jackson snags one more dough ball. "There. Now it's an even number."

Fiona pretends to scowl, but I see relief in her eyes now that the rows have been evened up. "Fine. Come on, Hud." Fiona is amazing with him and begs us to let her babysit. That comes in the form of us going upstairs and letting her have some solo time with her brother, but one of us is nearby in case she needs anything.

Fiona scoots out of the way so Hudson can clamber onto the stepstool next to her. His eyes are big and blue like mine, and he stares up at his big sister like she hung the moon.

I rub a hand over my belly, wondering if our little girl will look at Hudson the same way. Probably. Definitely.

"C'mere, take a load off." Jackson herds me slowly up the stairs.

"I didn't get a blob of cookie dough," I gripe, shuffling down the hallway to the couch at the foot of our bed.

Jackson sits at my feet and slips each of my Birkenstock sandals off of my feet. "It has raw egg. Not good when you're pregnant."

I don't bother to argue that there's barely any raw egg in a ball of dough. I love that he cares enough to read all the pregnancy books. "Fine. Will you bring me a couple once they're baked?"

"You already know the answer to that." Jackson lifts each one of my swollen feet and runs a finger down the arch. He kisses the top of each one before moving up my legs, dropping soft kisses over my bare knees and along the tops of my thighs.

Sitting next to me on the couch, he turns my face toward his and gazes into my eyes. He blinks like I'm still new to him after all this time.

"I will bring you anything you want, anytime you want. I still pinch myself every day to be sure this is real." Still intense, still the

"It's real," I assure him. "But I feel the same way."

He still begins every kiss with a brush of his lips against mine, a promise of more. And he always delivers. Even with a big belly between us, it feels like nothing really separates us as his mouth claims mine, and our kiss deepens.

I want to kiss him forever.

Good thing. Because I think I'll get my wish.

# Acknowledgments

Without you all, this book would just be a pile of pages—or string of words—on my computer.

Readers, you are it for me—I couldn't do this job without your support and love. And your beautiful edits and reels make me swoon!

Nicole McCurdy and Amy Vox Libris, you kept me out of the quicksand and made this book so much better with your edits.

Echo Grayce, holy crap, your covers are perfection, and I owe you big for not one, but two, gorgeous covers.

Erica, PA extraordinaire, I'd be sunk without you keeping me on track and thinking of everything I'd forget—ie most things…

Thank you to every blogger, IG-er, TT-er and FB-er who championed this book and helped get the word out—I am beyond grateful.

And to my boys who haven't read my books (and probably shouldn't), thanks for encouraging your mama to make that extra cup of coffee and keep going. Love you more.

# About the Author

Stacy Travis writes sexy, charming romance about bookish, sassy women and the hot alphas who fall for them. Writing contemporary romance makes her infinitely happy, but that might be the coffee talking.

When she's not on a deadline, she's in running shoes complaining that all roads seem to go uphill. Or on the couch with a margarita. Or fangirling at a soccer game. She's never met a dog she didn't want to hug. And if you have no plans for Thanksgiving, she'll probably invite you to dinner. Stacy lives in Los Angeles with her two sons, and a poorly-trained rescue dog who hoards socks.

Facebook reader group: Stacy's Saucy Sisters

Super fun newsletter: https://geni.us/travisNL

Email: stacytraviswrites@gmail.com - tell me what you're reading!

facebook.com/stacytravisromance

instagram.com/stacytravisauthor

bookbub.com/authors/stacy-travis

goodreads.com/stacytravis

tiktok.com/@stacytravisauthor

*Also by Stacy Travis*

**The Summer Heat Duet**

1. The Summer of Him: A Mistaken Identity Celebrity Romance

2. Forever with Him: An Opposites Attract Contemporary Romance

**The Berkeley Hills Series - all standalone novels**

1. In Trouble with Him: A Forbidden Love Contemporary Romance (Finn and Annie's story)

2. Second Chance at Us: A Second Chance Romance (Becca and Blake)

3. Falling for You: A Friends to Lovers Romance (Isla and Owen)

4. The Spark Between Us: A Grumpy-Sunshine, Brother's Best Friend Romance (Sarah and Braden)

5. Playing for You: A Sports Romance (Tatum and Donovan)

6. No Match for Her - an Opposites-Attract Friends-to Lovers Romance (Cherry and Charlie)

**San Francisco Strikers Series - standalone novels**

1. He's a Keeper: A Grumpy-Sunshine Sports Romance (Molly and Holden)

2. He's a Player: A Second Chance Sports Romance (Jordan and Tim)

3. He's a Charmer: A Brother's Best Friend Sports Romance (Linnie and Weston)

**Buttercup Hill Series - standalone novels**

1. Love You More; A Single Dad Grumpy-Sunshine Small Town Romance (Jax and Ruby)

2. Love You Anyway; A Brother's Best Friend Small Town Romance (PJ and Aidan)

Printed in Great Britain
by Amazon

33329596R00158